Into the Room

ENDORSEMENTS

Into the Room is a unique story that follows Ben Cahill on his reluctant journey on a twelve-day tour of the Holy Land. Steven Rogers does a superb job of allowing the reader to be drawn along into this journey of a man who is a slave to alcohol and has lost everything—his wife, family, job, home, and dignity. The main character's brooding introspection coupled with his dry humor made me laugh out loud, a balance in an otherwise compelling drama. The author has created characters who have flesh and realistic locations, with an overlay of the divine. He has fashioned a well-written work of fiction—or is it fiction? You be the judge.

—**Brent Brantley**, author of *You Cannot Grasp the River*

Into the Room tells the story of an amazing journey to Israel with people chosen by God to love one lost man. A man named Ben. His self-inflicted deep wounds, resulting from a lifetime of bad choices, are uncovered layer by layer as he struggles with God. Strangers become family as Ben opens his heart to God's unconditional love and steps "into the room." Thank you, Steven Rogers, for your well-written story which will touch the hearts of the lost and refresh the moment faith opened the hearts of believers.

—**Billie Fulton**, author and speaker. *Faith Is Not Silent* and *Just A Moment: Changes Life Forever.*

Into the Room by Steven Rogers is both intriguing and compelling. I did not want to put it down and, when I had no choice, the storyline and characters called me to return. I connected with Ben as well as the other characters, feeling like a friendship had formed by the end of the book. Rogers had me with the coveted "what happens next?" every author hopes to consume readers. If you are looking for a great read and longing to grow your faith too, *Into the Room* is for you.

—**Shelley Pierce**, author, award-winning devotional *Sweet Moments, Insight and Encouragement for the Pastor's Wife* and the middle-grade series, *The Crumberry Chronicles*

Into the Room is an inspiring story of a man who encounters the transformational power of the Messiah Yeshua—Jesus—in the Holy Land. The author Steven Rogers is a living testimony affirming the truth that, when you take a pilgrimage to Israel, you'll never be the same again.

—**Paul Klassen**, Tour Facilitator, President of Aliyah Foundation. Aliyahfoundation.org, Aliyahtours.org.

INTO THE ROOM

STEVEN ROGERS

ELK LAKE PUBLISHING II.

PUBLISHING THE POSITIVE
Plymouth, Massachusetts

Copyright Notice

Into the Room

This is a work of fiction. Names, characters, businesses, places, events, locales, and incidents are either the products of the author's imagination or used in a fictitious manner. Any resemblance to actual persons, living or dead, or actual events is purely coincidental.

Scripture quotations marked (NIV) are taken from the Holy Bible, New International Version®, NIV®. Copyright © 1973, 1978, 1984, 2011 by Biblica, Inc.™ Used by permission of Zondervan. All rights reserved worldwide. www.zondervan.comThe "NIV" and "New International Version" are trademarks registered in the United States Patent and Trademark Office by Biblica, Inc.™

Scripture quotations marked (KJV) are taken from the Authorized (King James) Version of the Holy Bible. In the public domain

Cover and Interior Design: Derinda Babcock
Editor(s): Michele Chynoweth, Deb Haggerty
PUBLISHED BY: Elk Lake Publishing, Inc., 35 Dogwood Drive, Plymouth, MA 02360

Library Cataloging Data
Names: Rogers, Steven (Steven Rogers)
Into the Room / Steven Rogers
288p. 23cm × 15cm (9in × 6 in.)
ISBN-13: 978-1-64949-264-7 (paperback) | 978-1-64949-265-4 (trade paperback) | 978-1-64949-266-1 (e-book)
Key Words: Contemporary Christian Fiction; Christian Fiction Books for Men; Christian Redemption Novels; Faith Based Fiction; Faith Travel Fiction; Addiction Fiction; Israel Fiction
Library of Congress Control Number: 2021939711 Fiction

DEDICATION

To Kathy. My best friend.

ACKNOWLEDGMENTS

In 2016, my wife and I traveled to Israel. On the flight over, I received the inspiration for Ben Cahill's story. We traveled with a group of thirty or so friendly and welcoming individuals. I will be forever grateful for the way their faith and love inspired my writing.

Thank you to Michael Compton for his thorough and sometimes hilarious editing input. Gratitude is owed Jenny Fairchild for her beta reading, plot "brainstorming," and amazing patience with my somewhat limited technology skills. I'd also like to thank my other beta readers: Corynne Arnett, Steve Foster, Mark Rogers, and Tom Wohlfarth. Your input made this a better story.

Three wonderful authors, Heath Hardage Lee, Brad Parks, and Adriana Trigiani offered encouragement and advice as I've strived to improve as a writer. Thank you.

John DeDakis, writing coach extraordinaire, has an amazing ability to identify strengths and weaknesses. In addition, his input is always provided with tact and grace.

To Michele Chynoweth, Cristel Phelps, Derinda Babcock, and Deb Haggerty at Elk Lake Publishing, Inc.— working with you has been a graduate course in the craft. Thank you for believing in me and in this book.

Noah Downs provided legal and marketing assistance. Thank you. I'm appreciative of Sawyer Wilkins's insights into some important plot points and character traits. I offer sincere gratitude for the stalwart support of my brothers, Mark and Chris Rogers. Our three children, Erin, Andy, and Leland, inspire me in more ways than I can explain.

Finally, thank you to Kathy. On a June night in 1985, she agreed to marry a self-proclaimed "wack job." I'm deeply grateful for her honest editing and unending patience with my insecurities.

DAY 1

There's nothing worse than Holy Rollers on a roll.

Yet here I am, on a bus bursting with Christians, all of them using their outdoor voices, enthusiastically talking about the upcoming pilgrimage. The excitement is lost on me. To take a pilgrimage, there needs to be a purpose, and as far as I'm concerned, this trip is simply filling time.

Also, to take a pilgrimage, you need to know who you are and what you want to become. I'm confident I couldn't give a sincere answer to either of those questions.

Who am I?

My name is Ben Cahill, and I'm taking this trip because I have no place to live, unless I camp on my brother's couch, which, at forty-two, is not something I want to do. The trip leader, the guy everyone calls Pastor Marcus, got me in at the last minute after Nick, my brother, pulled some strings and talked me onto the roster. Nick's half a Holy Roller himself.

Unfortunately, no matter how far away I go, I can't get away from myself.

I was, until recently, a highly regarded commercial real estate developer, arguably the best dealmaker in the city of Richmond, Virginia, and wealthy. Most of the fortune is gone. I told the lawyers Sarah deserved all of it, and all I wanted was seed money and the old Camry. I got $50,000, and after paying for this trip, there's $46,000 left.

Sarah is my soon-to-be ex-wife, an angel on earth who, for whatever reason, still loves me. I believe, however, she will never, under any circumstances, take me back. A woman will forgive all transgressions except one—there is no exoneration when she's convinced her children are in danger, no grace granted for subsequent good behavior.

We have two children. One is a beautiful little girl, eight-year-old Olivia, and the other is a strong-willed, determined thirteen-year-old boy named Zach. Zach has become his mother's and his sister's protector.

Three weeks ago, I graduated from the Seasons of Hope rehabilitation facility. My time at the Outhouse, as we called the place, was wasted—on the way home, I drank myself into oblivion.

Still, with all the mess I've created, all I want is a bottle of Absolut, a short glass, and a couple of ice cubes.

I've got things under control, though. Once I get through this trip, return to work, and re-establish my routine, all will be fine.

On to Israel.

$$\infty \;\; \infty \;\; \infty$$

The bus carnival is over, we're all on the plane, and there's been lots of talk about blessings and faith and praise. I once thought along those lines, but never with any sincerity, and I definitely don't now.

Don't misunderstand me. I've been religious my whole life, a good check-the-box Episcopalian. I sang in the choir, led committees, spoke to the men's group, and sponsored a kid for confirmation. Looking back now, I realize I was putting on a show—appearing faithful as a kid was one of those parent-pleasing behaviors, and after reaching adulthood, was helpful in business.

I flip through the folder Pastor Marcus gave me while the guy next to me, Joseph, scratches away in a journal. The folder has flight details, hotels, schedules, and places to take notes. As an added bonus, there are daily readings included in a section called "Devotionals for a Blessed Trip."

Yeah, I'll get right on that.

When the flight attendant comes by with the drink cart, my lips quiver, and before asking for a beer, I make sure the Holy Rollers aren't watching. She hands me the can, and as my palm touches the condensation, I imagine the first sip.

Joseph nods at the can. "Are you sure you want that?"

His accent is unusual, a Greek/Turkish mix.

"Uh, yeah, I do."

He shrugs, responding, "Suit yourself," and returns to his writing.

I'm annoyed this stranger would ask, but not enough to distract me from my beer. I take a small taste, followed by a gulp, before draining the can. I hit the call button and order another. The second one goes down fast too. I keep ordering. With the third, I start to feel comfortable. The fourth brings hopefulness, a feeling of optimism about the trip. After the fifth, all is right. All I needed was five beers over the course of about seventy minutes to convince myself I'm not such a bad guy after all.

The flight attendant returns and I take one more beer, making an even six pack, and also purchase three of those mini-bottles of vodka, tucking them away for later. I nurse the beer for a half hour and reach for the call button. Time for number seven.

"Stop, my friend."

Joseph, my intrusive seatmate, has decided to get involved again. This time his voice is firm, and he moves my hand back to the armrest. I should be irritated, but I'm not. I don't know why.

∞ ∞ ∞

On the way to Tel Aviv, there's a layover in Vienna. A few Holy Rollers have introduced themselves, but I already can't remember their names.

The good feeling from the beer is gone, replaced with nausea, parched skin, a headache, and intestines that are full but won't let me empty them—the byproduct of a drunk sleep, eating awful food, and hurtling through time zones in a metal tube.

Joseph sits down and gives me a cup of thick European coffee, looking as though he's returning from a day at the spa, and asks, "How are you doing, my friend?"

"Lousy."

"Would you prefer to talk? Take your mind off how you feel?"

"No."

"Suit yourself."

I inhale the aroma of the rich, dark liquid, and mull over Joseph's question. There's nothing to say about my physical condition, and if history is an indicator, I'll be okay soon enough. There is, however, the other side of the equation—all the destructive, deceptive things I've done. Do I want to explain how I frittered away the greatest life a man could ask for? Do I want to try and rationalize why I couldn't resist getting a buzz for one night, surrounded by people praying and praising God? Do I want to disclose how, when I stop drinking, I feel more worthless than before I started? Do I want to tell a virtual stranger any of this?

Of course not.

All I want is a nip of vodka and to make this pain go away.

PROGRESS REPORT # 1

Peter,

Your communication has been received, and I have arrived, eager to begin my work.

My preliminary appraisal indicates you have assigned an interesting case. There is little doubt our subject is firmly in the grips of his earthly vice. In addition, he is, as we thought, in a dark place. Perhaps beyond our early estimates.

The day, which consisted entirely of travel, was spent mostly observing. He had little contact with others, and those interactions were superficial. I tried several brief exchanges and was, for the most part, rebuffed. Interestingly, he did respond to one firm suggestion. This signals a possible hidden desire for change, and perhaps, we will draw this desire to the surface.

Speaking of time, you have clearly communicated the necessity for acute therapy. As a loyal servant, I will do my best to accommodate. However, and as you know, our stated objective sometimes takes many worldly years to accomplish. Much depends on our subject's willingness to understand and react to the cues he will be given.

With all that said, I am honored to be trusted with such an ambitious project and will, of course, exert every effort to ensure success.

I wish you mercy, love, and peace.

Joseph

DAY 2

We've landed in Tel Aviv. Pastor Marcus informs us the time is two in the afternoon, and the day is Sunday. As wrung out as everyone appears, I'm certain I come across the worst.

Passport Control is as quick and efficient as in other countries. I was expecting extensive document scrutiny, piercing questions, and a strip search.

"Security was easier than I imagined," I say to Pastor Marcus, who's tying his shoe.

"On paper, you're pretty harmless. Plus, and don't take this the wrong way because I'm in the same boat with you, but one glance will tell anyone you're spent. You look too haggard to be a threat."

He's got a point.

Pastor Marcus continues as he stands. "Don't be fooled, though. Behind the scenes, they go as deep as they need to, and if they had any concerns, you'd know."

We stop to let everyone catch up. When one of the women suggests we pray, the group joins hands, and a guy standing across from me starts by requesting wisdom for our trip's leaders. The woman next to him asks God to provide our traveling band with peace and fellowship. The man beside her, who I assume is her husband, says thanks for the safe travel. When the guy to his right starts talking, I realize they're moving methodically around the circle, in order, and each person is taking a turn.

I do a quick count. I'm four away from having to offer something. They pray for the Israeli/Palestinian conflict, our relatives at home, and those who are in pain.

After someone offers hope for Christians who are persecuted, my turn arrives. I bow my head, letting a silence build, frantically searching for a phrase or suitable platitude.

All I drum up is a picture of my Grandmother's favorite needlepoint trivet, and I recite the quotation. "There is a time for everything, and a season for every activity under the heavens."

I hear a whispered "amen," and as my neighbor squeezes my hand, I'm uneasy about the dampness in my palm. I'm vaguely aware of the subsequent prayer, something about resisting temptation, but in reality, I want to know the Steelers' score.

As we move through the airport, Pastor Marcus nudges me. "Now there's what I call security."

I'm not sure how I missed the overt police or maybe military presence. Whatever they are, they're heavily armed, carrying assault rifles and holstered pistols, standing near doors or moving around in groups of four.

I decide I should pay more attention and take a look around the place. There are huge electronic screens listing flights, a Duty-Free Shop, electronic kiosks for printing documents, and the ubiquitous McDonald's. The signs have three languages. One's English, and according to Pastor Marcus, the other two are Hebrew and Arabic.

At baggage claim, a growing number of people have a Middle Eastern appearance, or at least my pre-conceived notion of one—stylishly dressed, light brown skin, neatly manicured beards, and a lack of extra body fat. Several of the men and boys are wearing a yarmulke. Otherwise, I see a typical collection of businesspeople, tourists, exhausted parents pushing strollers or chasing kids, and love-struck young couples.

About twenty feet away, there's a group of men dressed in black suits and open-collared white shirts, their heads covered with black hats. All of them have beards, and several faces are framed by curled strands of hair.

I had expected this to be all I would see, along with women wearing modest dresses and sensible shoes, their faces framed by simple kerchiefs. Instead, most of the women milling about are dressed in everything from jeans and sweatshirts to stylish ensembles. I guess I've been watching too many old movies.

∞ ∞ ∞

We shuffle outside to another bus that, apparently, will be our daytime home for the next ten days.

As most people in our group of around twenty-five settle into the first dozen or so rows, I walk past them all, mumbling something about not feeling good, choosing a seat close to the rear.

Joseph joins me, saying, "I enjoy sitting back here too, my friend."

Pastor Marcus takes the front seat on the left and another guy, who I haven't seen before, takes the right. As the bus starts moving, he introduces himself as Avi, our Israeli tour guide, and reviews the places we'll visit, pointing them out on a map hanging from the windshield.

Our tour starts right away. No rest. No food. No coffee. No chance to freshen up. We're headed to Joppa, which used to be called Jaffa. The folder tells me it's Old Jaffa but Avi speaks again and says Joppa. I settle on Joppa, which Avi tells us is a Mediterranean seaport, has been since the Bronze Age, and is close to four thousand years old.

He moves on to what he calls our general orientation, starting with, "Israel is a safe place. Feel free to walk anywhere you want, night or day."

Pastor Marcus jumps in. "Regardless, please don't go out alone. Make sure you're with somebody at all times. We don't want to lose anyone in the Middle East."

Avi adds, "You do not have to worry about getting Israeli money. Your American dollars will be fine, and credit cards are accepted most everywhere."

He explains the Israeli currency, the shekel, which I thought was real only in the movies. I picture the stereotypical Jewish tailor urging his family to "save a shekel here and there."

Switching topics, Avi gets animated. "You are visiting at an exciting time for Israel, or at least the 'regathered' Israel, because 2018 marks its seventieth anniversary."

Everyone else on the bus regards this as exhilarating.

At Joppa we stop at a place called Abrasha Park. The short uphill walk is like the Bataan Death March, but I make it by watching for Avi's safari hat and the unkempt brown hair sticking out at various angles. At the top, we stop at a circular patio made from large white bricks, and Avi stands between two ivory-colored stone pillars with a block of the same size resting across the top, all covered in carvings. "This is the Statue of Faith, a symbolic gate, meant to illustrate God's strength and love for Israel. This pillar shows Abraham binding his son Isaac, preparing him for sacrifice to God. On the other side, the engravings show Jacob's dream about a ladder to heaven. Here, across the top, this is when Joshua and the Israelites conquered Jericho. Together, these events represent God's fulfillment of his promises to Israel."

I remember hearing these stories over the years, but the details don't stick with me, and at this stage of my life, they've become more mythology than history. I do study the statue, running my hands over the etchings. They are impressively done.

Drawing our attention to the opening in the sculpture, Avi points out a view of the Mediterranean. The gate frames the scene, with lots of green trees, vegetation, office buildings, and blue water. I'm reminded of my family, all of us going to seaside resorts for vacation.

I notice, as part of the impeccably sculptured landscaping, a lantana plant, the reddish-orange flower accented by yellow petals in the middle. I used to plant the same flower at my house. Back when I had a house.

Time for a drink.

"You okay, sweetie?" I hear a genuine southern accent and turn toward the voice. To my left is one of the Holy Rollers. Her nametag tells me she's Gerri.

"No problem. I'm fine," I answer.

She doesn't respond but doesn't leave either.

We turn our attention to Avi, and I notice his broad shoulders and thin waist hiding underneath a nondescript golf shirt and wrinkled khaki pants. His watch, with its cheap leather band and simple analog clock face, is street vendor quality. He's chattering on about Jonah, who, when he disobeyed God, hopped a ship in Joppa. As we know, the situation got complicated, with the whale and all.

Pastor Marcus takes over. "Time to dig into the New Testament. Let's talk about Cornelius, who sent for the Apostle Peter. At the time, Peter was in Joppa."

Pastor Marcus asks me to read a section from the Acts of the Apostles. While a cold-sweat forms, I notice everyone else has a Bible out, open, and ready to read. I rummage inside a nifty little backpack Avi gave us, shuffling stuff around, pretending there's something to locate.

Gerri hands me a book. "Here, honey, use this one."

"Thanks."

She smiles. "Anytime, sugar."

Gerri turns forward, and I notice she's older. Not old, but maybe a dozen years further along the life curve than I am, a smattering of gray in her tousled red hair.

I have no clue how to spot the passage—I've never bothered to learn much about the Bible. Instead, when I needed to find my way around the thing, I'd cheat by reading along with the person next to me or asking for a page number.

After a few seconds of fumbling, Gerri reaches over and gently flips the book open, whispering, "Big numbers are chapters. Little numbers are verses."

I glance down. There's a bold number ten staring out from the page and smaller numbers are sprinkled throughout the paragraphs.

I feel as bad, or worse, than I did when we landed in Tel Aviv, and though I enjoy reading, both silently and aloud, the last thing I want to do right now is recite words to a bunch of strangers. However, they're all waiting for me to start, so after clearing my throat, I read from the little one through to the little forty-eight before Pastor Marcus tells me to stop.

Turns out this Cornelius was a Roman Centurion, and he got a message from God to send for Peter. When Cornelius and Peter met, Peter relayed the story of Jesus, the Holy Spirit made an appearance, and everyone in Cornelius's house was converted.

After I finish, Pastor Marcus talks. "This is an important event, because the story of Jesus is brought to a non-Jew.

Peter's Jewish friends were definitely not happy when he preached the Good News to a group of Gentiles."

He gives us a few minutes to "reflect on and consider the word of God." With nothing else to do, I follow his suggestion. I read again and realize, if the story is true and Peter is real, he was here within my circle of vision.

I'm not expecting what happens next. My head clears and I feel better, experiencing a different good than I'm used to, a whole-body tranquility. The sensation stays barely long enough for me to notice before I feel lousy again.

I hand the Bible to Gerri. "Uh, here's your book back. Thanks."

"No, you keep it, darlin'. The book wasn't a loan but a gift."

"What will you use?"

"Oh, I brought another with me. See?" She shows me. "I always carry a spare in case there's a need."

I'm not going to try and understand why a person would haul two Bibles on a six-thousand-mile journey. After all, I can't remember the last time I opened my Bible. I'm not sure I could even find the thing anymore.

∞ ∞ ∞

Finally, we're headed to the hotel. Avi reviews logistics, including the meal plan—a buffet dinner, breakfast at each place we stay, and lunch on the road. I'm half listening, but do hear we need to be in the lobby, ready to go, at eight in the morning.

At the hotel, there's a carafe of lemon-flavored water. My body absorbs the liquid like one of those crusty sponges buried under the sink. While I finish off my fourth glass, I hear a clinking off to the right, along with the low murmur of conversation and soft music. Taking a peek, I recognize the mellow bronze lighting, and my mouth waters. A bar. *How will I drink without our little entourage knowing about it?*

"Hey, let's meet for a Happy Hour before dinner." I estimate the woman speaking is under thirty and definitely the youngest member of our group. She's got a long ponytail and her nametag says Addy.

Holy Rollers celebrate Happy Hour? While on a pilgrimage? Who knew?

Apparently they do, making me realize I don't know much about Holy Roller rules. Maybe the cult's not too bad after all. Plans are made to gather in fifteen minutes.

Should I join them? I preferred either secret or anonymous drinking, at least around people who know me. Unless, of course, I was with Sarah or the kids—I'd drink all I wanted in front of them. As I drag myself down the hallway, I figure, since I'm about a million miles from home and won't be associating with any of my new friends after the trip, I'm fine to indulge.

The minute I step through the door to my room, my worn-out body must know the initial travel part is over—fatigue fills my bones, nausea assaults my stomach, and every muscle starts to shake.

I have just enough presence of mind to notice Joseph, dressed in a fresh pink button-down shirt and jeans, organizing a pile of clothes on one of the beds.

He breaks into a broad smile, his white teeth illuminated against the dark of his beard. "Welcome, friend. I'm glad to be sharing a room with you."

I drop my bag and head into the bathroom, sit on the toilet lid, and fight the tremors, swallowing saliva to keep from getting sick. I use the mirror to study my pale, pasty skin, my chapped, quivering lips, and the dark caverns under my bloodshot eyes. The flight must have taken more out of me than I thought.

While what I need is a shower, I hear the quiet conversations from the bar and the sound of glasses hitting each other. My mouth waters, knowing relief will come with a cocktail, or two or three.

As I step out of the bathroom, Joseph is sitting on his bed, reading a magazine called *Fine Woodworking*. I give a nod, tell him where I'm going, and head out the door.

I'm the first one down and grab a stool, order a vodka on ice, and rest the glass against my forehead. As the first sip slides over my tongue, my muscles let go, and a long, satisfied breath escapes. The soothing has begun.

"Hey, there, pilgrim." Gerri, the Bible lady, and Addy, the ponytail woman, are waving to me. "C'mon over here, why don't you?"

Shifting in my stool to shield their line of sight, I empty my glass and join them in the lounge area. We order two red wines and another vodka and start chatting as Pastor Marcus and one of the married couples, who introduce themselves as Ruth and Jeb, roll in. Pastor Marcus is a beer man, while Ruth asks for white wine, and Jeb settles for a tonic and lime. We get to know each other.

Addy's an emergency room nurse, twenty-eight years old, and distressed there's no husband yet or, at the moment, any reasonable prospects. Gerri, a retired teacher, is Addy's godmother, and they take a trip together every couple of years. Ruth is enjoying her grandchildren after being a stay-at-home mom since her eldest, who is now thirty, was born. Jeb is a retired lawyer. We all know Pastor Marcus works at the church when he's not visiting the Holy Land. I tell them I'm in real estate, without offering any additional details.

The second drink is gone and I'm gauging how long to wait before ordering a third, when we decide to head for dinner. As we're standing to leave, I notice the nurse,

Addy, catch the eye of a tall, lanky guy whose nametag I can't see. After he quickly looks away, her mouth turns into a tiny smile. Her expression reminds me of the first time I saw Sarah, in the bookstore at Lehigh, as she picked out a hyper-organized notebook "system." My heart skips a beat. I shake my head and push the image away.

On the way out, I down a quick shot of vodka, settle my bill and arrange to have two Goldstar beers delivered to my room. Ten minutes later, I've got a steaming lamb meatball caressing my lips. The second before my incisors make contact, Pastor Marcus taps a fork against his glass and folds his hands. "Let us pray."

Uh-oh. As heads bow and eyes close, no one sees me shrug and lower the fork. I notice the married couple, Ruth and Jeb, holding hands.

Pastor Marcus says thanks for the food and the "privilege of seeing this special place." The meatball is headed back into my mouth when there's an insert from Jeb about walking with the Holy Spirit. I hope no one sees me roll my eyes. When Jeb's done, I chew the meat and silently add my gratitude for the bar and the essential sustenance it provides.

∞ ∞ ∞

As I return to the room, Joseph sits up and turns on the light. "How was the food, your first in Israel?"

I mumble a sentence about dinner being pretty good and disappear into the bathroom, eager for sleep. Between the overnight flight, the stop at Joppa, the vodka, and dinner, I'm done.

Joseph is waiting for me when I come out. "You're tired, my friend, aren't you?"

"Spent."

"Sit. Close your eyes. It is time to rest."

He's right. I need to sleep, but when my eyelids drop, everything inside me is still moving, racing around to get things done, trying to keep the factory going. I should have had more vodka.

There's a knock on the door. I groan, lifting myself off the bed, and am greeted by a room service guy with two bottles on a tray. "Your beers, sir."

I had forgotten about the Goldstars. Mumbling a thank you, I place one on the nightstand. The other is half empty before I'm back on the bed.

"Do you have a family, Ben?"

I swallow another mouthful. *Do I have a family?* I know I am the father of two children, and I love their mother. *Are we a family, though?* I offer a partial answer. "I have two kids."

"Is there a wife?"

"Technically, yes, but the marriage will probably end soon."

"I am sorry."

By now the bottle is empty, my neurons are slowing down, and since I'm starting to feel more social, I ask, "What about you, Joseph? Do you have a family?"

"I did. But they are gone from this world now."

As I'm twisting the cap off the second bottle, I struggle with what to say, but, thankfully, Joseph changes the subject.

"Ah, Goldstar. You enjoy the Israeli beer?"

"It gets the job done."

I tip the long neck, saluting him before taking another swallow.

Joseph keeps talking. "An interesting phrase. Gets the job done."

19

I mutter a swear under my breath. *Do I have to explain myself?* "It's a common expression."

"Suit yourself." Joseph stretches under the covers. "Time for me to rest, my friend. Good night."

He turns off the light and, from what I hear, is asleep before the bulb's out.

I stay propped against the headboard, in the dark, considering my choice of words. I remember, in college, after five cans of the cheapest brew available, we'd toast each other and say something along the lines of, "Yep, tastes like swamp water, but gets the job done!"

Honestly, I wasn't remembering my student days when I used the phrase with Joseph. I had reflexively responded to his comment because for me, at night before sleep, alcohol shuts down my system, holding back the invading armies as they pour over the wall and set up shop with whatever demons decide to visit once the noise of the day subsides.

I take my last pull of the Goldstar and start to drift off. *Who the heck is this Joseph guy?*

PROGRESS REPORT # 2

Peter,

Following the normal protocol, today was invested in foundational work. I managed to engage Our Man in a few moments of basic conversation and observed his daily habit. He employs a long-established routine, which on initial evaluation, explains his ability to function despite the depth of his earthly vice. I also observed his human vessel is resilient and capable of rapid recovery.

He engaged in the first substantial exchange with a subgroup of his traveling companions. For this encounter, I chose to utilize a time and environment where he is comfortable—in the lounge, immediately before the evening meal. This strategy proved effective and will be employed in future interactions.

From a spiritual perspective, we continued exposure to prayer, engaged him with the Word, and provided a copy of the Book. Most importantly, there was a brief but noticed visit from the Spirit. All are developments on which to build.

For tomorrow, the plan is simple—move to a full schedule and begin developing an overall approach.

I am, as always, a servant.

Joseph

DAY 3

It's 6:34 a.m., I'm wide awake and, after a shower and shave, don't feel half bad.

As I exit the bathroom, Joseph greets me dressed in another crisp button-down shirt, this one white. He's holding a steaming mug in his hand. "Good morning, my friend."

Why does he keep calling me friend?

"Are you drinking coffee?"

"Yes, I sure am." He nods to the room's electric tea kettle and packets of instant coffee. "The water's still hot." After I fill a mug and settle into an easy chair, Joseph adds, "I must say, you seem refreshed on this fine day."

I smile and toast him before taking a sip.

He's right to say I'm feeling rested. Having always been, undeniably, a morning person, all I need is a block of uninterrupted sleep, regardless of what happened in the shadows of the previous day. Of course, last night I only had five drinks, spacing them over a few hours, making travel lag the bigger threat.

I ask if he's going down to breakfast.

Joseph shakes his head, pointing to his suitcase. "No, I've brought along energy bars and nuts. I'll be sure to eat before we start the day's activities."

There's one reason the guy's fit. Not I-pump-iron-at-the-gym fit, but an honest fit, a man who uses his body to earn a living.

"Joseph, what do you do when you're not traveling to Israel?"

He scratches the bridge of his nose before responding. "A good question, my friend. What do I do? First and foremost, I delight in building tables, cabinets, and chairs." I again notice the copy of *Fine Woodworking*. "I also do various consulting jobs. Assignments designed to help people."

I'm curious. "What do you help them with?"

"Whatever they need. The organization I work for is excellent at getting to the core of a problem."

"What's the name of the company?"

"Ah, enough about work." Joseph springs from the bed. "We're on a trip. Let's enjoy. I'm planning to take a short walk, get some fresh air. When are you heading to breakfast?"

I check the clock on my nightstand. "I'd say fifteen minutes or so."

"Excellent. I'll see you on the bus."

After he leaves, I decide to check out Israeli TV. I scrounge around for the remote and plop down onto the bed, feeling the Bible from yesterday shift inside my backpack. I remember how the woman Gerri gave the book to me and I read about the Centurion. *What was his name? Cor something. Corbin? Corbett? No, not Cor but Corn. Cornell? Cornwall? Cornwallis? No, no, and no. Cornelius? Yep. Cornelius.*

Before I hit the power button, there's an involuntary urge, an itch, and I drop the remote onto the bed, move the backpack to the floor, and reach inside. *Really? Is this what I'm going to do?* Out comes the book.

I hunt through the pages, trying to locate the passage from Joppa, searching out the big numbers and the little numbers. I eventually get there—chapter ten in Acts of the Apostles. *How far did I go? Forty-five verses, maybe?* Close. I read forty-eight, all in a row, commencing at the beginning of the chapter. I spread the Bible open on my lap.

It starts as a half-hearted effort, and I'm skimming along, until near the end, a phrase slows me down. It's in a section bridging verses thirty-four and thirty-five. I study the words and say them aloud. "... God does not show favoritism but accepts men from every nation who fear him and do what is right." My finger moves to the last five words. "... and do what is right."

My shoulders fall. *Have I done what's right?* Absolutely not. In fact, I have no business asking the question. I'm a guy who once sat in the backyard, alone, stewed out of his mind, smoking a cigar instead of attending my five-year-old's dance recital. As my grandmother used to say, I behaved badly.

Regret simmers. My brain, in a matter of seconds, has turned my regret into guilt, my guilt into resentment, and my resentment into a simmering cauldron of anger. The thoughts don't surprise me—I'm used to this cognitive progression. On a normal day, however, the flow doesn't begin until later, allowing me time as a functioning adult.

My hands grip the edge of the Bible. *Seriously? Is this what I felt compelled to read? God won't accept me? Meaning what, exactly? Eternal damnation? Judgement from all the sanctimonious Holy Rollers?* I question whether there's a shunning in my future, if I will be banished by the elders, similar to an Amish teenager who watches TV or uses a cell phone.

I read the forty-eight verses again, focusing on the part where angels speak to Cornelius, followed by Peter having a bizarre hallucination. *Angels? Visions? Sure. Whatever. This tale belongs in a college Greek Lit seminar, including the classic Deus ex Machina.* I decide not to burn emotional energy worrying about a story I consider more supernatural than real, a faith-based myth.

I perk up, feeling good again, and head to breakfast.

∞ ∞ ∞

On the bus, Joseph and I sit in the back, grabbing the same two seats as yesterday. Before we get going, a woman I haven't seen before takes the microphone. Turns out she's from the US but now lives in Israel and, along with her husband, runs a congregation full of completed Jews. As she talks, I figure out this means Jewish people who believe Jesus is the Messiah. I didn't know you could do that.

She welcomes us to Israel and offers an eloquent prayer, first in Hebrew, then in English, expressing gratitude, asking for safe travels, and praying for peace.

As we pull away from the hotel, Avi greets us, saying "*boker tov,*" explaining it means "good morning" in Hebrew. He talks about Israel, breaking out the population of 8.5 million people into groups: 6.5 million are Jewish, about 1.8 million are Muslim, and the rest consist of Christians and members of the Druze religion.

Someone in the front shouts out a question. "What the heck is the Druze religion?"

Pastor Marcus stands to answer. "Druze beliefs are a hybrid of any number of religions. There are numerous theories about how the faith began. The Druze people have been persecuted relentlessly, although they are accepted here in Israel. They embrace the concept of God appearing to man and believe in reincarnation or the transmigration of the soul in continuous, successive cycles. At the end the soul is united with the Cosmic Mind."

Right. Glad we're all clear on the Druze thing.

Avi takes over again, running his hand along the map and explaining the country is three hundred and twenty miles long from top to bottom and seventy to eighty miles wide, and has been since the Six-Day War in 1967. According to Avi, precise dimensions depend on your stance concerning what actually constitutes the Israeli state, although he supports the most expansive interpretation. Regardless, for all the news this place generates, Israel's not particularly big.

Our first stop is a place called Caesarea Maritima, a seaport nestled against the Mediterranean. The deep blue water, contrasted against the sand, stone, and occasional patch of grass, creates a striking visual which, along with the pleasant ocean breezes, makes me want to develop a bunch of townhouses and upscale retail here. I could make a killing.

Avi gives us a quick overview, first pointing out a series of aqueducts, the system the Romans used to collect water, and an old stadium called a hippodrome. This was a place for chariot races, gladiator fights, animal shows and, at least in my imagination, sacrificing people to lions. He finishes with, "This is an ancient city, built over the ten-year period from 32 BC to 22 BC. Herod the Great had a summer palace here."

He points to a collection of ruins overlooking the Mediterranean. Even in ancient times, the rich preferred waterfront property.

We walk over to an outdoor theater which has ascending rows of benches forming a semi-circle in front of a large stage. The place is made of, I'm guessing, limestone, and everything is the color interior decorators call "greige." We climb, settling into the "nosebleed" seats.

Avi points out a couple of rows near the front with slightly different coloring than the rest. He tells us these are original benches, and they existed at the time the theater was used. The others have been reconstructed based on archaeological studies.

Singing drifts up from below and I turn facing the stage and spot a group of about twenty people, all dressed in black and all wearing hats, the men in fedoras, the women in those fancy wide brimmed ones ladies used to wear to church. A man stands in front of them, dressed the same except for a white shirt, directing. The words are in a foreign language, but, thanks to my half-hearted participation in the church choir, the tune is familiar. They're singing "How Great Thou Art," and I notice two things—they're good and the acoustics are fantastic. No one would have needed a microphone in Herod's day.

Pastor Marcus, who is next to me, comments, "They can't do this at home."

"Do what?"

"Sing in public, proclaiming their faith in Jesus. Those folks are a group from China. There're a growing number of Christians there, but they have to be careful."

I reexamine the little choir, noticing for the first time they're Asian, and ask, "Careful about what?"

"Being fully transparent, moving outside of Communist Party guidelines for worship."

"So they came here?"

"Yep. They came here. Lots of Chinese Christians do. Primarily, for two reasons. First, they get baptized in the Jordan River and openly declare their faith. An option, by the way, we're going to offer later in the week if you're interested." *For the record, I'm not.* "Secondly, they're allowed to honor God with as much joy as they want. Their enthusiasm is impressive, don't you think?"

I have to agree. Their faces jump with excitement, and the guy conducting could easily be standing in front of a group at Carnegie Hall. *The energy is springing from the ends of his fingers, his entire body drawing power from every voice. Where does his passion come from?*

After the song ends, the tune is stuck in my head. *Great, I'm walking around Israel with an ear worm.*

Avi leads us to a spot near the stage, and we each personally test out the acoustics. Pastor Marcus explains the Apostle Paul was imprisoned in Caesarea, where he gave a passionate testimony about Jesus during his trial. He references the biblical account beginning in Acts chapter twenty-three.

While I don't know the story, let alone anything about chapter twenty-three of the Acts book, I do know about Paul. I remember Sunday school and pictures depicting him being knocked to the ground, blinded, and, afterward, following Jesus, which was not a good strategy for a Jewish leader. Of course, those were the days when I was still trying at church, before I started drinking. Boyhood heroes tend to stay with you.

Avi takes over. "We don't know the exact place Paul spoke from. Possibly, he preached here in this very theater."

There was a time I would have been jumping up and down, testing the sound, searching for the exact spot, but I'm not a boy anymore. There's no need to chase down a fairytale.

∞ ∞ ∞

As we head across to see the remains of Herod's palace, Avi gathers us in a circle around a white stone. "This is called the Pilate Stone. It was discovered back in 1961 by Italian archaeologists who were excavating the site of the theater."

The woman Ruth—I remember her from the Happy Hour group—kneels and traces the letters on the stone. "What do these words say?"

Pastor Marcus squats next to Ruth. "They're a dedication to Augustus, and the stone was probably placed in a temple in honor of the Roman Emperor Tiberius. Augustus was his stepfather. Which is all well and good, but this stone is important because it specifically states Pontius Pilate was the prefect of Judea. Which ..."

"... proves Pilate actually existed." Ruth finishes the sentence.

Pastor Marcus claps his hands. "Exactly. The actual stone—this is a plaster replica—is kept in the Israeli museum in Jerusalem. The original limestone dated back to the first century."

As the group moves on, I sit on my heels, pretending to read the worn-out Latin letters. *Does this mean there are historical records, information outside the Bible, verifying these people existed?*

∞ ∞ ∞

The desert's rolling by the window, and I'm dwelling on Peter and Paul. I've only been in the country twenty-four hours, and we've already visited places where I'm told they actually walked and spoke. I've seen Pontius Pilate's name on a stone. The people around me are downright giddy about what they're seeing. I have a tiny sense there's something genuine behind the stories.

My thoughts stop there. I'm not exactly sure why, but Avi's talking about a man back in ancient times who got lost in the desert and died from diarrhea. This makes sense to me, especially when you take into account primitive medical practices. There's also the absence of ready water supplies, and no technology available to get help. The result was the guy emptied himself until he died.

Tapping my forehead with a closed fist, I realize I did the same thing—sent my whole life down the toilet. Which means I shouldn't care if there's any truth behind all this Bible stuff or not. I've traveled down a path far removed from the main road, so far away there's no benefit to me investing in this trip. Even if he's there, God couldn't possibly have room for me. The door's been shut.

The itch starts. *I want a drink.*

∞ ∞ ∞

Our next stop is Mount Carmel, which Avi explains is about eighteen hundred feet above sea level and made primarily of limestone. This last fact is not a surprise. Based on my observations, the whole country consists of limestone formations, man-made limestone structures, or limestone ground into sand, all baking in an open oven.

As we move onto a large concrete platform, Pastor Marcus gives us the historical background. "Mount Carmel was significant in Old Testament times. A hugely important place. Below us is the beautiful and enormous Jezreel Valley, the site of twenty-one Old Testament battles. Interestingly, at the turn of the twentieth century, it was a swamp. There are old pictures of water buffalo lying in marshes."

One of our group members, his name tag says Caleb, steps forward. "In the early 1920s the Jews in Israel began buying the land and planting Eucalyptus trees, which helped drain the swamp. Then along came intricate irrigation systems. Take a look, my fellow travelers. These are superior farmlands, among the most productive in the world, a shining example of how the Jewish people created prosperity out of nothing."

I peer over the edge and agree the place appears fertile. There's plenty of cultivated land with lots of green surrounding the roads, jagged rocks, and buildings.

As I pull myself back, I figure there's no way we're getting away from here without a Bible lesson. Turns out I'm right. Avi asks Addy, the nurse with the ponytail, to read. She goes through a long story about the prophet Elijah challenging the prophets of another god, Baal, right here on Mount Carmel. Elijah has the Baal prophets kill a bull, cut up the carcass as a sacrifice, and put the bull on an altar. They call on Baal to light a fire and burn the meat. Of course, nothing happens. Elijah does the same, using a different bull, only he douses the animal in water three times before calling on the God of Abraham. As you would expect, fire descends from heaven. Case closed on Baal.

The same guy, Caleb, is animated when Addy stops reading. "Those events happened here! On this mountain! One of the stories proving our God is *the* God, the only God."

As the group wanders off to take pictures, I notice Caleb sit down to read his Bible, which is unexpected given the image he projects. With the camera hanging around his neck, mesh baseball hat, baggy pants, New Balance sneakers, short sleeve T-shirt, and one of those vests covered in pockets, you'd consider him the typical snap a picture, read a plaque, get a snack tourist.

I stroll out to the main courtyard and, after studying a large white statue of Elijah, walk around the whole place again, contemplating what Addy read. I'm not sure why, but I don't instantly dismiss the story as a tall tale.

There's no chance to figure out why I'm intrigued. Pastor Marcus calls us and we load onto the bus. Lunch time.

∞ ∞ ∞

We stop at the Israeli version of a diner, which means no waitress and a cafeteria line, putting the order together as you move along. In line, Addy is talking with the same gangly guy she spotted in the bar last night. They're discussing types of food and personal favorites, and she gives a small chuckle after he makes a joke.

I get lamb and a bunch of Middle Eastern fixins' wrapped in a pita and sit at one of the wood veneer tables, joining Ruth, her husband Jeb, Caleb, and the tall lanky guy who was in line with Addy. I'm next to Jeb, who's having a conversation with Caleb.

"I've waited over forty years to come back," says Caleb.

"Back?" responds Jeb.

"Yep. Lived here until I was thirteen."

"Wow. What're you hoping to get out of this?"

I don't want to intrude on their conversation and turn to my left, toward gangly guy. After a handshake and a few pleasantries, I learn his name is Daniel and discover he's an IT architect at a bank.

When I ask him the bank's name, he shakes his head. "No work discussion for me right now. I'm ruminating on this morning."

I'm hesitant, but decide to engage. "What did you think?"

Daniel chews his pita bread, scratching the scruff on his chin. After the food is swallowed, he responds. "This morning was clarifying."

"Clarifying?"

"Yes. I spend substantial time in the Book"—he's holding a Bible—"trying to discern."

"Discern?"

"Yes, I believe life is about the discovery of purpose."

"What we did this morning ... uh ... clarified your purpose?"

"No. No. Nothing so monumental." He takes another bite, and starts talking around the food in his mouth. "When I say clarifying, I mean this morning put a picture to what I've read in the Book. I should add, I'm also including yesterday at Joppa. Being physically placed in a biblical setting is helpful. Similar to high-definition television."

I guess he's done talking, because he shifts his gaze forward again and concentrates on the food.

We've got an earnest one here. I glance around at the crowd and absorb the mall-food-court volume level. Around my table, everyone's involved in their own side discussions so I decide to reengage with Daniel. Unfortunately, his Bible's open and he's moving a finger across a paragraph while he chews.

I'm alone with my food which, I should add, is excellent.

Ruth, who is sitting directly across the table, breaks from her conversation and makes eye contact. "Tell me, Ben, what do you do back home?"

Uh-oh. That's a tricky answer. The way I see it, there are three options.

I could describe how I construct a façade of normalcy, competence, and good community citizenship, working tirelessly to deceive, hoping to make people believe I'm anything other than what I am. I label this the Overall Psychological Evaluation, although it's probably a tad early in our relationship to share my amateur conceptual theories.

A second choice is to explain how I do my best but sometimes need help dealing with life and, occasionally, will use alcohol to take the edge off. I label this one The

Small Reveal. It's also a load of garbage and, I'm sure, would lead to more questions.

A third alternative is to be candid and admit how, while there are other things in life, I've made alcohol consumption the sun at the center of my universe. This would require explaining how, in order to feed my habit, I go to rehab without any intention of making a serious effort, destroy my family, mislead work colleagues, and toil relentlessly to give away all the good in my life. I label this one The Real Answer, knowing I'll never divulge it out loud, and certainly not to anyone else.

Instead, I keep it simple. "Commercial Real Estate."

Caleb interjects. "Development?"

"Uh, yeah."

"Interesting line of work."

I nod.

"How'd you end up with our merry little band?" he asks.

"My brother ... he knows Pastor Marcus ... and, after a few calls, here I am."

Caleb presses. "What made you want to come?"

Is because I had no place to live a good answer? Ah, no. "The timing ... was right."

"Enjoying the trip?"

I use my standard response when I don't want to answer a question. "So far, so good."

Jeb takes his turn. "You work for a real estate company or are you in business for yourself?"

"Right now, neither. I'm kinda between jobs."

After the table goes silent for a minute, Caleb tries to get the conversation going again. "You have a family, Ben?"

Oh, man.

Ruth comes to my rescue. "Maybe we should leave poor Ben here alone. It's early in the day for the Grand

Inquisition." Her kindhearted tone, combined with her reaching across the table and gently squeezing my hand, has my blood pressure falling. "I'm glad you're with us Ben. I'm happy to be sharing this trip with you."

∞ ∞ ∞

Our first stop after lunch is at a place called Megiddo, a bunch of ruins sitting on top of a high hill. After we look around for a while, Avi pulls us together to provide background. "This is not a natural hill but one of our Tells."

I don't know what he means by the word Tell, but I don't want to look ignorant and nod along.

"This is a place archaeologists love to study and will be visiting for years." Avi opens his hands, directing our eyes to the ground. "Under our feet are the remains of twenty-six settlements."

"Why so many?" asks Ruth.

Avi explains, "This is a critical location, guarding a pass through the Carmel mountains, part of the famous *Via Maris* trade route."

"The Way of the Sea," says Daniel.

"Huh?" I ask.

"The Way of the Sea is what *Via Maris* means."

Avi overhears Daniel and nods before continuing. "Dating back to the Bronze Age, the *Via Maris* connected Egypt to the Northern Empires, countries such as Mesopotamia, Syria, and Anatolia. Because of its strategic importance, numerous battles were fought here. Perhaps more than any other site on earth."

He adds more about the place, telling us the peak of activity here was during King Solomon's reign in the tenth century.

Marcus herds us to the edge of the ruins. "This whole area you see below and in front of us is the Jezreel Valley. We looked down on the same valley earlier at Mount Carmel. According to the Book of Revelation, this is the supposed site for one of the final battles, if not THE final battle."

Final battles? Does he mean the end of the world? As Marcus continues on, I conclude his definition of final battle is the Big One, Armageddon. I study the beautiful landscape in front of me, wishing the flames and fury and smoke and destruction could happen right now, creating an expedient escape from what I've become.

∞ ∞ ∞

By three p.m., we're in Nazareth. What I'm seeing is inconsistent with my preconception of Jesus's hometown. Multi-story buildings, some old, some new, push against the sidewalks and funnel the crowds snaking along beside the jammed streets. People are wearing everything from long robes to casual clothing to full business attire.

Avi leads us to a building nestled in the middle of a city block. Climbing to the second floor, we enter a modern visitor's center, complete with scheduled tours, gift shops, and a rack overflowing with brochures. Again, not what I was expecting.

After a short wait, they lead us to watch a movie and meet our tour guide, who provides basic information on Nazareth. The population was probably four to five hundred people in Jesus's time and is roughly eighty thousand today, a mixture of Muslims, Christians, and Jews.

Outside, there's a replica of New Testament-era Nazareth. We walk along a dusty path between a collection of scraggly olive trees which look a billion years old. We press through the heat, stopping to interact with historical interpreters.

The first, with his full-length robe, staff, and standard shepherd head covering, perfectly fills the role. We also see a wine press unearthed during a 1996 archaeological dig, a replica of Jesus's tomb, and an olive press. Our guide explains the different types of olive oil and their uses, from cooking to perfumes to soaps to lamp oil.

When we get to the carpentry shop, things pick up. The white-robed interpreter is banging away using a wooden mallet and gives us all a big smile before he starts showing us the various tools, demonstrating how they work. He's got a saw, a hatchet, chisels, and instruments used to sand down wood. While they're unrefined and clearly hand-made, I'm amazed at how the basic design hasn't changed over the years. The exception is the drill, which is a small bow with a string attached. The bit is secured in the string, penetrating the wood as the bow is manually moved back and forth. A guy from another group volunteers to try. He's pretty good.

Joseph's next to me. This is the first time I've noticed him off the bus, except in the room at night, and as he's watching all of this, his eyes are alive, dancing. His hands are moving in sync with the interpreter, directing the tools.

Whenever the carpenter guy isn't talking, the guide provides a running narrative, explaining how carpenters in ancient Nazareth would swing this, lift that, cut by hand, and gather their own wood. He describes a physically demanding job.

"Our Savior was one buff dude!" After Caleb is rewarded with a laugh, he keeps going, "Yes, sir! I don't presume there was much need for a gym membership."

The guide restores order with a sweeping gesture, telling us we're standing in a courtyard designed to be a workspace. Behind the courtyard are replicas of the living areas which include the original rooms plus others added after sons reached adulthood.

Gerri murmurs. "My Father's house has many rooms." She sees me glance over and explains. "The Gospel of John, chapter fourteen, verse two. His daddy adding onto the house is probably not what Jesus had in mind, but, gosh all, the verse seems to apply right here and right now."

We start walking, and when I respond, I try to make it sound as if I'm half joking. "Have to be a pretty big house to fit the likes of me in there."

"Oh, don't fret, sweetie. There's a room for everyone. Your role is to accept the gift."

I don't know what she means and am not interested in delving much deeper.

We're in another outdoor courtyard, a place where raw wool is spun, stretched, and braided. The guide is providing more detail, but instead of listening, I'm watching the interpreter. Her name is Hannah, and she's sitting—wrapped in a band of sunlight sneaking under the wooden roof above her loom. The sun's glow illuminates her tanned face, exposing a lifetime of wrinkles, while she tenderly works the fabric.

After the guide is done explaining what Hannah is doing, the old lady stands, smooths the creases out of her gray robe, adjusts the purple head covering, and speaks to us. Avi translates. "Thank you for coming to see me today. I am privileged to share time with our visitors from around the world. This is my eighty-third year. My life has been a joyous ride doing my best to serve our Savior. I pray each of you are able to say the same. Blessings and peace. Someday, I will see you all again in heaven."

This isn't the first time I've heard people claim they'll find their way to paradise, and without exception, they make me scoff. To confidently state you'll cross through the gates is, if I'm being charitable, overconfident, and, if I'm being candid, the pinnacle of arrogance. This woman Hannah, though, makes her comment without a hint of pride or boastfulness. She simply ... knows. *Is this a glimpse at real faith?*

Our final stop is a full-sized replica of a first-century synagogue. The reproduction was built based on archaeological digs, primarily one in Magdala, and has a rectangular shape with three levels of stone benches along the walls, each joining with the white pillars supporting a thick log roof. At the front, there's a small table with a parchment resting on top.

Avi explains the typical service. There were seven readings, recited from scrolls which were stored in earthenware pots. He points to a few pots surrounding a nearby pillar and finishes by telling us only men were allowed to do the reading and attend the service.

"Figures."

Gerri claps her hands at Addy's comment and half shouts her agreement. "Amen, sister!"

Pastor Marcus asks if any of us know the story about Jesus preaching at the synagogue in Nazareth. I have a vague memory, something about Jesus speaking at his hometown church and getting chased away, although I can't remember why.

He passes his Bible to Ruth and asks her to read Luke, chapter four, verses fourteen to twenty-eight. When she's done, he invites a volunteer to interpret.

Gerri's hand shoots through the sleeve of her bright red paisley shirt. "The way this registers with me is Jesus came on home and read a prophecy from the Book of Isaiah about the coming Messiah. Afterward he said, 'here I am,' and they all threw a hissy fit and tried to toss him over a cliff. I'm thinking they couldn't accept this person, the little kid from down the street, had grown up and become all that. I get where they were coming from. One of my old students went to school at Yale. I told my principal I could remember him eating glue and keeping the messiest desk on God's Green Acre. I sure understand Luke's line where folks ask, 'Isn't this Joseph's son?'"

I notice Joseph, my roommate, listening. While his face is expressionless, his jaw muscles are working and his teeth are grinding away. No one else hears what he says. "Such a shame. To have the prize and not know."

$$\infty \quad \infty \quad \infty$$

Mercifully, the day's touring is over. While everyone is showing signs of wear, the fatigue level doesn't quell the enthusiasm for Happy Hour.

For me, this is good news. I'm at the time of day when the urges become obstinate, turning into relentless cravings. On certain days, and this is one of them, my hands have a mild tremor.

Everyone agrees to take a half-hour break before heading down for "appropriate Israeli adult beverages," as Caleb describes them. I'm in the bar in ten minutes, get a vodka on ice, and arrange an after-dinner beer delivery. Before the bartender has the order completely written down, I'm asking for my second vodka.

Addy comes in carrying a book, waving as she greets me. "Oh, hey, there. What a day, huh? Boy, this place is hot. I had to take a shower."

I smile and notice she's wearing a fresh pair of jeans, a simple blue T-shirt, hair tied in a loose ponytail, and Converse sneakers.

"I was going to have a glass of wine and read. Company is always good, though. Okay if I join you?"

I nod to the seat, order another drink and tell the bartender to add hers to my tab. As she climbs onto the chair, the book drops with a thud and I blurt out a reaction. "Jes—oh, sorry, wow, good thing you're reading a paperback. If not, a chunk of the bar would have fallen off."

The book is *The Source* by James Michener. I remember reading a few of his long, epic stories when I was younger.

"Yeah, this is a big one." Addy's smoothing down a crease on the cover. "I read a ton and tend to choose books set in places I've been or where I'm going. This one takes place here."

"Here? You mean in Israel?"

"Yep. It's about this archaeological dig through a Tell. As they discover artifacts, he writes a fictional chapter about each layer's time in history."

As she takes a sip of red wine, I remember Avi mentioning a Tell earlier in the day and not being sure what he was talking about. After swallowing half my vodka, I figure I should find out. "A Tell?"

"One of those artificial hills. We saw one at Megiddo. Actually, they're all over the place."

"Who makes the hill?"

"No one makes them. They're formed as people living in a place build and rebuild on the same spot over a long time. Around here, they're probably thousands of years old."

A few other folks are starting to trickle in. I toss back the rest of my vodka, and we join them at a table. Everyone orders drinks except for Jeb, who's having ginger ale.

When someone points to the book, Addy repeats her explanation, adding more flavor about the characters and plot.

Caleb, who apparently intends to spend every minute in the same travel vest with all the pockets, interjects. "I learned about Tells as a kid. They're tricky to work with. You've got layer upon layer, tons of sediment and trash and junk, all piled up over time, needing to be peeled away without hurting what's underneath."

Ruth is curious. "Is the peeling a delicate process? I've seen scientists dusting off dinosaur bones with a toothbrush."

"Sometimes, yes. Other times they dig down quickly, though, and uncover what's there, before figuring out the next steps."

"How do they choose an approach?"

Caleb shrugs. "I knew back in the day, but I can't remember. I guess they do an analysis of the area to figure out what's gonna work. Either way, they know how to get past the sediment and waste to the good stuff."

He stands and increases the decibels. "C'mon, people. Let's get us some good Israeli food."

∞ ∞ ∞

When I'm back in the room after dinner, the two beers are reliably delivered, representing my fifth and sixth drinks of the evening.

Joseph checks in with me. "What are your perceptions of today, my friend?"

What are my perceptions of the day? "We covered lots of ground, and I learned about Israel's past. Saw a group of Chinese pilgrims sing. Met a few people in the group. Got my system back on track after the travel."

"Ah, but this is the Holy Land, there must be more for you to say."

I empty the last beer before I respond. "I'm not sure there is. I don't believe, at least in any real sense. This is more of a historical trip for me."

He shakes his head. "You do, you know."

"I do, what?"

"Believe."

"Based on?"

"My friend, I don't know how you found your way here, but you would not have come otherwise. Whether they know why or not, people visit here for a reason."

"I'm here because I had no other options."

He turns off his light and rolls onto his side, offering one more observation before he's done for the day. "Ahh, as men our age know, there is always a choice. However, if you believe you didn't have one, I will not argue the point. Suit yourself."

Reaching over, I turn off my light and sneak to my luggage, taking out one of the bottles of vodka purchased on the airplane, leaving me two others for an emergency.

In the tick of a clock, the vodka's gone.

The only sound is Joseph's steady breathing. He's wrong. I don't believe, and if I did, I wouldn't. Because if I believed, I'm conceding there's something beyond me, something able to penetrate my carefully constructed and regularly reinforced shell. The shell, which at the moment is fortified by seven drinks, allowing me to endure what I am and, to a limited extent, bolster my self-image. When I'm sitting alone in the dark, marinated in vodka and beer, I'm almost convinced I'm able to handle my own problems.

PROGRESS REPORT # 3

Peter,

Today we followed a fast-paced itinerary, introducing a wide range of variables. As in all of these cases, we're never sure what strategy will best advance our objective. To narrow our options, we exposed Our Man to legitimate historical evidence generated from the secular realm, the concept of our Father having room for all, the faith of persecuted followers, accepting the Gift, and, of course, the Angel Hannah.

Our Man did experience minor episodes of acceptance. Perhaps acceptance is too strong a word. These moments would be better described as isolated instances of reduced cynicism. While they were short-lived, they could prove useful later in the process.

At the risk of being repetitive, I again urge caution concerning our timeline. We are working with a deeply despondent individual who dislikes himself immensely. The spiritual war rages hot and is overwhelmingly one-sided. I see him as a long way out.

At the end of the day, I planted a few ideas regarding participating in this excursion. We all know he could have, if motivated enough, pursued other options.

Tomorrow will involve more of the same. I do, however, hope he will spend time in the Book.

With the Spirit in my heart,
Joseph

DAY 4

As another day begins, Joseph and I are still sitting in the back, five empty rows behind the others, but a few people stop by to say hi. I don't hate it.

Pastor Marcus says a prayer. I hear the usual white noise until he finishes with "... and, Lord, if you want this day to change us in any way, please remind us change comes from the inside out."

I rewind to last night, skulking around the room, pulling out hidden bottles of liquor, and remember a poster outside the college chaplain's office. To be clear, I never visited the chaplain, but his office was on the way to a sitting area with big couches and comfortable chairs, a good spot to sneak a few drinks while I did my work.

The poster had a picture of a bearded guy with the quote, *"Character is what a man is in the dark,"* printed over the name Dwight L. Moody. At one point, I learned he was a famous religious leader back in the 1800s.

When I grunt and shake my head, Joseph responds. "What, my friend?"

"Huh? Oh, nothing."

"Suit yourself."

It's not nothing. I'm watching a slideshow, little images flashing back to last night and all the other dark places in my life, pictures I don't want to see, but I do. They're in the place Pastor Marcus, in his prayer, says needs to change first.

I face Joseph. "Maybe there's something." He turns and leans in. Our heads are close enough I can smell his breath. Peppermint. I'm pretty sure mine is coffee and eggs, but as I ask my question, he doesn't seem bothered. "What Pastor Marcus said. Is change, you know, from the inside out, possible?

"Of course, my friend. Anything you truly desire is possible."

I'm self-aware enough to know my behaviors are ingrained habits, developed over years of practice. To paraphrase a time-worn cliché, I'm too far along to learn any new tricks, and in reality, I don't want to anyway. I'm wishing I could rewind twenty seconds and not ask the question. Joseph's body language, however, clearly indicates he's expecting me to continue. I keep my response as simple as possible. "Not with me. I can't change my insides."

He moves closer. "Why not?"

A truthful answer would be along the lines of *I've created a person I hate, supported by a lifestyle I refuse to abandon.* However, I'm not feeling honest, and I barely know this guy. Instead, I try to get away with a boilerplate reply. "I mean, you know, at my age, life's too far along to make any fundamental changes."

Joseph shakes his head. "Ahhhh, my friend, we cannot be defeatist. Close your eyes." I comply. "Now, take in a deep breath and slowly let the air out." After I follow his instructions, he states, "For as long as you inhale and exhale, change is possible."

When I open my eyes again, he's reading a magazine. I silently ride along, wondering if he's right.

After Avi outlines our itinerary for the day, Caleb booms out his opinion. "We're getting serious now, folks!"

As the bus rolls along next to the Sea of Galilee, Avi tells us the Sea's thirteen miles long and, at the widest point, about eight miles across. "Back in the first days of Israel, the Sea, which is actually a freshwater lake, was the only water source."

"The lake's harp-shaped, you know." I jump at the voice, which belongs to the lanky guy, Daniel. He must have moved into the seat across the row while Joseph and I were talking.

"Harp-shaped?" I ask.

"Yes. Certain scholars say the lake's Hebrew name, Kinneret, is derived from the Hebrew word for harp, *kinnor*. Actually, I'm being too precise. A *kinnor* is an ancient instrument resembling a harp and is mentioned forty-two times in the Old Testament." His cadence is deliberate, something I also noticed during yesterday's lunch. "Of course, there are other scholars who view the connection as a myth."

Now there's more than I'd ever need on the all-important lake/harp/kinnor discussion.

A minute passes before Daniel changes the topic. "What are you all about, Ben?"

I look at his face, noticing the two-day stubble of dark brown beard. His T-shirt, resting untucked over a pair of worn jeans, bears the emblem of a Christian summer camp with a Bible passage printed underneath. I'm struggling with how to respond. "Uh ... yeah ... I don't know. I'm about all kinds of stuff."

He continues. "You sit back here—away from the crowd. You're not a rude man, not at all, but you don't say much either. When we make our stops, you're interested but not,

I don't know, enthusiastic. Overall, I'd characterize you as a minor enigma."

Does he study everyone else this much?

"When we get done today," he continues, "let's meet for a pre-Happy Hour. We'll get to know each other. I'd be happy to buy you a drink or two."

Not bad. Now I'm getting free drinks from one of the Holy Rollers. A development I never would have predicted.

∞ ∞ ∞

The first stop is Capernaum and we file in through a white wrought-iron gate, past a sign reading: "WELCOME TO CAPHARNAUM, THE TOWN OF JESUS."

Avi pulls us together, and I listen to him while admiring the trees, stone walkways, and the Sea of Galilee's deep blue water. "This was Jesus's base over the last eighteen to twenty months of his life. He performed more miracles here than anywhere. Capernaum is where he called four fishermen, James, John, Peter, and Andrew, to join him and become 'fishers of men.' Another disciple, Matthew, was a local tax collector."

Caleb's voice booms. "Yet the local people didn't repent. They saw the man, walked with him, witnessed miracles. Still, in the end, most of them didn't get with the program."

"And you, Capernaum, will you be lifted up to the skies? No, you will go down to the depths." Gerri, who I've nicknamed the Bible Lady, delivers the words softly, before adding, "The Book of Matthew, chapter eleven, verse twenty-three."

There's no book open in front of her. *Wow.*

Avi takes us to the ruins of a synagogue the Romans built for the Jews. I observe more space, taller columns, and higher quality building materials than the church in Nazareth. Definitely what you'd expect from the Romans, given their wealth and extravagant style.

Pastor Marcus explains what we're seeing. "This is two synagogues, one built on top of another. The new synagogue is made of limestone and the older one black basalt. The darker stones make up the foundation for the newer structure."

"Hmm. A good way to describe Christianity."

The guy next to me is Ruth's husband, Jeb. I give him a once over. He's tall, over six feet, with thinning hair and a tangle of broken blood vessels on his cheeks.

My response isn't exactly profound. "Huh?"

He tries to smooth the wrinkles from his untucked cotton golf shirt, which is draped over a modest belly. "I see Christianity as building a new life on top of an old one."

Now there's an unsolicited piece of information, and based on my quick analysis, I'm not sure how he's connecting a couple of Jewish temples with being a Christian. I'm beginning to believe these people will reason their way to any conclusion they want.

We move on to an oddly shaped building, a pentagon type structure with floor-to-ceiling windows resting on big concrete supports and hovering over the archaeological ruins. I theorize an alien spacecraft landed and decided to stay. Avi tells us the building is a Roman Catholic church, explaining there's a large glass pane built into the floor, enabling a person to look down into Peter's house.

The actual house is imbedded in an expanse of ruins stretching across the flat ground. I study Peter's dwelling, which blends in with the surrounding neighborhood, trying to get the gist of what I'm seeing—stone walls weaving here and there, following no apparent design, producing a maze leading to a round room.

The layout must make more sense to Gerri and tears glisten in her eyes. "He was here," her words are a silk scarf drifting to the floor, "my Savior was right here. At this very spot." I know she means Jesus. "He probably used this house as an escape, to get away from the swarm of folks followin' him around and to rest from all the miracles he did in this town. Heck, he cured Peter's mother-in-law of a fever."

I figure I should say something. "We know he cured her?"

"Sure do. The story's right there in Luke, chapter four. Of course, the story's in Mark one and Matthew eight too, but I prefer the Luke version. He says Jesus 'rebuked the fever.' I'm partial to the word rebuked."

I have to ask. "How do you know so much about the Bible?"

"Oh, darlin', the Bible or books written to help me study the Bible are about all I read. Oh, I've spent time with those Mitford stories and the Francine Rivers novels, dabbled with Karen Kingsbury. I'm fond of them all and one of my good friends swears by 'em. Ever since I was a girl, though, all I've ever wanted to read was the Good Book."

Who are these people?

We're awarded free time which most people are using to go inside the church, stand over the glass floor, and get a bird's-eye view of Peter's house.

I ramble around, first checking out a big bronze depiction of Peter. He's holding a staff in one hand, a large medallion in the other, with a fish resting at his feet. His face is surrounded by bushy hair connected to a magnificent beard, projecting confidence and triumph. This guy's ready to lead the fight. The statue reminds me of those paintings from the Middle Ages, where all the faith heroes seem way too put together.

Out of the corner of my eye, I spot the tall guy, Daniel, and the nurse, Addy, sitting on a park bench leafing through their Bibles, pointing towards Peter's house. She motions towards the Bible passage on his T-shirt, and, I'm guessing, asks a question. He nods vigorously, turns a page, points at the words and, with the help of deliberate hand gestures, provides what I assume is an explanation. Satisfied, she bounces to her feet, joining Gerri as she heads into the church. Daniel, for his part, follows her with his eyes. I want to tell him reading the Bible together isn't the most effective way to attract a girl and recommend he buy her a cup of coffee or a glass of wine. Then again, these are Holy Rollers. I'm not versed in their mating rituals.

I shrug and turn the corner, finding a spot with grass and trees abutting the Sea of Galilee. There's a breeze coming off the water—a good place to get away from the heat and avoid the people poking around the ruins.

Settling onto a flat rock, I watch the water gently rolling to shore. This woman, Gerri, intrigues me. She's made what she calls the Good Book her life's work, an endeavor I can't begin to imagine.

Without giving my surroundings much thought, I take out my Bible, and after tracing the gold letters with my fingertips, randomly turn to a section called "A Roman Centurion Demonstrates Faith." I see a big number eight, little number five, and the name Matthew across the top margin.

I decide to read.

In the story, the soldier had a sick servant and asked Jesus to heal him while at the same time saying he wasn't worthy to have Jesus enter his house. Jesus remarked he'd never seen a greater faith and declared the servant healed, and at little number thirteen, Matthew confirmed he was.

The book rests on my knees. *Is this true?* I remember, from my history classes, the Romans ruled Israel and there were definitely centurions here. As you would expect, the Jews hated the occupation. Could this person, a Roman soldier, have actually existed and become a follower of Jesus? For argument's sake, I assume he did.

He'd have a lifelong base of beliefs and prejudices with no Jewish faith to frame what he was seeing and hearing. Despite this background, he believed in Jesus. Earlier Jeb compared Christianity to building a new life on top of an old one. *Is such a thing possible?*

The leaves rustle. Along with the warm Capernaum air, I inhale a rush of "good," an optimism, a buzz without the booze fog. The sensation, which is the same feeling I had in Joppa, stays for a moment, before riding out on a flood of thoughts.

The centurion, whether fictional or real, was probably a decent man, living a good life, who happened to be on the wrong team. Signing him up probably didn't take much effort. Me? Any sincere change would be more difficult than turning a tractor trailer around on a packed city street. I am, after all, the guy who, while my new wife slept, snuck down to the hotel bar on our wedding night. The one who, an hour later, stumbled back upstairs drunk and threw up because a bar patron, upon discovering I was celebrating my wedding day, insisted on buying me the best Irish Whiskey in the house. I hate Irish Whiskey and Irish Whiskey hates me, but I accepted his hospitality.

Yeah, as far as I'm concerned, this new life concept is a fairy tale.

I head to the bus and bump into Gerri, who is exiting the gate at the same time. "I saw you sittin' over there. Contemplation time?"

I'm not sure why, but I don't deflect my answer. "I read for a little bit in the Bible you gave me."

I tell her about the passage and she reacts with "Mmm. I love that one." Her comment means nothing to me because, in my experience, Gerri loves everything in the Bible. "Did the story speak to you, honey?"

"Speak to me?"

"You take anything away? Find a nugget?"

The reflexive "no" is about to leave my mouth before I stop and describe the short moment of serenity, including how quickly the tranquility went away.

Her head bobs. "Ah, a God whisper."

Here we go. Holy Rollers unleashed.

I don't have time to reframe the response before she elaborates. "Sometimes, when God speaks, He starts with a whisper."

Back in my seat next to Joseph, I close my eyes. *A God whisper? God speaking to me? No. No. No.* First off, what God? Secondly, he'd get a better result dialing up anyone else on this bus. Sure, maybe, for a brief instant I felt a modicum of peace, but a shot of Absolut would be much more efficient.

$$\infty \quad \infty \quad \infty$$

After lunch, we take a short ride to our next stop and begin boarding a boat tethered alongside the Sea of Galilee. The boat is made of a dark brown wood, has a deep hull with benches running along each side, and a canvas roof to protect us from the sun.

At the dock, there's a sign prohibiting, among other things, fishing. This, to everyone else, is utterly hilarious because, as Pastor Marcus points out, "several of the disciples were fisherman right here on this body of water."

You have to appreciate good Holy Roller humor.

Caleb, while he fiddles with his vest, provides additional perspective. "For goodness sake, people, we had Peter's fish for lunch—tilapia—the species swimming around underneath us. You'd think they'd let us throw a line in the water."

There's no mystery to this part of the day. We've arrived at walk on water time. Caleb is standing on the bow, his hairy arms pumping the air, threatening to jump the minute we pull away from the dock. The whole way out, the group speculates about who's going to step over and "test their faith in God."

When we stop, however, Pastor Marcus wants to talk about a different story. He asks Ruth to read Luke, chapter eight, verses twenty-two to twenty-five. Gerri helps me find the page.

> One day Jesus said to his disciples, "Let us go over to the other side of the lake." So, they got into a boat and set out. As they sailed, He fell asleep. A squall came down on the lake, so that the boat was being swamped, and they were in great danger.
>
> The disciples went and woke him, saying, "Master, Master, we're going to drown!"
>
> He got up and rebuked the wind and the raging waters; the storm subsided, and all was calm. "Where is your faith?" he asked his disciples.
>
> In fear and amazement, they asked one another, "Who is this? He commands even the winds and the water, and they obey him."

When Ruth's finished, Avi interjects. "These sudden storms, they happen here. They start from over there." I'm not good with the points of the compass and don't know which direction he's indicating. "I must add, these storms are not mild. Sometimes, they are severe enough to threaten a boat, put lives in danger. Our good captain will confirm this has happened to him a number of times."

The guy driving the boat nods and replies in broken English. I assume he's expressing agreement.

"Now there's something new to me," comments Ruth. "I've never thought of a squall as being particularly harsh. However, based on what Luke wrote, I'm guessing the storm was pretty severe."

Pastor Marcus responds to Ruth's comment. "Agreed. According to the passage, the boat was being swamped."

"Those poor disciples must have been terrified."

Now Caleb jumps in. "I bet they were, Ruth. Until Jesus shut those waves down."

We sit in silence, with only the sound of the waves slapping against the boat's hull, until Addy stands and moves to the middle of the deck. The breeze is blowing her ponytail around. "This is the first Bible story I remember ..." We wait for her to continue. "I was young—"

"You're pretty young, now. Especially compared to us fossils," interrupts Caleb.

"I mean I was a girl. Nine years old on a cold Saturday in February. Except for Gerri," she offers a head nod, "I've never told anyone this. I remember exactly when because my parents had recently split, and they hated each other back then. Every time they were in a room together, there was screaming and fighting and doors slamming and they'd swear out loud right in the open. Not the little curses but the major swears. All the turmoil would make my baby sister cry."

She wipes a tear away. "I would read her this story, telling her we'd be okay. We studied the pictures in our Children's Bible and she'd ask me if Jesus could help her not to feel sad. I'd say yes, if we believed, Jesus could do anything."

The boat rocks. I close my eyes and see a little girl, wise beyond her years, holding a smaller girl, the two of them cloaked in fear and uncertainty, desperate for comfort, guidance, and, I don't want to consider this but I do, someone to save them. In response, they turned to a book.

Where would I turn? I don't finish the thought. There's no reason to ask a hypothetical. I've answered the question a million times.

Everyone else is either reading their Bibles or gazing over the water, lost in their own reveries. Addy, eyes closed, is silently moving her lips. She must be praying.

I wonder if I should try reading.

There's a split-second chill in the breeze before the first punch comes, hitting me with disgust, followed by the second, delivering a blow of worthlessness. The third punch obliterates my defenses as guilt, shame, and fear crash through, mix together, and boil into anger.

I have no doubt where all this originated. *The Holy Rollers.* They're making me feel this way with the whole wide-eyed kid act, prayer times, and story sharing. *Whatever. I'm me and they're them.*

As the boat turns back, heading to shore, music drifts out from the loudspeakers and I hear "How Great is Our God," a hymn we occasionally performed in the church choir. People start singing along.

Outstanding. More pious music.

I slump in my seat.

Caleb stands halfway across the deck, leading us, singing in full voice, which, undoubtably, is causing the birds on shore to flee for cover. He moves in close to me, waving his hands, trying to get me to join the chorus. When he sees I'm not singing, he shrugs and moves away, happy to charge up everyone else.

Joseph places his hand on my shoulder, the sleeve of today's immaculate button-down rolled tightly to the elbow. I hear him clearly, despite the cacophony of noise. "You okay, my friend?"

"I'm tired."

"We have had a busy day."

"No, I mean I'm tired of the prayer, tired of the readings, tired of seeing these," I make air quotes, "'magnificent holy sites.' I'm tired of faith."

"I must disagree. I don't believe you're tired of faith. I submit you're tired of *their* faith. You see, my friend, we all have faith. We all turn ourselves over to something, and as long as we sincerely believe in whatever we worship, we will remain true."

I ignore his comment, studying the horizon as we chug back to where we started. While we move along, I convince myself of one truth—a bottle is always better than a book.

∞ ∞ ∞

I stay tired.

We stop again, tour the area around a big house, and Avi shows us the hill where Jesus supposedly delivered his "Sermon on the Mount," describing the acoustics of the natural amphitheater. The hill's blocked off and we can't actually walk out there, but Pastor Marcus finds a shady spot and has someone read pieces from, if I heard right, Matthew's Gospel, chapter five. I sit on a bench, Gerri's Bible secure in my backpack, eyes closed, daydreaming about vodka over ice. I hear the words poor, meek, hungry, and merciful, knowing I don't feel any of those. I certainly don't believe I'm blessed.

∞ ∞ ∞

I'm desperate for the day to end, but there's one more set of archaeological ruins to scrutinize. We file out of the bus at a place called Magdala, and I stagger along to a spot where they've excavated an actual first-century synagogue.

Pastor Marcus takes the lead. "Magdala is where Jesus drove seven demons out of Mary Magdalene, meaning we know he was here. There's a high probability he preached in this synagogue."

The archeologists did a heck of a job on this site and in a better mood, with a stronger belief system, I'd be impressed. Instead I shrug, uninspired by my third synagogue of the week.

The rest of the group is enthralled and there's animated conversation along with all the picture taking. I must give the impression I'm fatigued because Addy hands me a bag of Peanut M&Ms, which is empty in three handfuls. The sugar helps, and I'm hopeful we'll get to the hotel before the cravings become debilitating.

∞ ∞ ∞

At the hotel, I dump my bag in the room and race back down to the bar. I finish my first drink in one overloaded swallow.

I'm working on another when Daniel saunters in, orders a Rum and Coke, and gets right to work. "What did you think of today?"

One-and-a-half drinks isn't enough to loosen my tongue or mitigate a crabby mood. "Long."

He watches carbonation escape from the Coke. "I agree."

"I'm guessing the pace was probably easier for you and the others."

"Easier?"

"Sure. Being lifelong believers and all."

"Lifelong believers?"

"Yeah. Aren't you all, you know, cradle to grave whatevers, depending on which church you go to?"

Using a finger, Daniel stabs at the ice in his glass. "I won't speak for everyone, but you're not describing my experience."

"What do you mean, did you move between different churches?"

"No, I've only belonged to one church."

"What do you mean then?"

My drink is gone. He signals for another. "I can't answer the question without telling my story."

Uh-oh. I've been around enough church folks in my life to know there's a testimony coming, and I don't want to hear Daniel's. On the other hand, an enduring backstory is a small price to pay for free cocktails. *Why not?* When my next vodka arrives, I offer a toast. "Cheers. Tell away."

"The long and short of it is, I didn't follow Christ until I was thirty-one years old." *Okay, there's an unexpected start.* "After college, I began my career in Manhattan. Wall Street. Worked for a small but powerful investment house. Twenty Ivy League MBAs, all blessed with magnificent abilities, scouring the market and doing analysis, all day, every day. They hired me right out of college to be their IT person. I took care of the phone system, the mainframe, the laptops, and fixed spreadsheet problems. The compensation was lucrative, even for New York, and there were bonuses after every deal. I had over six figures in the bank."

"Pretty heady situation for a recent college grad."

He squeezes the space between his eyes and keeps going. "I lived at a frenetic pace. All work. Days in a row with only a few hours of sleep. I didn't care. I had determined I could put away a million-and-a-half dollars by thirty-five and I was ruthless about getting there. They brought in other IT guys to help out, and I'd drive them away within weeks. More bonus for me."

From what I've observed, Daniel's always either reading the Bible or contemplating the Bible, unless, of course, he's cogitating on the places we've been visiting. I can't picture him as a hard-charging career guy.

He continues. "My plans were on track. Until this one particular deal. A big one. My potential bonus was enormous. Big enough to alter the timeline. One of the Managing Directors pulled me in and asked me to gather intelligence on the target company."

"Gather intelligence? How?"

"I'd hack into their investment banker's system. Try to locate one specific piece of information."

"Hack?"

"Yes."

"Isn't hacking a system illegal?"

"Quite." He shakes his head. "I agreed right away, especially after he told me he'd double my usual bonus percentage."

Other members of the group trickle in, waving as they gather, but not motioning for us to join them.

"What did you do?"

"Wanting to keep the electronic trail away from our system, I waited until one o'clock the following morning and went to an internet café. Paid cash for a coffee and found a terminal away from the other customers. To be safe, I pulled the rim of a Yankees hat down to cover my face." He hides behind his hand. "I should have known to stop right there."

"You didn't?"

"No. I didn't. The infiltration itself was relatively easy. Before any misgivings could develop, I was traveling around their system and quickly got to the CEO's email account. He was, and continues to be, one of those famous deal makers. He's a minor celebrity and also publicly transparent about his faith in God. I once read in an article his favorite Bible passage was Psalm 91, verse eleven. His password wasn't difficult to figure out."

Another vodka appears and I wait for him to continue.

"I started scrolling through the messages, and as I did, I noticed one from a woman who I assumed was his wife. The subject line read 'Don't forget.' I opened the email, not because I thought it was connected to our deal, but because I thought I could use a laugh, maybe see a reminder about getting bread and milk or a weekend 'Honey Do' list."

Daniel's giving himself a neck massage. "There wasn't a list. The message was a Bible verse. 'He who loves money never has enough. Whoever loves wealth is never satisfied with his income.' It was from the fifth chapter of Ecclesiastes, verse ten."

Now he's kneading both temples. "I stared at the words until I saw another message with the same subject line, 'Don't forget.' Inside was another Bible verse. 'Dishonest money dwindles away but he who gathers money little by little makes it grow.' A passage from Proverbs chapter thirteen. The eleventh verse. I scrolled further, curious as to whether there was a third 'Don't forget.'"

"I'm guessing you found one."

Daniel turns. His eyes are lasers. "She wrote: 'Remember, my dear, the wisdom of Proverbs 15:27— 'A greedy man brings trouble to his family, but he who hates bribes shall live.'"

I break the stare.

"I was all alone in the café, sitting in the dark, surrounded only by the glow from the computer screen. After I read and reread the verse, imprinting it on my brain and doing the same with the other two, I logged out and went over to the office. The time was around three-thirty in the morning, and surprisingly, no one was there working. I cleaned out my cubicle, walked out and never went back again."

"Just like that?"

"Just like that."

I hypothesize there's more and since Daniel and I are now, apparently, confidants, push for particulars. "You're saying you read three Bible verses in a few emails, and bang, you quit your job and changed your life?"

"Yes." Daniel's drawing figure eights on a bar napkin. "When I read those passages, the words steamrolled over me. At first, I wasn't sure why, but as I walked back to the office, I realized if this man, a legend in the industry, a person wealthy beyond all reason, was operating within a set of parameters, and, believe me, I had no idea what they were at the time, then maybe I should too."

I must look confused, because he tries another angle. "Maybe what I'm saying would make more sense if I summarized it this way. I knew I had no guardrails and that he did. I didn't get any further at the time, but I was far enough along to want a change."

"And you became a Christian?"

He shows a small smile. "Ah, no. I had found the starting point. There was considerable work and struggle afterward, including discovering where those guardrails came from. At first, I assumed they originated with his wife, but eventually I accepted they were provided by a source outside the man himself and shifted my focus."

Whether I want to or not, I'm hearing a testimony, and I'm reminded of the conversation with Joseph about changing from the inside. "How did all this happen?"

"We'd need about three more drinks worth of conversation for me to provide an adequate answer." While this isn't an unappealing prospect to me, Daniel doesn't offer to invest the time. "At a high level, I went through a period of study and soul searching and introspection. Figuring out who I was. Eventually, I found my faith. Now I work to support my daily needs, read the Bible, and try to honor God by the way I live my life. Part of my journey included getting a Master of Divinity degree."

The vodka is working, and as my frustration with the day clears away, I'm feeling magnanimous. "Wow, impressive story."

"No, there's nothing remarkable here." He waves me off. "My story is more disappointing than anything else. I took too much time discovering my path."

Daniel doesn't expect a reply, and after we both watch the bartender mix a fancy green concoction, he abruptly shifts focus. "I'm curious about you, Ben."

"In what way?"

"What brings you to us?"

"A, uh, complicated situation."

Daniel spreads his arms. "Was the story I just told you simple?"

"Yeah, I mean, no, but I'm not much of a church guy. I don't have a story. At least not a faith story."

"With respect, I disagree." He motions at the others in our group. "Everyone has a story."

"Do you know theirs?"

"For several of them, yes. I won't share the stories, though. They're not mine to tell."

"I'm confident mine's not worth telling."

"At the right time, all stories are worth telling. Maybe yours is still under development, evolving. As with all of us."

Daniel stands and walks away, presumably to get dinner. As he does, I realize he didn't take a single sip of his drink.

∞ ∞ ∞

Two beers drip condensation onto the night stand. Joseph is in his usual end-of-day spot, propped against his pillow, reading yet another carpentry magazine. "You enjoy your libations in the evening, don't you my friend?"

"They help me wind down."

"You do this every night?"

"Since I was about fifteen." The answer jumps out of my mouth, making me wonder exactly how many drinks I've had. I'm clearly over my limit.

"Such a young age."

As Joseph goes back to whatever article he's reading, I pour more beer down my throat, and, despite the conscious thought to stay quiet and drink, begin to elaborate. "I started out with those little airplane-sized liquor bottles. My dad would get them in gift baskets at Christmas. He'd mix them in with his collection, a bunch of scotch, bourbon, gin, and vodka in one of our kitchen cabinets. A high one. You had to stand on a chair to reach inside. On the night of my Grandmother's funeral, I got curious, snuck a bottle, and drank my first vodka right before bed. In an instant, I was hooked. A few weeks later, after I'd had about half a dozen, I started refilling the empties. Either from the larger liquor bottles or from half-empty wine bottles."

Joseph puts his magazine down. "Your parents never suspected you were doing this?"

66

I shake my head. "Mom and Dad were regular drinkers and there was always company hanging around. They never missed the booze or noticed if I snitched a beer."

"And you kept on drinking?"

"Every night, before bed. Right to this day. Vodka and beer are my favorites. For me, the dark whiskies are no good. They make me sick."

I finish the first Goldstar and start to reach for the second, but the bottle's cradled in Joseph's hands, the label facing me. "This is an important ritual for you, no?"

I wouldn't label a couple of drinks at night a ritual, but decide not to quibble over vocabulary. "It's a part of my day."

"You believe in this, don't you?" He's tilting the bottle towards me.

Believe. Joseph needs to choose his words better. "I'm clearing my mind, sweeping off the decks before sleep. Nothing more."

He hands me the bottle. "Suit yourself." After I take the beer, his side of the room goes dark.

I gulp the beer and brood over all the meaningful dialog this evening, utter a two-word curse, and close my eyes.

PROGRESS REPORT # 4

Peter,

I must begin with gratitude. Your gentle reprimand regarding timeline concerns was, of course, completely warranted. I have a single responsibility—to fill my role. He Who Is Above will determine the direction of events and ensure the components fit together. Given the various experiences of my own earthly life, this reminder should be unnecessary, but alas, there are moments of weakness.

The day was full. Both from a touring perspective and in relation to what was learned about Our Man. There are a few key items to note.

Our Man received another short visit from the Spirit. The encounter occurred after interaction with the Word and had a significant impact. He mentioned the interaction to one of the caretakers. She provided a strong response, provoking a series of follow-up thoughts. They were, however, quickly defeated when layers of negative human emotion diverted any productive thought pattern. Not an unexpected development this early in the process and, for me, not discouraging. I am pleased a brief foothold was achieved.

There was a lengthy exchange with one caretaker who, as we continue our work, will serve as the primary guide. He introduced his story, an impressive account of rapid conversion. I'm confident the conversation resonated, establishing an initial layer of trust between the two men. I also have no doubt the interaction was impactful, and suspect Our Man, having learned not all souls begin their human experience as faithful followers, will benefit greatly.

I completed a measure of direct work on his earthly vice, which proved to be an informative exercise. Our Man is ensconced in a regular, long-term routine, and he is faithful to the ritual. Any eventual break will be painful in both the psychological and physical sense. While we are equipped to guide him through, extra planning will be necessary.

Concepts introduced: building a new life on the old, changing from the inside out, and realizing there's always a chance.

A final note: Our Man is cerebral. A thinker. This should prove helpful in revealing cognitive themes to be utilized for the good. Of course, this trait will also make him more susceptible to spiritual warfare.

With faith in our success,
Joseph

DAY 5

I'm awake early, not certain about much, other than knowing there's another eight or nine hours of Israel ahead.

When I slip off the bed, my body objects, and a shower is entirely ineffective. Sure, I'm clean, but I'm no closer to waking up and am surprised all the cracking and popping hasn't woken Joseph.

In the dining room, Caleb waves me over. He alternates between writing in a journal, sipping light-colored tea, and working his way through a plate of fruit. I hover over a cup of thick black coffee, impressed with his productivity.

He smacks the pen down. "You know what I think?"

I don't bother with a guess.

"This whole Jews hating Arabs and Arabs hating Jews situation is overrated."

They have cable where you live, Caleb old buddy?

"Of course, yeah, there's legitimate tensions," he concedes.

I'm no history expert, but I've heard about more than tensions. *Doesn't Israel have nukes?*

"What about the people, though?" He's on a roll. "The people on the ground every day. I've been talking to the locals, using my Hebrew and Arabic."

I decide to engage in the conversation. "You speak Hebrew and Arabic?"

"Yep. Learned them when I was a kid. They came back pretty quickly. A skill I have. I get by in German and Japanese, too."

On any regular day, this would be remarkably impressive, but I'm too busy trying, desperately, to get stimulants into my bloodstream.

"I look around and, hey, this guy's an Arab, this guy's a Jew, and they coexist every day, getting along fine while they live their lives." While Caleb's monologue builds, I'm picking at a chocolate croissant. "The problem is the leaders! The leaders! The Bozos at the top create obstacles where they don't exist. They keep stirring the pot. I say, live and let live."

Now, I know the circumstances are more complicated and I suspect Caleb does too, although, despite my fog, I respect his passion.

"Real estate, huh?" he asks.

There's no moss growing under this guy. "Yeah."

"Funny, you're not the typical real estate man."

I'm too lethargic to care, but I bite. "What's your picture of the typical real estate guy?"

"You're a developer, right?"

"Yeah."

"When I've worked with those guys, they're tall, have a paunch, puffy face, and receding hairline. They always seem to be wearing tan Dockers and a golf shirt with the logo of their college or a fancy country club. Slap-you-on-the-back, drink-you-under-the-table, get-a-deal-done types."

I've got the drinking part down.

"You, you're average height. Always wearing those lightweight fishing shirts with the cool pockets and loops. Where do you get those?"

"Either L.L. Bean or Cabela's. I follow the sales."

Caleb nods. "Right. Anyways, you've got no belly to speak of. Have all your hair. Your appearance is more scholarly, especially with the wire-rimmed glasses."

"I was an English major in college. English and Philosophy."

"Ah! A literary man. You probably appreciate poetry."

"Depends on the poet."

His probe persists. "How'd you end up in the land and building business?"

"Had to get a job. Started out selling houses and worked construction. One job led to another, and bingo, a career happened."

"Not your intent?"

"No."

The conversation stops for a minute and I remember my pre-college goals. The plan was simple—get my degree, go to grad school, teach English, and write the Great American Novel.

Caleb starts talking again. "What do you do when you're not playing the real estate game?"

I'm quiet while I consider a reasonable answer. There's no socially acceptable way to explain how I love to drink or how my "hobby" destroyed my career and ruined my family.

He pushes for an answer. "Come on now, you don't work all the time, do you?"

Actually, I don't and there is one other activity I sincerely enjoy. "I read to seniors."

"Seniors?"

"The elderly. I visit a nursing home near my house and read to them."

Caleb puts his fork down. "Now there's a decent way to spend your time. How does a real estate guy begin reading in a nursing home?"

"When I was a kid, my grandmother lived with us, one of those little apartments over the garage. I'd spend all kinds of time with her playing cribbage and helping her cook. After she had a stroke when I was about twelve, she had to move into a nursing home. I'd go see her every day, feed her a sweet treat, and read to her from books and magazines. After she had a second stroke and died when I was a teenager, I started reading to the other people in the place she lived."

Caleb gives a nod, and a second or two passes before he asks the next question. "What do you read to them?"

"Novels, mostly. John Grisham, Baldacci, James Patterson. They enjoy the lawyer and thriller stories."

"How often do you do this?"

"I used to go by twice a week, right after lunch, and read to a small group. About half of them would have a copy and follow along, and about half would listen. They're from a generation of excellent listeners."

"Used to?"

Yes, sir, Caleb. Getting arrested and my court mandated vacation in the Outhouse disrupted the flow. "I've been somewhat, ah, distracted for the last couple of months. Maybe I'll get back in the loop when this trip is done."

After he eats a few strawberries, Caleb reopens the conversation. "Dry cleaning myself. Three stores."

I ask a question to keep him from hopping to another topic. "Your family go straight to the US after you lived here?"

"You bet. We emigrated. Opened for business. I found Christ."

"Your dad started the business?"

"Him and my uncle. I run it now. I didn't have any cousins and both my brothers are hot-shot lawyers in DC. They're happy to pay me a salary, have me take care of the day-to-day, and collect their share of the profits."

There's a modicum of caffeine working, and I rewind to his earlier comment. "You found Christ?"

"Oh, yeah. Only one in the family. Had the big experience around nine on a Thursday night. A light in the room. Collapsed to my knees, grabbed my head, felt the Spirit enter my body."

"The Spirit?"

"The Holy Spirit. Practically knocked me over. Got baptized the next weekend and been a follower ever since."

"Pretty quick conversion." I'm guessing he notes my skepticism.

"Sure was. Until the light, I didn't know if he was there or if there even was a 'he.' Since the light, I'm sure."

"Who's there?" I ask, fairly confident I know the answer.

"Him. God. Yahweh. The Man Upstairs."

His conviction leaves me slightly envious. "Did your, ah, conversion, cause any strife in the family?"

"Not too bad. My parents believed in religious freedom. Plus, I was still in the Judeo-Christian family, so to speak. The only real issue was the logo."

"The logo?"

"Yeah. The business logo. After my dad and uncle died, I added an anchor. Chose it as an emblem, a nonverbal cue."

"An anchor? For dry cleaning?"

"In the early church," he responds, nodding, "the anchor, as Hebrews says, is 'firm and secure' for the soul, a symbol for safety and hope. Using one as our logo is a statement of faith. Seemed better than the usual Jesus Fish. Too many of those for people to notice. My brothers, both nonpracticing Jews, hate the darn thing. In the end, though, I'm the CEO. The decision is mine."

He pulls out a business card. Sure enough, next to the name "Roth's Cleaners" and slogan "Our Customers are our Family," there's a simple black anchor designed in the shape of a cross.

I sense movement to my right and notice people gathering for the bus.

Caleb stands and gently squeezes my shoulder, his mouth leaning into my ear. "He's there. Trust me." His voice booms. "Hey, people, we all ready for another big day?"

$$\infty \quad \infty \quad \infty$$

Pastor Marcus volunteers a front-of-the-bus traveler to say the prayer and Avi takes over with his usual review of activities, explaining we're going for a scenic ride before visiting the Dead Sea Scrolls and stopping at an oasis.

The oasis concept intrigues me. We are, without a doubt, traveling through a desert. Everything is the color of coffee lightened with two or three creamers. When we've moved around outside, the heat sleeves our bodies, the dirt crunches under our feet, and a film of sandy dust clings to our shoes and lower legs.

As the bus climbs a hill, Avi gives us a history lesson. "I want to talk to you about modern Israel. What we call the New Israel. For this to exist, there had to be large-scale Jewish migration, although we don't call it migration. We call it *aliyah*, which means ascent. Aliyah is the reversal of what is known as the diaspora. Diaspora is the dispersion of Jews away from Israel. Those driven out, sent into exile, all through history."

Caleb interrupts. "When I was a boy, they taught about aliyahs. They happened in waves from 1880 until roughly 1960."

Avi nods in agreement. "The first of these were in the late 1800s and early 1900s from Russia and Eastern European countries. You see, as they conquered new territories, the Russians wanted to move out the Jews they found living there. They would conduct pogroms—"

"Which were nothing more than organized massacres." Caleb stands, his voice louder than usual. "The Russians would kill the Jews, destroy their towns, drive them away. Groups of refugees found their way here. Frequently, they were sixteen to twenty-year-old boys called Zionists, relocating against their families' wishes, which is a big deal. Jewish families stay together, they don't split up. For most, their parents warned them—if they left, they would be dead to them. My line goes back to 1902. An eighteen-year-old Russian refugee."

Ruth studies the unhospitable terrain passing by her window. "They left their families for this? Did they know what they were getting into?"

"I'd say, for the vast majority of them, no." Avi shrugs. "Many arrived expecting a land of milk and honey. As you've observed, this is a harsh place and the unprepared often faced catastrophe. Overall, though, we Jews are a sturdy people. We found ways to survive and now, thanks to our hard work, we thrive."

Jeb, who normally doesn't say much when we're on the bus, offers a question. "It was after the Holocaust, wasn't it?"

Gerri's head pops above the seat. "What was?"

"When your family did their *aliyah*." As the sentence comes out, Jeb nods towards Avi.

Avi says yes and elaborates. "My grandparents arrived here in 1948. Alone. Everyone else was dead. Their parents, their siblings. All victims of the Nazis. They came here and started again, building a new life and making a new family. In the process, they taught us one lesson above all others."

Ruth prods. "What was the lesson?"

He hesitates, ponders, and squares his shoulders. "We are Jews *and* we are Israelis. We will not surrender our land again." He waves his Bible. "If, as the book tells us, the world ends here, then so be it."

∞ ∞ ∞

When the bus stops climbing, we are far above the Dead Sea. Avi talks about length and depth and the salt content as compared to the ocean. He urges the group to enjoy the view of the endless desert sky and the hills surrounding the valleys below. As he ushers us along, I notice Daniel maneuver and get next to Addy. While I can't hear exactly what they're saying, these two aren't having a simple, polite conversation. The tone implies more than a casual acquaintance. I'm convinced Daniel is attracted to Addy. He keeps checking her out, and I can't blame him. Her brown hair, always in a ponytail during the day, clear skin, and blue eyes produce the universally recognized "wholesome girl" look. Ten years ago, assuming I was available, Daniel would have had to compete with me.

Watching the two of them together generates additional memories of Sarah. After our first encounter in the Lehigh bookstore, I was happy to discover she was in one of my classes, a standard writing course they made all freshman take. I found Sarah at the desk next to mine and was thrilled with the coincidence, although Sarah later confessed she orchestrated the whole thing. Through casual chats, we learned each other's names, where we were from, and other superficial details. We discussed my love of books and her self-described obsession with oatmeal raisin cookies. I would spend most of the class sneaking peaks at her glossy black hair, brown eyes, and fair skin. My goodness, she was beautiful.

Of course, I was clueless and didn't comprehend she was broadcasting signals—the sideway glances when the professor told a bad joke, asking what I was doing for the weekend, and checking on how my other classes were going.

Watching Daniel and Addy, I see a similar dynamic, although they're old enough to actually know what's going on.

I start to refocus on the Dead Sea when Avi points out spots where the shoreline is receding. From our high vantage point, I see where the water level was before the retreat, reminding me of low tide at the ocean. Here, though, people are concerned the water's not coming back.

"The Jordan River empties here," Avi explains, "and much of the river water has been diverted to support agriculture and human settlements, leaving less water flowing into the Sea, causing the level to decline. Now, this leads us to an interesting development. At the places where the Sea is withdrawing, there are what we call sinkholes forming and a subset of these sinkholes contain fresh water, fish, and plants."

Pastor Marcus gathers us around. "Eventually, according to one specific prophecy, fresh water will flow, cleansing the Dead Sea, and allowing life to flourish."

"Ezekiel, chapter forty-seven, verses eight and nine." Gerri strikes again.

Amazing.

We're driving in and out of Palestinian territory and the bus stops at what I'm assuming is a military checkpoint. There's a small building, more of a toll booth, with four Israeli soldiers stationed there. Assault rifles are draped over their shoulders and they're wearing vests packed with God knows what. One approaches the bus and two others stand a few feet back, ready to react if anything goes off kilter. The fourth is in the booth watching what's happening and, I'm guessing, prepared to call for help. I notice they're not all guys. Two of them are women. Their body language tells me they mean business. I wouldn't mess with them.

As you'd expect with a bus carrying mostly middle-aged American tourists, the stop is uneventful, and we're quickly on our way again.

Avi is walking down the aisles handing out hats with the name of his tour company on them. When he gets to me, I ask a question. "Were you in the military here?"

He nods. "National service is part of being a citizen."

I'm aware of the obligation, but don't know specifics.

"All of us over the age of eighteen are required to serve. Well, most of us. Arab citizens don't have to, but there are those who do. Also, the so-called Religious Jews are exempt."

"Religious Jews?"

"They are our Jewish scholars. The ultra-orthodox. They devote their life to studying the Torah and praying to God. You see them in the conservative dress, wearing beards and the long side curls, although others also dress in the same way." I remember the men I noticed in the Tel Aviv airport. "For many, the wives support the families, and the men are free to study. Work is beneath them. I, myself, do not agree with this lifestyle. A man needs to be a man, and all true Israelis have a duty to their country."

I'm surprised at his disdain. The men he describes are, based on my perceptions, the stereotypical Jewish persons.

"For those who honor their commitment, the men serve for three years, women for two, officers for four. There are variations for combat and non-combat roles, but those are the overall rules."

My mind switches back to his comment about the Religious Jews. "Are you a practicing Jew?"

"I am half a Jew. I believe in Christ as the Messiah." This makes sense given the nature of our tour. "Most importantly, I believe Israel comes first, ahead of all other priorities."

He balances himself using the seatback and, after the bus comes to a stop, heads to the front. We're at our lunch destination.

∞ ∞ ∞

I order a lamb meatball wrapped in pita bread, along with a Coke Zero. Caleb comments about how I always order "pretty much the same food." He's got a point. Given a choice, I'll always choose lamb.

The place is loud, and there's not much chance for a group discussion. Next to me is Addy, who's dressed in her usual stylish jeans, V-neck T-shirt—this one is black—and matching Converse sneakers. She's got sunglasses pushed back on her head and her light brown hair is, as always, in a ponytail.

What the heck do I talk to her about? While I remember learning she isn't married, I'm not dumb enough to explore the topic. I also recall she's a nurse, which represents a much safer subject matter.

Before I start talking, her head bows, eyes close, and lips move silently. She prays long enough for me to wonder if she does this in public all the time.

When she finishes, I try to start a conversation. "You're a nurse, right?"

"Sure am. An emergency room nurse."

"Do you enjoy what you do?"

"I do. Very much."

"Rewarding?"

She takes out her phone and starts reading messages. "Uh-huh."

"Where do you live?"

"Pittsburgh. I work at UPMC."

"UPMC?"

"University of Pittsburgh Medical Center."

"You go to school in Pittsburgh?"

"Ah, hold on, gotta reply to this." After the message is sent, she answers my question. "No. JMU."

"James Madison?"

Another uh-huh. Another tap on the send button.

I'm a lawyer peppering a witness. "Why'd you choose nursing?"

"I didn't. Nursing chose me."

Her response slows me down. The lull doesn't bother Addy, who keeps clearing out her inbox, or texting her friends, or doing whatever the heck she's doing.

"It chose you?" I ask.

"Yes. I have a calling."

"A calling?"

The phone goes down. "Yes. A calling."

"You were called to be a nurse?"

"No. I was called to be an emergency room nurse."

"How would you know you were called?"

Addy must sense the shift in my tone from "I'm trying to make conversation" to "I don't understand this but right now, at this moment, I'm curious about what you're saying." Her legs swing to the side of the chair and she faces me straight on. "He let me know."

"Seriously? Is the he who I think he is?"

"Who do you think it is?"

I point skyward. "You know. Him."

Addy gives a small smile. "Yes, Ben, he is who you think he is." She turns in her seat, takes a bite of food, and resumes thumbing her way through messages.

I chew my pita bread, recalling my conversation with Daniel. He claimed everyone has a story. I watch Addy. Now she's back staring at her phone, and she's become every other twenty-something I know, saying "you did not!" to the screen before typing in what I'm sure is a snappy comeback. I try to reconcile this person to the one from a few moments ago when she was talking. Without a doubt, there's a story there.

A question pops from my mouth. "How did you know?"

Addy's eyes move my way. "Know what?"

"What God wanted?"

She goes all mature again, reminding me of Jekyll and Hyde, except there's no bad version. "When I was seventeen, me and my best friend were in a car accident. She ran a stop sign. I was fine but she was hurt—she's okay now—and I rode along in the ambulance. At the hospital they wouldn't let me in the room, but I watched through a window, saw the nurses work, saw them save her life. They were angels to me, the way they moved and talked and cared for her. I'm sure there were doctors in there too, but I didn't see them. At that moment, I knew."

I'm moved by the story, but can't connect what she's saying to receiving a calling from above. "I'm not sure I understand."

The phone hits the table again. "Let me explain this way. I'm one of the lucky ones." Her hands rest on her lap. "God didn't have to break me. I was with him from my earliest memory. I've spent my whole life trying to make sure I follow his will."

"You've faced hardships, though."

She knows I'm talking about the story on the Sea of Galilee. "We've all had those. The difference is, God didn't have to use them to get me into the tent, so to speak. Instead, he made use of my faith to help my little sister."

I'm in too deep to climb out. "Are you saying everything ... all of your actions ... are, uh ... directed by God?"

"Yes. If I listen and seek his guidance, God will lead me."

"His guidance?"

"Yes."

"God talks to you?"

"In a way."

I lean back, spreading my arms wide. "Come on. Honestly? How do you know God is talking to you?"

She doesn't flinch as my voice rises. "I ask for guidance. I wait. I listen. The answer, most times, comes as a feeling. Every once in a while, he uses a more tangible approach. One time he made a bird sing, and another, I dropped my car keys into an aquarium."

"You're sure you're hearing from God?"

"Yes."

"How do you know?"

She nibbles what's left of her pita. "I asked my grandma once how she knew who to marry. She told me, 'Honeybuns, when you get to marrying age and you're chewin' over if a guy is THE guy, he's not. When he is, you won't be asking any questions. You'll know.' With God, I just know. I don't feel the need to ask any questions."

Gerri sticks her head between the two of us. "How about ice cream, little girl?"

Addy claps her hands and jumps to her feet. "Only if there's mint chip, big girl!"

"I don't know about mint chip, but let's try rustling around in the cooler over there."

They bounce off like a couple of schoolkids on their first trip out of the house.

∞ ∞ ∞

A few minutes later, we file out of the restaurant. Addy is practically skipping along beside me, eating a pre-packaged ice cream parfait.

I continue our conversation. "Do you plan on being a nurse for your whole career?"

"Not my decision." She licks chocolate sauce off a stubby wooden spoon.

"It's not?"

"Of course not. I follow God."

Gerri overhears the conversation. "Amen, little girl."

Addy stops me, gently grasping my upper arm. "Do you have a strong faith, Ben?"

Seriously? I'm standing in a parking lot, somewhere in Israel, having a discussion about faith with a twenty-something nurse who I've known for, what, five days? Actually, she's a twenty-something nurse I've been *acquainted* with for five days. The absurdity of the situation persuades me to answer. "No, I don't."

"The way I see things, my faith only allows me to take care of the here and now. God leads by showing, at the most, one or two steps at a time. Which is all fine by me. I'll know what to do when he wants me to know."

I hear Gerri over my left shoulder. "'Therefore, do not worry about tomorrow, for tomorrow will worry about itself. Each day has enough trouble of its own.' Matthew, chapter six, verse thirty-four."

This could become irritating.

The two of them head for the bus as I stay put, and despite my innate sarcasm, I admire these two women and what I'm learning about them. I can't drum up any specific words to characterize who or what they appear to be, other than to say they're self-assured, but not cocky, and certainly not overbearing.

Gerri's talking to the driver and Addy's climbing aboard when I half shout a question at them. "How do I get a stronger faith?"

Addy moves the wooden spoon away from her mouth. "Step into the room, Ben. With God. Ask him to help you."

∞ ∞ ∞

We're heading to a place called Qumran, which is the home of the Dead Sea Scrolls. On the way, Avi provides backstory. "These Scrolls, they are significant in world history. The first were found by a group of shepherds in late 1946."

Shepherds? With all the rocks, sand, and only occasional scrub brush, I try to figure out what sheep would eat in this place.

"Initially, they found seven Scrolls in a single cave. Eventually, over nine hundred documents were discovered."

Caleb adds his usual color. "Those documents weren't folded and wrapped in plastic, preserved and ready to read. Pieces, people, they were in pieces."

Avi goes on. "True. Most of what they found were fragments. Scholars estimate as many as fifty-thousand individual pieces. Please, look out the window on the right side of the bus. Most of what you see is limestone and along the hills you will notice the caves."

All I see is the barren alien planet in a science fiction movie. Eventually, though, I spot a solitary dark hole. It's hard to determine the size of the cave's opening, but I'm guessing I could walk through or at least stoop and get inside.

"Between the first discovery and 1956, they found eleven caves where the Scrolls had been stored. The caves were both natural and artificial. Made specifically for the Scrolls."

Ruth asks a question. "What were they stored in?"

"Mostly clay pots."

I count six more apertures before we pull into the site.

Avi leads us to the remains of a settlement. Similar to the other excavated areas we've seen, there are original ruins and refurbished facsimiles. Pastor Marcus and Avi take turns explaining them, showing us living areas and cattle pens. I try to listen but am distracted—the heat makes pulling oxygen from the air like trying to quench your thirst with hot water.

I get interested when they start talking about the aqueducts, a series of paths used to funnel rainwater from the hills and into cisterns for storage. *How many people were killed by these conditions before they figured out how to survive?*

"Who lived here?" asks Gerri.

"Most researchers agree the residents were a group called the Essenes," answers Avi. "They were a scholarly Jewish sect, living in shared community, perhaps similar to our *kibbutz*. The Essenes were dedicated to studying and preserving God's Word, a devout people."

He points to a set of stairs descending into a rectangular area, maybe eight or nine feet across and five or six feet deep. "These are baths. The Essenes followed the ritual Jewish bathing tradition. They probably immersed themselves in here once each day."

Gerri remains curious. "When were they here?"

"Ah, an interesting question. It's hard to say exactly, but we know they were in this settlement during the last century BCE and the first century CE."

Those are new terms to me. They must be new to Jeb, too, because he wants to know what BCE and CE mean.

Daniel pipes up. "It's the same as the traditional Before Christ, what we call BC, and *Anno Domini,* what we call AD. BCE stands for Before the Common Era and CE stands for the Common Era. They changed the words to avoid a direct link to Christianity in the reference."

Jeb's displeased. "What a shame. From my perspective, at least. Getting back to the, ah, Essenes, how do you know they were here then?"

"Coins," replies Avi.

"Coins?"

"Yes. When archeologists dig, they frequently discover coins. Based on what or who is on them, we conclude people were around during the era they were made and used. The coins discovered here confirm the settlement was here, at a minimum, during those two centuries."

We enter a concrete and stone building, passing under letters spelling out "The Secret of Qumran." Everyone perks up in the air conditioning.

Avi's ongoing explanations and a short movie inform us the Scrolls were written on either parchment, which is made from untanned animal skins, or papyrus, which is made from a plant with the same name. Archeologists discovered documents related to every book in the Bible except Esther. Since I didn't know there was an Esther, this doesn't concern me in the least. They did, however, come across a complete version of Isaiah, and, skeptic or not, Isaiah is hard to ignore. I listen closely. Apparently, the manuscript discovered was a thousand years older than the previous version.

In a circular room, there are facsimiles of the Scrolls along the walls and on an elevated platform. All of them are behind glass. I read about the originals being housed in Jerusalem.

I peruse the reconstructed parchment on the wall, the product of a painstaking process involving fifty thousand separate fragments which were pieced together to create over nine hundred coherent documents. My hand goes to the glass, curious what language is written there. I know from the video the Scrolls were created using Hebrew, Aramaic, Greek, and Latin. Tracing the letters with my index finger, I'm forced to accept these words, true or not, as the source material for what millions of people regard as the Word of God. This is ground floor stuff.

I consider the local climate, the relentless heat and dust, the pervasive sand and stone. *Why would a sane people choose to live here? Why would they take the step of digging caves into limestone hills to preserve and store all these documents?* I guess Addy would say they had a calling. Regardless, these individuals demonstrated an impressive level of commitment. They clearly didn't believe the stories, which were passed down, either verbally or in written form, over thousands of years, originated from a myth or folktale. They were convinced there was something real behind them.

Along with the thought, the "good" feeling, a repeat of the ones from Joppa and Capernaum, comes back.

Returning to the bus, I glide along, lost in my thoughts, and don't talk to Joseph when I'm back in my seat. As we pull away and Avi begins to describe our next stop, I don't hear any details. I've opened my Bible and I'm reading the first chapter of Isaiah.

When the bus stops, I'm rested, peaceful, and ready to go.

The venue is pretty cool. Literally. I have no idea where we are and don't bother asking. The freshwater lake, surrounded by rocks and trees, with a couple of small waterfalls cascading into turquoise colored water, is all the information I need.

We didn't drive far, certainly not far enough to leave the desert. This must be the oasis Avi mentioned in the morning.

While folks either swim or sit with their feet in the water, I settle on a nearby hill, enjoying the serene feeling, watching families having fun. While I'm aware we're getting close to the time I should be wanting a drink, for whatever reason I don't. With the sounds of water splashing, kids laughing, and the feel of soft grass after days of dust and pebbles, I see no need to consult my watch.

I'm not surprised to see Addy and Daniel sitting next to each other, their feet dangling in the water as they share an inside joke. He pushes the hair from in front of her eyes, and she playfully splashes water on the front of his shirt. This potential romance is starting to gain steam.

Between my placid mood and watching the two of them interact, I'm reminded of the first time I met Sarah's parents. When her father, an engineer, found out I was going to major in English and Philosophy, he couldn't control his reaction—a half-frown, half-grimace, eyebrow-raised expression. Sarah had prepared me for her father's reaction, and we both laughed. When he asked what was funny, we shrugged and shared an "in the know" look. I enjoy the memory.

The moment doesn't last. Quiet and contemplation aren't good for me, at least without a drink or two to buttress the demons trying to slither forward.

I scan my memory banks, stopping at the nights I had choir rehearsal, singing with vigor, pretending to feel the words. Some evenings, I would offer the closing prayer, piously beseeching God for mercy and grace, thanking him for all our blessings. When we were done, I'd go out, because the choir always went out after practice, and sip a Coke Zero while everyone else had a glass of wine or beer or a frozen fruity drink. I'd walk out to my car, stone cold sober, a respected man, a leader, someone who projected moderation.

I'd drive home, my lips quivering and my hands shaking, thankful I was close to the time I could drop the façade. Sarah and Zach would still be awake, and before saying hello, I'd bolt down two quick drinks, each loaded with extra vodka to achieve maximum impact. After my emergency ration, I'd have a couple more regular ones and start with the judgment, the yelling, and the verbal abuse. Telling Zach five A's and a B weren't good enough, watching his cheeks redden underneath the close-cropped black hair. I'd notice his forearm muscles tighten, impressed, despite my bad mood, with his fit, lean build. After I was done with Zach, I'd interrogate Sarah about time management because my favorite shirt wasn't back from the cleaners, gripe about not having time to myself, or fuss over the size of the grocery bill. When we'd go to bed, I'd pressure Sarah to be a wife, trying to get her to express a love that couldn't possibly be there, especially in the moment.

This was the routine any night I came home late. The other nights weren't any better, except I'd begin with less potent drinks, spreading them over a longer period of time.

All at once, I want to stop watching people swim and resent hearing the sounds of fun. They make me remember the mornings when I'd listen, half a house away, to everyone having breakfast. I'd swear to myself I was going to stop, convinced I would, until the day moved along and I wore down. Not the week or the month, but the day. Actually, the hours.

I watch the families playing in the water. Dads are heaving small children into the air, their laughs piercing as they fall with a splash in a spread-eagle landing. Others dive for rocks or ride on shoulders. I'm reminded of our trip to Disney and the pool in the afternoons, when I was able to sneak in a few drinks while the kids splashed the heat away.

My thoughts tumble further down the rabbit hole, and I'm standing in front of the judge again, listening to the harsh words, the restraining order, the "rehab or else" ultimatum. I remember I left the court, went to a sleazy motel and drank, hoping to generate a good buzz before flying out to rehab. How I held the bottle of vodka, knowing what had happened should have been enough to make me put the stupid thing down. For good. Instead, I took a swig, knowing I felt bad but, in the moment, not bad enough.

Turning my wrist, I peek at my watch. 4:22. The day's slipping away. Time to get a drink.

∞ ∞ ∞

While we're heading to the hotel, there's talk about Addy losing a necklace. She's pretty upset, and because Holy Rollers pray constantly, the whole bus beseeches God, who I'm sure has more pressing matters, for help finding the necklace. They also mention thanks for the day, peace for the Middle East, and safety for families back home. I'm not in the mood and pretend to doze.

An hour later, we're checking in. I'm anticipating Happy Hour, but the crew's going swimming in the Dead Sea, which, apparently, is out the other side of the lobby. After their salty dip, everyone's heading straight to dinner.

As I watch them making plans to meet, observing their excitement, marveling at their energy, I know I don't belong with them. I've made too many mistakes and hurt too many people to earn a spot in their world.

Since there's no Happy Hour and no place for me with the Dead Sea crowd, I'm left with my default option that, in actuality, is the one I prefer. Being alone, far away from home, means I'm free to drink in public—all I want.

After dropping my bag in the room, I take the elevator back down, charge out of the hotel, and work my way into town, stopping at the first bar I see. Time to tie one on.

"To the greatest country on earth!" The guy next to me, a scotch drinker, clinks his glass against my Goldstar bottle. He throws back the dark shot in one swig before concluding his toast. "I don't mean this rathole, either." He points to the American flag planted firmly in the middle of his shiny, white baseball hat. "I mean the good ol' U S of A."

He's a few drinks ahead of me, but I'm catching up and feeling good again, especially when another Goldstar and another shot appear.

"I didn't want to come. My wife made me. She's probably back in the room, writing in her fancy journal notebook. Not me. I ain't relatin' to the Holy Land."

He's fond of his little saying and repeats the words before going on. "Plus, I gotta get the heat and the dust out of my mouth." He downs the rest of the shot and starts motioning for another. "Why you here, Ben?"

"Because I'm homeless."

"Homeless! Hah! You're kidding, right? You came to Israel because you have no place to live? You should have found a box."

My scotch-drinking friend orders two more. "Add my buddy here on my tab. He's homeless!"

I put my hand on his left shoulder, staring through a haze, smiling as if we've been cronies for twenty years. "No, no, no, you don't have to pay. I've got money, see?" I show him a small wad of US dollars.

The guy smiles back. "Don't worry, pal. I made a killin' in my forties. Car dealerships. Been living off the money for eighteen years. I could buy every day and not know the cash is gone."

This is a good development. I've found myself a Sugar Daddy.

"One condition, though." His body language tells me we're negotiating a contract.

"Anything for my new friend."

"If I pay, you drink what I drink."

Twelve ounces of beer ago, there's a strong possibility I would have declined. However, free booze is free booze. Bring on the scotch.

∞ ∞ ∞

Oh God. Oh God in Heaven, help me.

The contents of my stomach are on the sidewalk. The red spots in my eyes and the black taste in my mouth are dwarfed by the involuntary heaving—dry, violent lurches stretching from my shoulders to my lower back. After about ten or twelve of them, they begin to subside, but I stay the way I am, bent over on my knees, head hanging, guzzling mouthfuls of air.

I hear people wandering by, chattering in the street, and wonder if anyone sees me. I roll onto my butt and lean against the wall. I'm around a corner in a type of alley, out of any direct line of sight. I close my eyes, trying to remember how I got to this spot. I can't.

"Ben? Ben? Do you hear me?" I open my eyes and see Jeb, his face a foot in front of mine. "This is bad."

I catch Daniel's voice. "Should I get medical help?"

Jeb leans in and sniffs. "No. I don't think so. We need to get him get out of here and back to his room. Grab an arm."

After I feel the lift and land on my feet, a cloth wipes my face, and they lead me onto the main street.

I shake my arms free. "I got this. I'll stand."

"You sure?" Daniel doesn't sound convinced.

I hobble forward, heading, I believe, towards the hotel.

Jeb turns me. "Whoa, there, buddy. This way."

My eyes see an impressionist painting, and to adjust course, I follow a blur I assume is Jeb's finger.

When we go through the sliding doors at the hotel, the brightness of the lobby is shocking. I sense Daniel move away, but Jeb stays at my side, while Addy and Gerri watch me shuffle across to the elevators.

I'm expecting anger or disgust or resentment and am surprised there isn't any. As we travel to the ninth floor, Jeb makes sure I stay upright. Once we're in the room, he ensures a soft landing on the bed, being careful to align my head with the pillow. He whispers a few words about sleeping things off and quietly exits.

"This is not a good night, is it?" I respond to Joseph's question by shaking my head while he covers me with a blanket. "No, there is nothing to be done for you right now. Sleep, my friend, sleep."

He turns off the light, plunging the room into darkness.

PROGRESS REPORT # 5

Peter,

I begin with positive news. Two concepts seem to have resonated with Our Man.

First, he appreciates empirical, worldly evidence supporting the Word. Please don't chuckle. We've discussed, endlessly, how this should be effective in all cases. These humans, however, are a tricky lot and, for reasons I don't understand, tangible proof does not always have an impact. Regardless, an introduction to the famous Scrolls was a meaningful experience.

Secondly, we put forth the concept of the "room" or "tent," using it as a proxy for being present with Him Who Is Above. One of our caretakers deftly introduced the subject. I am confident this will become a primary theme in our work.

In addition, we presented the idea of calling. This, most assuredly, will not prove useful in the short term. However, given the complexity of the topic, I welcome the opportunity to insert basic information when possible.

Beyond these developments, there were several meaningful events today.

The Spirit appeared once again, bringing a few moments of peace. A short but violent spiritual battle ensued, and human regrets and misgivings quickly overwhelmed Our

Man's tranquility. This led to complete submission to his earthly vice. Not a pleasant scenario, but informative nonetheless. My personal intervention, when necessary and at the appropriate time, will need to be direct and dramatic.

Our Man asked for help, saying a desperate prayer under physical duress, a crass plea made as an afterthought. Not wanting to waste an opportunity, I made sure he received an answer, sending two caretakers to assist. He could, in the future, recognize this occurred. We both know, however, whether his awareness occurs at the conscious level or not, all responses from He Who Is Above serve as important building blocks.

A word on caretakers. Your team has assembled an exceptional group of faithful individuals, each blessed with excellent instincts and an uncommon ability to discern. On a more personal note, they are an intriguing crew, and I regret my assignment is short. It would be interesting to better understand their earthly journeys. Perhaps on another occasion. For now, I will thank you for their presence and utilize them as effectively as possible.

On an overall basis, I'm afraid we overloaded Our Man today. As alluded to above, he fell and fell hard, although this is not a discouraging event. All of us know human failing induces transparency and vulnerability, which, with many of our subjects, proves invaluable. I will observe early tomorrow and determine what, if any, opportunities have been created.

With gratitude for your guidance,
Joseph

DAY 6

I wake up, pain stretching across my forehead. As my body drops to the floor, I curse, ejecting the smell of open sewer lines through parched lips. The glow from the clock, which reads 4:17 a.m., guides me to the bathroom, where I pull myself up and click on the light. The flash knocks me back, I hit the door, and bang against the wall.

Out comes a second curse, one you can't say on TV. I peek out to see if I've disturbed Joseph, aware there's no need to worry. Joseph doesn't wake up unless he wants to wake up.

With an unenthusiastic spirit, I face the mirror.

The glare from the fluorescent tubes is merciless. My gray pallor, combined with chapped dry skin, a day-old beard, small specks of residual vomit, and eyes embedded in dark caverns, has me staring at a creature from a zombie movie. My clothes are equally disgusting.

Where do I start with this mess?

I take a tentative first step and brush my teeth. When I rinse, I start drinking, inhaling the toothpaste with the water, trying to quench my thirst. I pause for a breath and see a bottle of Excedrin which must belong to Joseph. I can't imagine why. He never gives the impression he's uncomfortable, let alone in need of painkillers. I consume four.

Okay, what next? Right. Clean up. The hot water must relax my muscles, because, as soon as I'm done showering, my system evacuates my digestive tract, only I don't throw it up this time. Afterwards, I take another shower, shave, and sit, wrapped in a towel, on the toilet seat.

This is bad. I can't remember the last time I got sloppy drunk with people who know me. *Who saw?* If I recall, there was Jeb and Daniel outside on the street, plus Addy and Gerri in the hotel lobby. Joseph in the room. I turn off the light, burying my head in my hands.

I'm not sure how long I've been sitting on the toilet when I hear a click, and a band of light sneaks under the door. Stepping into the room, I see Joseph, propped up in bed, holding a newspaper. I glance at the clock. 5:13 a.m. *Where the heck did he get a newspaper at this hour?*

He appears happy to see me. "Ah, my friend. You are up. Feeling better?"

With the Excedrin, shower, and intestinal purge, my body, which has been through this drill before, should be ready to go. On the interpersonal side of the ledger, though, last night is hanging there, not in the background, but right in front. A big, fat, albatross between me and whatever interactions occur throughout the day. *No, Joseph, I don't feel better, thank you very much.* Instead of answering, I shake my head.

He nods to my nightstand. The coffee is in a ceramic mug, an improvement over one of those thin Styrofoam cups. This hotel must be a step up.

I show a minimum of gratitude. "Thanks."

After a few minutes, the mug is empty. Time to get dressed. Rummaging through my luggage, I spot the two remaining bottles of vodka from the airplane, and my mouth starts watering. As I close my hand around one of them, I briefly pause and consider a change in approach. I reject the idea, though, convinced one drink, this one, will help me deal with any negative reactions when I see the rest of the group.

I take the bottle, along with my clothes, into the bathroom. As soon as the door shuts, I twist the top, draining the vodka in two gulps. I finish dressing and walk back into the room, smiling.

"Yep," I say.

Joseph is puzzled. "What do you mean, my friend?"

"My answer is yep. I feel better. Ready for the day."

I exit the room, not worried about the albatross, prepared to face whatever's before me.

∞ ∞ ∞

I get to the lobby a few minutes before six in the morning. While there's hardly anyone around, and breakfast isn't going yet, there must be coffee available because I see Daniel—off in a corner, drinking a cup, and reading.

I lower my head, moving in the opposite direction, when he sees me. "Good morning, Ben."

I turn. "Hey, Daniel."

"Care to join me?"

Only if the root canal slot is filled. "Uh, I don't want to mess with what you're doing. You're busy. There're plenty of other spots."

He closes the book and gestures towards an empty chair. "I'm not busy. I'd enjoy starting the day with you."

He would?

Daniel directs me to a table holding coffee and light food.

A minute later, I'm sitting, cup in hand, along with a small plate of fruit. They're either figs or dates. *Does anyone know the difference?*

We drink in silence. While Daniel appears comfortable, I'm not. Less than twelve hours earlier, the guy helped drag my drunk carcass off the street.

I fidget, not willing to address what needs to be addressed, drink half a refill, and, because I can't stand my uneasiness, cough out a stupid conversation starter. "I'm sorry to interrupt your reading."

"No worries there. I'm brushing up, doing a refresher to get ready for the day."

"Refresher?"

"Yes. We're going to Ein Gedi this morning. Second stop, I believe."

I don't know what Ein Gedi is and don't want to ask, figuring I've done enough to alienate him. He, however, keeps speaking, scratching his stubbly beard and studying the wear in his jeans. "You can learn about Ein Gedi in the first book of Samuel. David hid there after Saul became jealous of David's, shall we say, growing popularity. To avoid being killed, David found his way to Ein Gedi and lived in the caves."

A memory stirs. I must have heard this one somewhere along the line. "There's something about a robe in there. Something gets cut off."

Daniel nods. "Saul and three thousand of his men tracked David down. He, Saul I mean, went into a cave where David was hiding and David snuck up and cut off a corner of Saul's robe." *A bold move. In David's situation, I'm guessing I would have opted to take the King out.* "There's a fairly intense conversation after, but, in the end, Saul was relieved he hadn't been killed and tells David he knows David will be king someday."

I guess Daniel figures he's covered the topic and sips away, studying the people who've started milling around the lobby. I fidget again, assessing if he's owed an explanation for what happened, before squashing the idea. My drinking is none of his business. Besides, I hadn't asked for any help and am confident I would have found my way without him and Jeb.

I'm not safe, though. Daniel introduces the subject. "Last night was interesting."

Interesting is one word to use. "Uh ... yeah ... I had too much to drink, on an empty stomach. I'll be more careful."

He twists the overgrown whiskers on his chin. "No, I believe there was more going on. There's good in the world, and there's bad. The bad is always trying to get to us. Last night was spiritual warfare."

Here we go.

I push back. "You're overcomplicating what happened. I made the mistake of accepting free scotch. Scotch doesn't agree with me. You saw the results."

Daniel's either ignoring or unaware of my end of the conversation. "I was watching you yesterday. You were more relaxed than the other days. Until you weren't." He swallows a mouthful of coffee before continuing. "I believe in Satan. I believe he saw movement away from him and decided to get his hands on you, provide a measure of temptation."

Daniel was watching me? What, making sure I behaved okay? And now, the Devil? He's saying the guy with red horns and a pitchfork is watching me too?

I'm on my feet. "Who the heck are you? What about all the things you did? Big things. Illegal things."

"This isn't about me."

"Finally, you've made an accurate statement. Sure, I made a mistake. Me. Alone. I didn't hurt anybody, and I didn't cause an international incident. Don't turn this into the final battle between good and evil."

Before he responds, I'm at the elevator, banging the UP button and headed to my floor. In the room, I pull out the last miniature vodka, empty the contents into my mouth, causing my cheeks to expand, and release the liquid down my throat. The relief is palpable.

∞ ∞ ∞

On the bus, people, including Daniel, are friendly and I don't detect any anger, disappointment, or resentment. Jeb goes out of his way to pat me on the shoulder. No one asks "Are you okay today?" or "How you feeling?" I was definitely expecting a different reaction.

I'm relieved but not surprised—I didn't make us all late. I've always been good on the rebound, and regardless of what I do to my body the night before, I show up.

As we rumble along, Avi offers one of his educational sessions. "Have you found yourselves any of our shekels yet?" A few people nod. "We've had them around here for a long time. In the book of Genesis, Abraham used them to buy a burial place for Sarah."

Gerri shouts out. "He paid four hundred shekels, to be exact."

Avi nods. "Yes. In those days, shekels were used as currency and as a unit of measure, linked to the weight of barley. As you would expect, there were changes over the years and the original shekel disappeared somewhere along the line."

Caleb raises his hand, talking at the same time. "Until 1980. I remember when the shekel came back, replacing our old currency which was called either the Israeli Lira or the Israeli Pound."

"However, the 1980 shekel is not what you get when you are here today," Avi continues. "There was big inflation and a new shekel was put out at the end of 1985.

Pick one up if you haven't already. A shekel would be a good souvenir for you to bring back to America."

∞ ∞ ∞

We unload from the bus into a furnace, settling onto wooden benches. There's a tarp keeping the sun off but, according to my soaked shirt, not the heat.

A woman in front of us holds a Bible and tells us we are going to see the tabernacle built by Moses to hold the Ark of the Covenant. "A tabernacle is a portable tent. The word also means 'place of dwelling' or 'sanctuary.' What you are going to see is an actual reproduction based on specific directives delivered from God to Moses in the Book of Exodus."

My mouth is a wad of cotton, and my stomach a roiling sea, churning with acid. I realize I haven't consumed anything but alcohol and coffee for close to fifteen hours. Maybe longer. *Gut it out, Ben, gut it out.*

She opens the Bible to chapter twenty-six and reads a meticulous list of instructions. I hear types of wood, learn a cubit is a measure about eighteen inches long, and endure numerous detailed parameters. The guide is delivering a college lecture. A long one. I'm desperate for her to wrap this up—I can't sit much longer.

Finally, she finishes. After standing, I feel slightly better and manage to dig a few peppermints out of my pocket. Sucking on the hard candy is temporarily refreshing.

We walk about twenty steps, and as we look around, the guide narrates. "We're in the valley of Timna. The area you see is the wilderness mentioned in the Bible. Not the entire wilderness, obviously, but this will give you an idea of the landscape. Moses and the Jews roamed through this and similar terrain for forty years."

I rotate in a full circle, not seeing much. There is a hill in the foreground which, according to Caleb, is named Mount Timna. Off in the distance, there are a few threadbare trees and more hills. None of the nearby modern upgrades, including the road, parking area, and visitor's center, distracts from what registers in my mind. Desert. The real desert. Hard ground, no clouds, direct sun, arid air. An oven stretching forever. *A whole people wandered for forty years in this?* Based on the way I'm feeling, I wouldn't have lasted a week.

She keeps going. "I imagine you're considering this is an inhospitable environment."

Caleb answers for all of us. "Uh, yeah, I'd say these are unfriendly conditions."

She nods, not missing a beat. "God, however, did provide. He sent manna every day."

Ah, manna. One of those cute Biblical legends.

She moves us along to the tabernacle, which is an oversized tent, similar to the ones they use for weddings, except there are thin pillars in front and a wooden frame under the canvas. Long ropes, staked into the stiff ground, hold the structure in place. According to the guide, the tabernacle was portable and would be disassembled and moved as the Jews traveled. I'm impressed. This is no two-man pup tent from Walmart.

She finishes with "as the Jews moved from place to place, God would guide them. He would provide a pillar of cloud by day and a pillar of fire by night."

I blurt out a question. "Then how the heck did they get lost for forty years?"

My inquiry is greeted with an awkward pause, before Ruth offers an explanation. "I'd say losing their way was necessary for the Jews—to prepare them to cross into Israel. They had to be provided the Ten Commandments, disobey God, be forgiven. Endure test after test after test. Sometimes they submitted, other times they rebelled. Through all the challenges, though, they were watched over, blessed by God."

"What you call blessings," I kick the dirt at my feet, knowing I should let this go, "I call magic. Maybe even myth."

I see shoulders tighten and eyes shift away. Except for Ruth. "Despite all the blessings, they still wavered. Don't misunderstand, I'm not being critical. We all doubt. At least I know I do. Maybe, without those forty years, the Israelites would have questioned more later on. Either way, why events happen is not for me to know. God does what God does. Sometimes we have to accept circumstances as they are."

Pastor Marcus responds. "Amen, Ruth, and thank you."

As the tour continues, I don't have to worry about bumping into anyone. The group is giving me plenty of space.

Inside the tabernacle are life size statues of guys in colorful robes sporting full, flowing beards. They remind me of a wax museum. The first room is called the "Holy Place" and contains the "Table of Showbread," the "Golden Lampstand," and the "Altar of Incense." The guide explains all of them, but I'm working to stay on two feet. When we move into the next room, which is called the "Holy of Holies," the guide gets excited. This has the Big One—a reproduction of the Ark of the Covenant. I ease out to the edge of the group, lean against a post, and hope to diminish the growing nausea.

When the Scripture reading starts, I decide to get out of there before I barf all over the Ten Commandments, although in reality, I've been barfing on them for years.

I kneel next to the bus, head between my knees, staring at the pebbles and sand between my feet, feeling the cold sweat, enduring the dry heaves. When I stand, the bus driver hands me a bottle of water, leads me around to the door, says a few words in Hebrew, and directs me on board. The first thing I notice is the air conditioning. The second is the water, a river of relief, sliding down my esophagus. My body stops revolting, and I lay my head on the window.

My fellow travelers exit the tent. Pastor Marcus points to the bus, and I guess they're heading over, but before they start moving, Ruth orchestrates them into a circle. Heads are bowed, and a prayer is said.

A few moments later, as the bus fills, Ruth makes a detour and comes to see me. "Is there anything you need?"

Shaking my head, I wave her off. "I'm fine, thanks. Headed in the right direction."

"I hope you continue to feel better." She heads back to the front.

"Uh ... Ruth?" I don't mean what I say next. "I'm sorry I didn't come out to join the prayer."

She smiles and comes back to my seat, putting her hand on my shoulder. "We were praying for you, Ben. You weren't invited."

While Ruth's words were delivered without judgment and in the same soothing tone she always uses, the sheer arrogance of her comment flips a toggle switch in my brain. *These presumptuous Holy Rollers need to pray for me? Seriously?*

"Are you angry, my friend?"

I don't remember Joseph boarding the bus or coming down the aisle, let alone sitting down beside me.

"I'm not angry. I'm ticked off."

"Ticked off? Are you using an American term?"

"Yeah. It's a popular American term."

"Perhaps we should talk about this?"

"It's them," I declare, saluting the front of the bus.

"What about them?"

"They're so sure of themselves."

Joseph is perplexed. "Sure of themselves?"

"My point is, they assume they know what I need. Get in those little circles. Ask God for whatever they ask God for."

"Perhaps you should consider their perspective."

"Whatever."

"Suit yourself."

Joseph starts reading one of his carpentry magazines but doesn't turn the page before he starts in again. "Ben, over the course of the last day, what do you think everyone saw?"

I don't answer.

"I'll tell you. They saw a man, a new acquaintance, hundreds of miles from home, foul with alcohol, sick in public, and unable to stay standing through the morning's activities."

I strike back. "I'm recovering from too much to drink. There was no crime committed, and I was perfectly capable of finding my own way back to the hotel. The situation was under control." My face is getting hot. "I certainly don't need a bunch of people praying for me."

Joseph lets me calm down before he responds. "Do you know what they prayed, Ben?"

"Probably a pile of nonsense about my salvation or them hoping I'll see the light of God and turn my life over to Jesus."

"What you describe was not the focus of their prayer."

Boy, I'm not in the mood for this. "They said what they said. I'm not sure I care."

"Ah, but you should at least know."

I give the old bring-it-on hand gesture.

"All they did was pray you would feel better and ask God to help you heal."

"Beseeching God didn't work. I feel awful again."

"Ah, but he provides."

Joseph reaches into his bag and pulls out a pouch of nuts, a handful of dates or figs, and a piece of pita. He also produces a bottle of Coke that, and I can't imagine how, is ice cold.

"Here, my friend, eat and drink. You will feel better."

I do and he's right. As soon as I'm done, there's a groundswell of weariness, and I have no choice but to lean my head back and close my eyes.

∞ ∞ ∞

"How long was I asleep?"

"We traveled about half an hour to get here," answers Joseph. Right before I exit the bus, he holds me back. "There's considerable walking at this stop. Are you able?"

The nap, the food, and the cold drink have all helped. I'm ready to participate. "Sure, fire away."

"Excellent. This is a special place and significant in Israeli history. You'll learn about our great king, David. More importantly, my friend, see and absorb what is here, appreciate the beauty."

When my feet hit the pavement, Addy is standing there with two white pills and a bottle of water. "Aspirin. Don't fight me on this."

I pop them in my mouth, draining the bottle in one long swallow.

After reaching into her pack and giving me more water, Addy's hands prod my neck, feel my forehead, and lift my eyelids, before she tells me to stick out my tongue. "Have you urinated today?"

"Excuse me?"

"You heard me."

"Ah ... I can't remember."

"Drink the bottle of water."

People are getting bossy around here. I do what she says.

"Did you sleep? Eat?"

"Yep."

"You should be okay. Take more water with you."

I comply with her directive, grabbing another bottle and joining the cluster of people around Avi.

∞ ∞ ∞

Avi moves his arm in a wide arc. "This is Ein Gedi." As my eyes follow the path of his hand, I observe lush plants, running water, patches of grass, and kids scampering along a path, a few of them wearing bathing suits, disappearing into clumps of trees. There's nothing desolate here. "We're going to hike in and be surrounded by the beauty of this wonderful nature reserve. As we do, I urge you to keep one thing in mind—what you will see has been here since ancient times."

Caleb cuts in. "Let's not forget David."

"No," Avi responds, "we will most certainly not forget David." He tells us about the cave and Saul, citing David as his favorite character in the Bible.

Ruth asks why.

"Because he was human. David committed adultery, stole another man's wife, lied, murdered. He was an imperfect man."

"David's misbehavior makes him your favorite?" Ruth sounds unconvinced.

Avi shakes his head. "No. David is my favorite because, through the failures in his life, he continued to reach for God, to ask for his forgiveness, to follow his will."

Gerri lifts her Bible. "As they say, David was a man after God's own heart. He's searching for God in the Psalms. The pain, the crying out, the joy, and the begging for protection."

Avi adds color. "A number of those Psalms were written right here, while David was hiding from Saul. Let us go see."

Walking is good. As we wind through a combination of trees and shrubs, we come to openings where steep cliffs ascend and small streams make their way to the Dead Sea, my muscles loosen and my legs stretch out. I speculate about the science—how this type of place, bounded by a desert, exists and survives. I watch my feet move along the dirt trail, picking their way around jutting rocks, up inclines, and around corners. Despite being in the shade, my shirt clings to my back. Sometimes a leaf tickles my neck or a branch needs to be held out of the way, and my mind empties.

Brains don't stay unoccupied long. Mine quickly fills again, inundated with memories of the last twenty-four hours, followed by disappointment. Not in my behavior but in my sloppiness. Alcoholics try to stop drinking by getting on a "program." I'm the opposite. My "program" is designed to hide how bad things are. When I went to the bar, I deviated from my usual agenda and risked being seen drunk. The result? I've let them witness me at my worst. I'm convinced people are judging my actions, analyzing "what's wrong with Ben?"

I need to get away from the crowd and pick up the pace. I ask Avi. "Is it okay if I go ahead on my own? Will I get lost out here?"

"No, feel free. Please, though, stop at the bridge ahead."

Legs sticking to the inside of my jeans, I jog for about a half mile, feeling winded along the way, until I arrive at the bridge. There's a long waterfall and the mist cools me off. The cascading water empties into a pool that, in turn, creates one of the streams we'd been hiking past.

With my elbows leaning on the wood railing, I watch a young girl and her mother playing under the waterfall. I also catch my breath and brood on my behavior.

Sure, this is bad, although in relative terms I've been through worse. Much worse. The splashing girl reminds me of Olivia and my thoughts race to a Saturday from a few years back. Sarah and Zach were out at a Cub Scout popcorn sale, and I needed to restock my Absolut.

Olivia, all of three years old, was in the bathtub. I completed a quick mental calculation and figured she could play for the fifteen minutes necessary to make a quick run. I told her to stay put, I had to take care of an errand, and I left.

I returned in twelve minutes that, despite my earlier conclusion, was not fast enough. As I pulled into the driveway, Olivia walked out from behind the garage, stepping in front of my SUV. She was wrapped in a towel, her miniature hands holding the front closed. As the vehicle bounced to a stop, my eyes locked on those two tiny fists. The look on her freckled face was a combination of fear and misunderstanding, a mask of confusion peeking at me through her strawberry-blond curls.

When I got out, she asked, "Where did you go, Daddy? Why did you leave me alone?" Her eyes were as wide as silver dollar pancakes.

I, in all my fatherly grace and wisdom, responded by making sure none of the neighbors were watching.

Afterward, I drank more than usual.

My devout friends are beginning to arrive at the bridge. I straighten and sip my water.

Avi explains he needs to make a phone call and offers us a break. The group mingles on or around the bridge. I'm content watching the waterfall. At the same time, I review Avi's comments about David being his favorite Bible character, despite David being a flawed man.

He couldn't have been as messed up as I am.

Gerri is on my left. "You okay, sweetie?"

"Uh, yeah, thanks."

"Good. I was afraid I was going to have to make you my Grannie's remedy. Glad I didn't. Not sure if I could dig up coke syrup, ginger root, molasses, and a raw egg in this part of the world."

A different voice sounds from my right. "We've been worried about you."

Jeb, whose wrinkled golf shirt looks slept in, is facing me, ready to talk. I figure I owe him something, considering he helped get me back last night. "Ah, hey, Jeb, about walking to the hotel—"

He waves his hand. "Let's not discuss that right now. Getting back on your feet?"

"Yep, on the road to recovery."

Jeb's eyes shift away before he responds. "There are lots of layers to recovery. Another topic for later on."

I'm not sure where he's headed, but my gut starts churning. I don't want to explore any further and turn to Gerri. Her Bible is open on the railing, presenting an easy path to a different discussion. "What are you reading?"

"About David. I share Avi's affection for the guy. He's one of my heroes."

Jeb warms to the new topic. "You on the good part or the bad part?"

"You know me, sweetie. If something's in the Bible, it's all good, but I know what you're getting at. I'm on Bathsheba."

I remember the name Bathsheba. She was a slave girl or servant who slept with someone. Gerri helps to set the record straight. "She must have been a beauty. David gets one eyeful of her sittin' in a bath, and he sends for her."

"I got Ruth the same way," says Jeb, "one look, a summons, and the rest is history."

Gerri reaches across and pats his hand. "Right, honey, I'm sure you're remembering exactly how things happened. Either way, David faced a more complicated state of affairs. First off, he gets Bathsheba pregnant. Secondly, she's married to a man named Uriah."

"David has him murdered, right?" Jeb's bumping a fist against his forehead. "Shoot, I can't remember the specifics."

"Oh, the details are worse than any old murder. Uriah was part of David's army, a loyal soldier. David had Uriah put out front during a fight and the rest of the soldiers backed away, leaving Uriah hanging out there to be slaughtered."

"I remember now." Jeb smiles.

Gerri keeps going. "What David did would get your hide whipped in my family, after which we'd tell you to get lost and never darken the door again. I know because my ex-husband got the boot, as they say. He didn't get anybody pregnant, but the unfaithful fool swapped me for a younger model. Of course, we've got one forgiving God, and David came through his trials okay. He got to stay around and married Bathsheba. They had a son, Solomon, who was the king after David. You set this story in a law firm or some of those glitzy Manhattan townhouses, and I'm paying good cash money to watch it on Netflix."

Gerri? Dumped? Learning this about her is surprising—she's funny, smart, and fun to be around. Then again, maybe the guy was tired of all the Bible verses.

We listen to the water for a minute before Jeb speaks quietly. "I'm no David, but in my life, God has made good out of bad."

"Amen. The Lord works with us where we are."

After Gerri's reverent response, I feel cynical again. They're relying on the hope God mystically orchestrates everything. *Please.* These two probably faced adversity and, when the worm turned, attributed their good fortune to divine providence.

Avi's back, and we continue along the path, walking with the cliffs climbing to our right, the continuity of the grayish white rock interrupted by an impressive number of caves. He points out a few. "When David was in exile, he hid in those caves."

"I'd hate to have to attack those!" Caleb's practically bellowing.

"Yes," agrees Avi, "they are strategically situated. Also, there's water, and food is plentiful. Fruits, dates, wildlife. God's protection and abundance have been here for thousands of years."

We're back working our way through a vegetative tunnel. Listening to the water moving along the small stream beside the path, I remember Avi's words when we first got here, Gerri and Jeb jabbering on about David, and the exchange about the caves. These Holy Rollers are certain. There's no one questioning what we're seeing or hearing. They're convinced.

We hit the top of the trail, and as we emerge back into the sunlight, I mutter a question. "How do we know this is where David hid?"

The words must have come out louder than intended, because Gerri answers. "The story's right here in the

Book. First Samuel, chapter twenty-three, verse twenty-nine: 'And David went up from there and lived in the strongholds of Ein Gedi.'"

"The Bible actually mentions this place by name?"

Gerri points to a pamphlet she's holding. "Spelled the same as you see on the brochure."

I have to admit, the long-term historical connection is impressive. *Of course, we could go visit Harry Potter world too.*

The rest of the short hike takes us to beautiful pools and more long waterfalls pouring down from what I guess are fifty-foot drops. I'm not interested, though. My stomach is growling for food.

∞ ∞ ∞

I'm swaddled in a post drunk funk, a pithy description for my mental condition after I get all tanked up, as the old timers would say. I think about how my post-drinking days follow a typical pattern—feel awful all morning, better but crabby in the afternoon, lots of overriding cynicism, and a decidedly short fuse. At work, I'd cover by isolating myself to do paperwork. If I had to interact, I'd march my way through the process, aided by a discreet sip or two.

It was different at home, though. If the funk happened on a weekday, the defenses went down once work was over. I'd walk through the door and see Sarah's expression, a combination of dreadful anticipation and a hopeful 'welcome home' smile. As soon as I saw her, whatever I was using to hold myself together was replaced by a tornado. My mood would rip through our family, a torrent of short answers, slammed doors, criticism, and yelling.

Sarah reacted by pleading with me to stop, yelling back if the kids weren't nearby, and eventually going all mama bear protectionist, sending me away. Which was fine from my perspective. I'd retreat into my little study, sit without a light on, and start drinking, stewing in guilt, shame, and how-dare-you-judge-me anger. Until the alcohol kicked in, and I'd settle down, believing I was okay. A good man.

The pattern was similar on the weekends, except the at-home cycle started first thing in the morning.

As the bus stops, I pull myself back to the present, and we file out. People have been pleasant, which makes me anxious. The group's small enough, meaning everyone must be aware of last night's events. For those who aren't, today's interchange with Ruth and the abrupt exit from the tabernacle happened in front of everyone. I'm expecting to be ignored, get a self-righteous lecture, be greeted with the cold shoulder, or be patronized with overly-sweet expressions of concern. The holier-than-thou approach. However, after we go into the restaurant and get our plates filled, I'm welcomed with smiles and an invitation from Daniel to "join us here" at a large, round table.

I've got an empty chair on one side and Daniel on another. The conversation is about kids and jobs and happenings back home. I join in, answering questions, and tell a stupid joke about a rabbi in a nursing home. The mood is light, airy, and pleasant.

"How come people aren't mad at me?" I ask Daniel quietly.

He shows me his knowing grin and answers with a question. "Would our anger do any good?"

"Any good?"

"Would us being mad make your situation any better?"

"I guess not, no."

"There you have it."

I push back. "This is all way too easy."

"Easy?"

"Yeah. How do they not react?"

"Ben, this group here, our happy little clan—they're a unique bunch. God walks with them in a special way."

I evaluate those around the table. There's Daniel, of course, the reformed corporate climber. In addition, I see Gerri—the Bible savant, Addy—a mid-twenties, enlightened nurse, Caleb—a boisterous dry cleaner and relocated Israeli, Ruth—the peaceful one, and Jeb—a retired lawyer whom I don't know much about yet. While there's no doubt I'm surrounded by an interesting group, I struggle with Daniel's comment. "Wait ... wait ... are you saying they're more spiritually evolved? Claiming they're better at this than other folks?"

"Not at all. I'm saying the opposite."

Okay, this light-hearted lunch gathering is starting to go deep. "You're gonna have to help me out here."

"They know how weak they are. They rely on God to help them fight the war."

"The war?"

"The spiritual war."

Uh, oh, here we go again. I tighten up. Thankfully, Daniel stops there and turns back to his food. We finish lunch with Gerri telling a story about how her Granny, while attending a woman's retreat, won thirty dollars in a poker game.

∞ ∞ ∞

"Okay folks," explains Avi after lunch, "time for a fun break. Snorkeling in the Red Sea."

Following a short ride, we're at the closest thing to a traditional tourist spot I've seen. People are clustered in groups, getting masks and snorkels, listening to safety briefings, and eating ice cream. I jump into a humid shower room and, surrounded by hairy men and hyperactive boys, change into my bathing suit.

Ruth has commandeered a picnic table and offers to watch our belongings. As I walk past, I notice a Bible open on the table. "Aren't you going to join us?"

"No. I'm going to read in the Psalms while you're all out there swimming."

I try to maneuver the conversation away from faith. "You don't enjoy snorkeling?"

"Oh, I love snorkeling—and scuba diving too. After Ein Gedi, though, I have an urge to spend time with David."

She starts reading, managing to focus in the midst of squealing kids running rampant, childless couples maneuvering toward the beach, and teenagers either snapping towels or holding hands. There are also a few grandmothers wearing long dresses, their heads covered by scarves, eating from plates of figs, nuts, and grapes, chatting away while their families are in the water.

Jeb approaches, wearing a black bathing suit, a mask and snorkel hanging around his neck. The usual rumpled golf shirt has been replaced by a beat-up T-shirt, and his face is hidden behind streaks of sunscreen. He asks Ruth, "Are you sure you don't want to come?"

"Believe me, I want to, but I got an urge."

He kisses her cheek. "I'm not going to argue with an urge. Hasn't worked before, and I'm sure it won't work now."

After Jeb heads for the beach, Ruth refocuses her attention on me. "He wrote about half of the Psalms, you know."

"You mean Jeb?"

Ruth smiles at my pitiful joke, probably because she's kind, and keeps going. "No, David."

"Uh-huh."

"I'm amazed at how much I learn from him." She has a finger marking her spot on the page. "Do you remember what Gerri said when we were at Ein Gedi? The Psalms cover the whole range of emotions. Praise, thanksgiving, anguish, fear. When I read them, I picture a man tortured, fighting the battle between his human failings, which were significant, and his desire to do God's will."

Oh, boy. I'm heading straight for another discussion about spiritual warfare. Time to extricate myself. "I'll let you get to it."

I'm about two steps away when she calls out. "Ben?" I turn. "It's okay to have questions about God. We all have in the past and, sometimes, we still do. If you didn't, you wouldn't be human. Remember the Jews in the desert? Wandering around for those forty years? I know I'm being repetitive, but maybe certain struggles are supposed to happen."

I give her the once over, trying to match her slim, seemingly brittle body with an active lifestyle. "I'm sorry, I can't picture you snorkeling or scuba diving."

"Open your mind, Ben. Preconceived notions get you in trouble."

She lowers her eyes and gets back to reading.

∞ ∞ ∞

The water's loaded with adults and kids, rubber flippers churning, their exposed backs and shoulders absorbing the sun. Scattered among the line of swimmers, mini-geysers spurt from the top of snorkels. I join them, moving steadily between two piers, being careful to stay inside the ropes creating a sea lane. Before we got in, they told us the rope line closest to shore protects a coral habitat. The outer rope, I assume, helps us avoid drifting away and never coming back.

I jump in, and it's cold enough to flush away the last tiny remnants of hangover. Bobbing along, I study the brightly colored fish congregating in schools and around rocks. After unsuccessfully trying to catch them with my hands, I drift, enveloped in the hush of the water. There's no contemplation of my life situation, no impulses to drink, and no fretting about the Holy Rollers. The current provides a peaceful ride to the second dock.

I hoist myself up the ladder, feeling cleansed. Joseph is there waiting. "How was your swim, my friend?"

"Good, Joseph, good. I'm refreshed. Feel the best I have all day."

"Ah. The great cleanser. Water brings life in all kinds of ways."

Moving along the platform, I see Jeb there, toweling off, and we decide to head back together. He's effusive about the snorkeling. "Boy, a good dunking was definitely what I needed. Too much walking and sand and dust and heat. It was good to submerge and get the all-around cool you only get in the water. Reminded me of when I was a kid in the county pool."

The late afternoon sun dries us off while we stroll along.

"Think my wife has finished her reading?" Jeb's query, which comes across as a random musing, doesn't register. "She'll sit there all day if she's not done. At least at home she would. I guess here, she'll keep going once we get on the bus."

The second part of Jeb's comment sinks in more. I had the impression Ruth was merely passing time while we went swimming. Jeb keeps going. "Sometimes, though, whatever she's pursuing is right at the beginning and she'll be done after a couple of minutes."

Now I'm curious. "She doesn't know what she's trying to find when she begins?"

Jeb shakes his head. "Not when she has one of those urges." I remember Ruth mentioning urges back at the picnic table. "Those urges, they gnaw at her until she acts. She describes them as an unrelenting itch."

I say nothing, knowing where this will head if I ask about where the urges or itches or whatever the heck they are come from. My silence doesn't matter. Jeb offers an unsolicited answer. "She has a good gut."

I consider Ruth's rail-thin body. "Based on what I've observed, she's got no gut at all."

Jeb, who's nibbling his right thumbnail while we walk, breaks into a smile, projecting his affection for Ruth. "Yep. Not much accumulated there." He pauses, and when he says the next sentence, I would swear he's awestruck. "What she has is an amazing gift, one she's had for as long as I've known her. Credits her missionary parents."

"Ruth was a missionary?"

"Daughter of missionaries. The family lived all over the world." Jeb's hand is rubbing the back of his neck. "Plus, she's brave enough to use the gift, to follow those feelings she gets, the impulses she feels. They're how she hears. Me? I'm useless. I miss most of what's being said. Too thick in the head. I've gotta get run over by a truck to get the message. Not my Ruth. As far as I'm aware, she's never overlooked or ignored one. She always follows through." He says the next sentence softly and I have to lean in to hear the words. "I admire her more than I can say."

Jeb's overly intimate comment compels me to move our little talk along. "Because she listens?"

"Because she hears."

"In my line of work," I reply, "hearing is a valuable skill. Understanding the other side makes a big difference in a deal."

"No, no ... I'm not talking about business." Jeb gives a head shake and points up to the sky. "I'm talking about him."

I'm pretty sure I know who the "him" is, and I know we're heading towards another testimony type conversation. I want to disengage, preferably by physically relocating. Unfortunately, I can't figure out any logical next step. "Him, huh?"

"Yeah, 'him.'"

After Jeb nods and points to the sky again, I give up. "You mean God, don't you?"

"I mean God."

"You're saying Ruth speaks to God?"

"To be clear, I believe he speaks to all of us. Ruth, though, she has an exceptional capacity to hear him."

"Because of the urges?"

"Uh-huh. On top of that, she does what they tell her to do."

We start walking again. While the sounds around us begin to creep back in, I remember Gerri, back in Capernaum, mentioning something about God whispers. I have an impulse to try and connect her comment with Jeb's observations about Ruth's urges, but I shake my head. I'm having enough trouble staying free of my hangover.

Jeb shifts topics. "This must have been a long day for you."

I'm not sure if I welcome the comment, but he's right. "Rough start, yeah."

"I'd say. The way you looked this morning, I thought you were exhumed from a crypt."

I peek over to see if he's joking. He's not.

Jeb continues, "Actually, I'm pretty impressed."

There's a turn I didn't expect. "Impressed?"

"Yep." He gives my right shoulder a mild slap. "Considering the shape you were in about ten last night, the fact you showed and didn't make us late tells me something."

What? I'm good at cleaning puke off myself and changing into fresh clothes?

Instead of elaborating further, he invites me for a drink. "We've all earned our rest tonight. How about we meet in the bar after we get to the hotel? Unwind after a busy day."

Sounds good to me. We're getting close to the time when I could use a drink or two. "Excellent idea."

∞ ∞ ∞

Throughout the day, Addy and Daniel have been side by side. He's cracking corny jokes, and she's pestering him about updating his jeans.

Right before we board the bus, Gerri taps my shoulder. "Those two are fun to watch."

"Yeah, in a way, they are."

"I tell you what, Benjie. I'm as close to Addy as anyone, and I've seen her get hurt more times than I want to talk about. This one, I believe, is different."

Since we're only on the sixth day of our trip, and as far as I know, they haven't even been on a date, I don't know how she arrives at her conclusion. I'm more interested, though, in her view of Daniel. "What makes you conclude he's different?"

"Daniel's got a gentle soul."

While I agree, I decide not to interject how, not long ago, he'd have cut your throat to keep his bonus intact.

"Also," she adds, "he's easy on the eyes."

Physical attractiveness is not the first characteristic I notice about a man. Unless, of course, he's "off the charts." The Ryan Gosling, Chris Hemsworth, Denzel Washington types. To me, Daniel's a guy who wears worn-out jeans, Christian themed T-shirts, and beat-up hiking shoes. I take a closer look and notice, despite his thin physique, he's pretty muscular, and his faced is nicely framed by a thick mop of what the fashion folks call "good hair." As an added bonus, when Daniel's not smoldering on a deep religious topic, he has an engaging smile. My response, though, is noncommittal. "Ah, if you say so."

Gerri laughs and punches my shoulder. "Typical guy. Afraid to find a man attractive." After a few more steps, she adds, "of course, they're both at their best right now. You never know if a relationship will withstand the grind of life."

Now there's a perceptive statement. I remember how Sarah, when we were dating, didn't understand the extent of my drinking. We were, after all, in college, and partying hard was not unusual behavior. Sure, there were times I got sloppy, but I could cover my behavior with a clever retort. My favorite was "I had a bad month last night." Plus, since we didn't live in the same house, I could escape into my drinking on days she wasn't around. When she was, my late-in-the-day beverage habit was part of playing house together. After college, when I moved to Richmond to be near her, we didn't share an apartment until we were married—Sarah didn't want to be disrespectful to her parents.

The thing is, when I wasn't drinking, I was, in Sarah's words, "sweet." Among the lessons my grandmother taught me was how to behave in regard to my dating life. "Benjamin," she advised me, "you'll never go wrong bringing a girl flowers." At the time, I was too young to understand, but I remembered her advice, and with Sarah,

I brought lots of flowers. I'd also let her pick the movie and always paid, two of my grandmother's other rules. I was attentive too. When Sarah's dad was in the hospital, I was at her side, holding her hand, fetching coffee, and running interference with overzealous neighbors. After we were married, though, the problem areas became more evident, and because of the pressures of life, my drinking got worse. Over time, my personality changed. As I look back, I started rotting from the inside out.

Working my way down the aisle of the bus, I realize I miss Sarah, and I miss the man I once was.

∞ ∞ ∞

One more short hop and the day is over. Though I've been able to rally, aches and fatigue accompany the late-day shakes. My body needs fluids, and not the hydrating kind. I figure a nap will speed up the ride and I'm dozing off when Pastor Marcus starts talking, using the bus microphone. "Hey, guys. What a great day! To top things off, Ruth has something to share."

Ah, the unrelenting Holy Roller chorus.

Ruth stands and says, "While you were all snorkeling, I spent time with the Psalms."

Am I allowed to sleep through this? My head burrows into the back of the seat, but her voice invades my solace. "Today, I was reading bits and pieces, here and there, of my favorites. After a while, I found my way to Psalm twenty-two. David's writings attract me, and I love the way they draw me deep inside his anguish. His cries to God show a humility I wish I had, revealing a raw vulnerability I admire. If you all don't mind, I'll read a few sections."

Caleb agrees for everyone. "Nothing like a little anguish to get the old brain working. Let's hear it!"

Ruth starts right in. "My God, my God, why have your forsaken me?" The next couple of lines slip into the background until one verse penetrates my pre-sleep murkiness. "But I am a worm and not a man."

My eyes open. "What Psalm is she reading?"

Joseph, who's also trying to rest, murmurs his answer. "Twenty-two."

I dig into my bag and pull out my Bible, fumble around for a few pages, and locate the Psalm, impressed I succeeded without any help.

At verse six, my finger stops moving down the page and I land on it. "But I am a worm and not a man."

Jesus. I murmur to myself.

Joseph's eyes open. "He is not here, my friend. I mean, of course he is here, but let's not bother him yet. Tell me, what troubles you?"

I reply by repeating the words quietly. "But I am a worm and not a man." Before I know what's happening, I'm reliving THE night, the last one at home, when I did what no man should ever do, the night I was worse than a worm. "Oh, God."

This time Joseph lifts his head. "What is it, my friend?"

"Not now, okay, Joseph? I need to rest."

"Suit yourself." He closes his eyes again.

I try to sleep, but my mind is swirling, as two phrases loop over and over. The first is Ruth's line from the Psalm, "I am a worm and not a man." The second is what Joseph said about Jesus: "... let's not bother him yet."

Jeb was right. I need to take the edge off.

∞ ∞ ∞

I arrive at the bar first and get a quick shot down.

When Jeb settles onto the stool next door, I order my second vodka and Jeb gets himself a tonic and lime.

We clink glasses, take our first sips, and I ask, "You don't drink?"

"Not now, no."

"Don't like it?"

"Oh, I like it plenty. Too much, in fact."

His answer hangs, waiting for a question I don't want to ask. I know his comment could dangle there all night because, as I'm learning more and more, Jeb is a patient man. He keeps sipping, his eyes studying the array of bottles behind the bartender.

I lob out small talk. "I'm surprised the others haven't come in for a drink."

"They're on the tenth floor, sitting around the pool, sharing a bottle of pre-dinner wine."

I'm ready to move upstairs. "We should join them."

"No, let's stay here." Jeb's shaking his head. "Talk for a while."

I remember earlier, at Ein Gedi, when Jeb didn't want to discuss last night "right now." Is this the 'right now?' Given Jeb's endurance, I decide to find out. "Any specific topic?"

After a sip of tonic and lime, he answers. "Do you want to go into the deep end or the shallow end?"

"Deep end or shallow end?"

"Of the pool."

Okay, what are we talking about here? Is there a good strategy for answering? I choose evasive. "I thought we were having a drink."

His head tilts back, ice bumps against his mouth, and Jeb lets out a small laugh before requesting another tonic and lime. "We're at a time, Ben, for more substance."

He goes back to being patient. I go back to my vodka. While we sit, I'm certain Jeb is willing to contemplate whatever he's contemplating until I either respond or we head to dinner. He must have been one heck of a lawyer.

As a distraction, I eavesdrop on a couple of middle-aged women talking about their kids—college, upcoming weddings, and first jobs. Nothing exciting. When they start in on how they wish their children had a stronger faith, I disengage and take a gander at Jeb. His demeanor hasn't changed, except he's rolling and unrolling his napkin, engrossed in his little miniature scroll.

I crack. "I know I told you this earlier, but I'm sorry about what happened last night."

"I'm sure you are. I was always sorry too."

Is he saying what I believe he's saying?

Jeb sips. "The catch is, for a long time I was never sorry enough to stop."

My brain tells me to keep my mouth shut, but my ego can't stand the silence and has to speak. "Yeah ... uh .... you know, I have my moments, but things don't go bad every day."

Jeb ignores my words, puts his glass down, elbows resting on the bar, and finally turns his head to look right into my eyes. "I'm a drunk, Ben. Have been since I was in my early twenties. I drank at work, I drank after work, I drank after dinner, and I drank while watching TV. I spent the better part of nine years pickled, deceiving everyone I knew, half-heartedly working my way through my career. I wasn't a cheap drunk, either. I spent most every penny of disposable income on the top-shelf liquor. Imported single malts, one-hundred-and-twenty-dollar decanters of brandy, and five-hundred-dollar bottles of bourbon. If I didn't have any money, I ran up the credit cards." He scratches the back of his head. "Along those lines, you do better than I did."

"Excuse me?"

He nods to my drink. "I've been watching you. No super extravagant tastes. Sure, you enjoy a good vodka, but you're not paying top dollar and indulging in the high-end, private reserve liquor. Other times I've seen you drink a beer. Beer's always economical."

I'm suspicious Jeb's trying for one of those private interventions and contemplate leaving, but he signals the bartender for another vodka. He must not believe I'm too bad off if he's ordering me alcohol, and since he's being reasonable about the whole situation, I should at least indulge his conversation. "I'm guessing you stopped drinking?"

"Thirty-three years ago. Thirty-four in two months."

What's the correct response? "Congratulations."

Jeb grunts. "Ben, me, personally, all I did was make a decision. Afterward, though, I got the help I needed from up there." He repeats what he did at the Red Sea and points skyward.

I want to run. I've been to this rodeo before. I know we're heading towards "Do you have a problem, Ben?" However, I haven't finished my vodka, and Jeb's settled into his stool.

"What made you stop?" I ask.

"You in the mood for a long story?"

"Long enough for another drink?"

"Sure."

He orders for both of us, putting me at four. A good number.

Jeb picks up where he left off. "I was pickled for the better part of a decade. Actually, from my twentieth birthday until about halfway through my twenty-ninth year. I never drank in high school, but I went to college with a bunch of Irish kids from New York. Freshman year, I tried beer. The taste wasn't for me. At all. In my sophomore year, I met this guy we called Jimmy O. He loved Jack Daniels, and his mission in life was to get everyone to drink. He got me to bet on a football game, which I lost. Had to take a shot of Jack."

He stops to swirl his tonic and lime, before finishing. "I loved the first taste and kept on going. One became two, two became three, drinking at night became drinking at five in the afternoon, then noon, then a shot before breakfast. I didn't become a drunk overnight, mind you, but over a few years. By the time I got out of law school, I pretty much had a steady buzz all day long."

I listen to his matter-of-fact delivery, wondering how he got from there to here, wondering how anyone does, and if I ever could. "And you still graduated and started a career?"

"Sure did. Also passed the bar. After I cleaned up, my career took off. Once I wasn't half-baked all the time, I was a pretty good lawyer and became a prosecutor. I put away drug dealers, drunk drivers, and people who sold to minors."

"What made you want to stop?"

"Let's be honest with ourselves, Ben. Although we all want to stop, we can't."

I have a *déjà vu* moment, reliving the endless aggravation of rehab. I didn't appreciate being part of a "we" at the Outhouse and I don't appreciate being part of a "we" here.

"For me," Jeb continues, "the end came on a dark, winding road. I was driving home from a business dinner and noticed a car in front of me, a blue Honda Accord. I saw two kids in the back, jumping around and being goofy, reminding me of the days before everyone wore seat belts. In the second before I rammed the car, they both looked at me, lit up by my headlights, smiling and waving. They kept grinning at me through the window while the Accord somersaulted, grinning at me through the window until the impact flattened the roof and the eyes went empty."

He gets quiet, allowing himself time to let his breath out. "The kicker is, there was no car."

My glass freezes in midair. "No car?"

"Nope. The whole scene was a hallucination. I stopped and ran back to where the Accord should have landed. There was nothing but bushes and croaking frogs."

"What did you do?"

"Got out of there as fast as I could. Picked my way home and sat in the driveway of my little bachelor pad townhouse, fighting tremors and sobbing like a baby. After I got myself together, I went to a midnight AA meeting, me and a bunch of college students."

"And you stopped?"

"Sure did." He tilts back and slaps his thighs with both hands. "Three days of tortuous withdrawal, an honest talk with my boss, and a treatment center later, I reintegrated back into the world. Of course, I'm only describing the first step. There's much more between then and now. Too much to cover tonight."

"Wow, Jeb, you've had a tough run." I run a finger around the rim of my glass. "Why'd you tell me this?"

"I want you to know."

"Know what?"

His stool swivels. "We're dealing with a disease here. To begin treatment, there needs to be a first step."

"Yeah, I know ... you think I need Step One, don't you?"

"Ben, how in blazes do I know what you need? Only one person knows the answer." He points to my chest. "I want you to understand, though, I was caught by it."

"It?"

He waves to the bottles lining the back wall. "The sickness that makes us love those."

I spit out the next sentence. "I'm okay. My life is under control."

Jeb shrugs. "You're the one who knows." He slips off the stool. "Time for dinner. Join me?"

As we walk, I have a question. "Why you'd meet me here? In the bar?"

"As opposed to?"

"Somewhere without alcohol. Knowing what you wanted to say to me, what I think you think I am, why give me the chance to drink?"

"Ben, I don't think you're anything more or less than what you are. Only you know your situation in life. However, suppose we had talked in the lobby. Was being out there going to stop you from having a few drinks? Or, if I wasn't here with you, would you be drinking?"

"No and yes."

"There you go."

∞ ∞ ∞

At dinner, everyone's tired and we talk about jobs and families and hobbies. Daniel's a fisherman, Gerri's a horse person, Addy a runner, and Ruth sews. Caleb tells us he raises bees, and while I've never met a bee keeper before, this makes sense. He promises us all a jar of honey when the trip's over. As I listen, I ruminate. Maybe I've been harsh calling my traveling companions Holy Rollers. Outside of their passion for God, they seem to live normal lives, including our daily Happy Hour celebrations.

Afterward, I'm alone in the elevator, chewing on the conversation with Jeb, especially his comment stating we all want to stop. The problem is, I'm not part of the "we." I can stop.

Can't I?

As the doors slide open, there's another thought—I want to stop, but I don't want to stop.

Joseph's in the room. "Ah, my friend, you've had a long day. Time to rest?"

"Yep. Time for a break, for sure."

I fall onto the bed, face down, arm hanging over the side. Joseph laughs and says, "As I thought. I will leave you to recharge."

I'm a sack of potatoes, not wanting to move, but not resting either. Fragments from the conversation with Jeb keep intruding on my efforts to shut down. I see the faces of those imaginary kids and him running back to look for the car. I consider how, based on a hallucination, he decided to quit. My own memories invade and overlap, creating a whirlpool of nonsensical but unpleasant images. A cycle starts—as I doze lightly, the thoughts and recollections come in a swirling tornado. I wake up, and they recede. With each sequence, the cycle gets more intense.

Time to change the channel. "Tell me about your family, Joseph?"

"As I told you the other night, they are gone now."

"You have children?"

"Oh, yes, we had several of our own and one who was more of a foster son to me."

Foster care. A complicated subject. "How old was he when he came to you guys?"

"Oh, he was born into the family. You see, my wife was pregnant when we were married. He was not my son, per se, but I loved her and wanted to honor her and chose to raise him as my own. Taught him my trade."

He tilts his magazine, showing the *Woodworker's Journal* title, but I only half notice. Instead, I'm curious about a specific phrase from his last sentence and probe. "He was not yours, per se?"

I'm not sure what Joseph is seeing, but his thoughts have taken him somewhere else. Closing his eyes, he shakes his head, his lower lip gripped between his teeth. When he speaks, the words come quietly. "He died. I wasn't there, but I've been told he experienced a horrible, painful death. Not what he deserved."

I have a sense of déjà vu and realize what I'm hearing is the same story I'd hear if I was talking to THE Joseph, the guy I heard about at church and in my Sunday-school classes—the man who was Jesus's father. Of course the scenario I'm imagining is impossible, but because my brain has become thoroughly saturated with alcohol over the past several days, my thoughts are too foggy to go any further, and I give up. Still, my heart goes out to this man who's been my roommate for close to a week now.

Although I've never been good at these types of conversations, always wanting to say the right words but never knowing what's appropriate, I try. "I'm sorry about your son."

"I am grateful for the words. We all must endure life. I get comfort knowing he was God's child." Joseph waves a hand and sits straighter. "Ah, my friend, let's not burden our evening with the past. We are all God's children, are we not?"

I remember the phrase from Ruth's Psalm, "I am a worm and not a man," and offer a rebuttal. "I guess we are, but I'm not a good child."

"We are all flawed. Thankfully, our Father is unendingly forgiving. Consider the Prodigal Son."

Joseph hands me a Bible, opening it to the Gospel of Luke. I've heard the story before, but I read anyway. Kid disrespects his dad, asks for his share of the money, blows the cash on women, gambling, and drugs, or whatever vices were available back in the day, before crawling home to a father who takes him in with open arms.

When I'm finished, I'm not reassured, and I don't want to talk. "Joseph, I'm beat up and tired. Do you mind if we go to sleep?"

"Of course not. Rest well."

He's slumbering before I get off the bed to change.

I stop cold. The beer. I forgot to order a delivery. I hustle to my bag before remembering all my emergency booze is gone. *Oh no, oh no, oh no.*

Jeb stopped drinking, but I'm not going to. Not tonight. I'm not ready to be the Prodigal Son, and regardless, my home and my family are in no mood to accept me.

Following the night I slept in a jail cell, when they let me out on my own recognizance, I found a twenty-four-hour bar and drank myself blind. Then I wobbled into the office and told my boss, the guy whose name was on the door and who had made me wealthy, what had happened. I provided a detailed account of the worst thing a man, a father, could do. He didn't know what to say, and as he stared at me, I sat—feeling smaller and smaller. I lashed out, verbally attacking him and his miserable little company, incinerating any chance of continued employment. I'll never understand my behavior. I loved him, and I loved his company.

I've got to get a drink.

Joseph stirs as I move towards the door. "Where are you going my friend?"

"Out. A short trip. I'll be back soon."

"Are you sure you want to?"

"Yes."

"Suit yourself."

The elevator doors don't open right away, and I head for the stairs. As I practically run down the cement steps, I hear the footsteps echo off the gray, bare walls. The sound reminds me of jail, stirring the memories of my inexcusable behavior, getting arrested, and standing in court. I replay the events again ... and again ... and again.

How in the world did I get here?

My wind is giving out, which is pretty embarrassing considering I'm going downhill, and I stop on a landing, a big "3" telling me what floor I'm on, and bend over to catch my breath. While I'm gulping mouthfuls of air, an honest thought, an answer to my question, squirms through the emotional muck.

I managed to get here because I drink, and despite all I've done, I have no true desire to stop.

"You okay, pal?" A man is walking up from, I'm guessing, the lobby. "Seriously, buddy. You don't look so good. At all."

He's no prize either, but I don't bother commenting. "Yeah, yeah. I'm fine."

"Okay, have a good one."

He trudges past me, lumbering up another flight before exiting into the hallway.

All I hear is my breathing.

Am I okay? Of course not. I'm tired, alone, and frantically hunting down a couple of cold beers before I sleep. To get them, all I have to do is travel a few floors down the stairway and sit at the bar.

I'm vaguely aware I could weigh the other option. Behind me, a few flights away, is my room, a safe place with a bed.

Suddenly, the lights go out. *Now what do I do? And where the heck are the emergency lights?* I sit on the landing, realizing how tired I am, exhausted all the way to my bone marrow, knowing there's no safe way to maneuver in this darkness.

I slide against the wall, crossing my legs at the ankle, and with the relaxation, the whole day comes back. David's sin, Ruth's reading, Addy's care, and the faith of the Holy Rollers. I again consider the term Holy Rollers, an unkind nickname for these folks. They've been good to me. Certainly nicer than I've been in return. They know who they are and what gives their lives meaning. Outside of my vodka, I don't.

What had Ruth said earlier? Sometimes all of us wander, imitating what the Jews did for all those years in the desert, adding she doesn't question what God does. Also, Daniel had talked about spiritual warfare, and Joseph told me about the Prodigal Son.

The phrase Joseph uses—"suit yourself"—echoes in my ears.

Does getting a drink right now suit me?

The lights come back on. I stand, blink into the glare, and ask again.

Does getting a drink right now suit me?

I say no and head upstairs to bed.

PROGRESS REPORT # 6

Peter,

As promised, I evaluated Our Man's state following yesterday's dramatic submission to his earthly vice. Despite the extraordinary resilience of his human vessel, a quick assessment indicated there would be a time of adjustment, presenting both physical and emotional challenges. Accordingly, I made two decisions. First, because Our Man's actions and subsequent mood could test anyone, including this group of gifted individuals, I injected our caretakers with additional grace and patience. Second, I continued to keep Our Man fully immersed in all aspects of this experience. The current environment is too rich, especially when combined with the strength of the Word, to do otherwise.

As previously reported, the "real" concept has connected with Our Man and today we added a small block to our previously laid foundation. Upon visiting the site of the Great King's exile, we connected the location in The Book with that in the present day, standing largely unchanged, and still called by the same name.

In addition, there were three important interactions designed to give Our Man a glimpse in the mirror.

With the first, I attempted to provide an alternative perspective by illustrating his appearance to others. The second was designed to lessen his cynicism by clarifying the contents of a prayer submitted on his behalf. The third exposed him to a caretaker's experiences with the same earthly vice from which Our Man suffers. The caretaker was masterful, presenting a fully transparent story and making sure to indicate how this particular problem stems from human illness.

I believe the reactionary emotions, feelings derived from deeper and more foundational concerns, will provide a primary roadblock to Our Man's ultimate success. I'm specifically referencing guilt, shame, and remorse. In response, we have continued with the notion that people of faith are not flawless. Today's exposure to the Great King David, with all his contradictions, combined with the more contemporary examples of our caretakers' struggles with greed and alcoholism, should prove fruitful as he progresses down the path. As you know, this group has more stories to tell.

While all of this represents continued progress, the most significant event occurred at the end of the day. Our Man, shrouded in temptation, was victorious in a spiritual battle. He received a small portion of help when I temporarily plunged him into darkness. However, he used the time wisely and, without any supplemental encouragement, considered various factors and personal observations. As a result, a decision to forego his daily habit was his alone.

Our next step is critical. While tomorrow's agenda should prove helpful, continued abstinence from his earthly vice will lead to severe physical distress, introducing an added variable. I am grateful you have provided a caretaker to assist with this eventuality.

As we know, there is opportunity here. Timing of any suffering could prove optimal, opening the doorway for my own direct involvement. I am hopeful this will be the case. We do, however, have mitigating plans in the event his restraint is temporary.

I close encouraged and hopeful,
Joseph

DAY 7

As I wake up, I'm traveling through one of those half-conscious visions, remembering the stairway and, again, deciding not to get a beer.

Did I miss my best friend alcohol?

I sure did as I went to sleep. Nodding off took forever, and I was restless all night, having a million little dreams while I rolled around, shivering one minute, overheated the next.

How about now? I'm experiencing an unusual level of first-thing-in-the-morning edginess, although four-thirty a.m. is still night as far as I'm concerned.

Swinging my legs over the bed, I reach for the wall, an attempt to control a sudden bout of nausea and my wobbly legs. The room's rocking back and forth, but I manage to steady myself and get to the bathroom.

A half-hour later, I'm clean, shaved, and down in the lobby. Daniel's there too, with his scruffy beard and worn jeans, reading the Bible. He's sitting in the same place as yesterday, but because of the time, we're alone except for the guy at the front desk. I forage around, discovering coffee but no food.

As Daniel motions me to the empty chair, I inquire, "Don't you ever sleep?"

"I get by on a few hours a day. Always have. Of course, I could ask you the same question."

He's got a point.

Daniel closes his Bible. "How goes your journey?"

"Having a good time, thanks."

He gives a small shake of his head. "I'm not talking about the trip. How's your journey with God?"

Yeesh. I know he's an A-list Holy Roller, but this guy is unrelenting. "Man, I'm barely awake, and as we've talked about, I have no journey—at least I don't have one that involves God."

"Ben, my friend, you are mistaken. The issue isn't whether you're on the journey, the issue is whether or not you decide to take the journey."

Whatever patience I have is shot. "I'm sorry, Daniel, but we all can't read a quote in an email and immediately be all in with the man upstairs."

"Is that your view of what happened with me?" His head is tilted, a bewildered expression on his face.

"Based on what you said the other night, yes."

"I'm not certain your perception is entirely accurate. I believe I characterized what I told you as the beginning of my story." There's no question Daniel's recall is better than mine, and I concede by staying silent. As I expect, he adds to the thought. "There's always a journey after you step into the room."

I vaguely recall someone mentioning a room a couple of days ago. Maybe Addy? Either way, I have no idea what Daniel means. "Into the room?"

"Yes. Sitting in that New York café, in the early hours of the morning, I stepped into the room."

"There's a room?"

"In my mind, yes. A figurative one. Once a person decides to step in there, their journey begins."

"How does someone take a journey if they're stuck in a room?"

He doesn't seem bothered by my sarcastic tone. "The step is only one step. There are others, lots of them. Both in and outside of the room."

Since I'm talking to Daniel, unless I remove myself, this conversation will continue. For whatever reason, I ask a follow-up question. "Who's in this room?"

"You and God. Nobody else."

I throw out a half grunt, half laugh, sit back, take a long swig of coffee, and decide to go on the offensive. "How about we talk about Addy?"

Daniel shifts in his seat. "What about her?"

"Ah, Daniel, my friend, you're interested in her."

"And you're concluding this based on?"

"I develop real estate and do deals every day. I earn my living reading the room."

Daniel broods for a moment before his expression softens and he changes from Bible scholar to sheepish guy. I'm watching Addy's Jekyll and Hyde transformation all over again, when she's a twenty-something kid one minute and all serious, telling me about her faith the next. "Okay, yes, I guess I am interested, although I don't believe there's much I can do about my feelings for her here."

"Why not?"

"For starters, the schedule is structured, and there's always a group hanging around. Plus, we're in a foreign country. I mean, we can't slip away for a movie or go see a show."

"You could ask her to eat dinner with you."

"What, move to a corner at the group table?"

I knock my knuckles against his forehead. "Hello, Daniel, you there? Find a table for two. Get her away from the rest of us."

He ponders, nods, and gets intense again. "How about we get back to talking about you?"

"I've got a better idea. Time for a coffee refill." When I stand, the nausea returns, along with a surge of dizziness. After I stabilize myself using the top of the chair, Daniel offers to help.

"Are you okay?"

"I'm fine." I snap back. "No problem."

As he eases me to a sitting position, I close my eyes and swallow hard, attempting to control the urge to heave.

"I'll get you the refill." Daniel heads across the lobby. Once he returns and the coffee is secure in my hands, he asks a question. "Something you ate, maybe?"

"Nope. I don't think so."

"Could you still be suffering from ..."

He hesitates, but I know what he's trying to say, and I finish his sentence. "From two nights ago?"

"Yeah."

"Nope, the hangover cleared out earlier yesterday. Heck, I didn't have a beer before bed last night."

This piques his interest. "You didn't drink last night?"

"Not after dinner. Not a drop."

"Tell me about that."

Although I hate the phrase, I still adhere to his request. "I was heading to get a beer but decided to hit the rack instead."

"Did you want one?"

"You know what, Daniel?" I don't wait for an answer. "Talking to you is like having a woodpecker on my shoulder. You keep jabbing away, trying to dig out whatever's behind the bark, and well, sometimes I don't want to talk. I mean, maybe I want to talk but not about what you want to talk about."

His response is to go back to reading the Bible.

I occupy myself watching the lobby come to life. A few people move around, the pastries are rolled out, and a woman asks a question at the desk. Daniel doesn't seem to notice the increased activity and is satisfied reading. We create a peaceful scene, me with my morning beverage and him with his book, but I fidget. "Thanks, by the way, for the cup of coffee."

His finger becomes a bookmark. "You're welcome."

We hear dishes and silverware start rattling in the dining room. I fidget again. "Last night wasn't a big deal. I wanted a drink, but a couple of things happened, and I decided to skip having a beer." *Or two, or three.*

"Interesting. Would you mind telling me what happened?"

The woodpecker's back at work, and if I had a miniature noose, I'd hang the thing. By now, however, I know the persistent little bugger is sincere. A gentle soul. I give in, telling Daniel about being on the landing, describing the man who walked by, our conversation, the lights going out, and my thoughts before heading back to my room.

When I'm done, he's animated. "Ah, excellent. A battle won."

"A battle?"

"In the war."

"The war?"

"The spiritual war."

Right. This is a theme with him.

"I see a development here," he adds.

I have to ask. "You see a development?"

"I believe you're on the threshold."

"Of?"

"The room. Maybe you're about to step into the room."

Breakfast is buzzing. Today we are going to visit Masada. I sit in complete ignorance, listening to the words, "siege," "Romans," and "suicide," getting the gist this is a Big Stop. I don't invest too much energy learning more. I'm busy trying to get food into my whirling stomach.

I'm shaky on the way to the bus, half collapse into the seat next to Joseph, and gingerly sip water, hoping to hold my food down. As we pull out, Avi starts our education. "Masada is one of three fortresses built by Herod, a paranoid man who needed safety. We're going to climb a plateau, to a spot about fifteen-hundred feet above sea level. It was built sometime during the thirties BCE. We're not far away, and I'm going to stop talking—allow you to enjoy the countryside while we ride."

The bus scales a hill, surrounded by the light brown Israeli desert, approaching a large, impressive fortress sitting, seemingly, on top of a table. Herod's stronghold is built stone on stone, and there must have been world class masons in his employ, especially to construct the guard towers overseeing the valley below. Working on this project could not have been easy.

The day is the hottest one yet. Avi tells us the temperature's thirty-seven Celsius, but I don't know how to do the conversion. Caleb tries to set us all at ease. "Don't worry, my fellow travelers. It's a dry heat."

The man's a riot.

As we pile out of the bus, my stomach is still doing somersaults, and I've got a mild case of the shakes. Dry heat or not, too much time in this outdoor kiln isn't going to be great for me.

Leading us through the fort, Avi points out a dark line meandering along the walls, identifying the areas below the line as the original, ancient ruins, and those above as reconstructed replicas. He shows us bathhouses, storage areas, and residences. There are two palaces. Herod lived in one, and the other served as the administration building. A system of aqueducts collected and stored water for everyone.

Under the relentless sun, my queasiness grows, my legs are heavy, and my body's not producing much sweat, causing me to lean against walls whenever there's a break. Addy's watching me, but I pretend not to notice, acting as normal as possible.

We stop and gaze down at the surrounding countryside.

"The area over there," everyone follows Avi's hand, "served as the Roman encampment." From where we are, I can't determine the size of the rectangle I see on the landscape, but I figure Roman soldiers and all the accoutrements must have needed space. "Come, let's learn about the siege."

We move to a small room, away from the direct sun. I'm planning to stand, but Addy, after I see her give me an unmistakable "nurse" look, takes my elbow and leads me to an open seat on a rock bench. I start to object but stop—her expression doesn't leave room for protest.

Avi starts talking. "In sixty-six CE, a group of Jews fled here from Jerusalem. This group, called the Sicarii, were an extreme sect of Jewish Zealots. They carried small daggers, called *sicae*, to attack Romans and those who supported the Romans' occupation."

"Yeah, probably not a good strategy."

I'm not sure anyone heard Addy but me, and certainly not Avi, who goes on with his lesson. "The Roman army followed them here and besieged the fortress. The Sicarii bravely held out. They were led by—"

"Elazar ben Yair!"

"Ah, yes, scholar Caleb. You are correct."

"My schooling here paid off."

Avi goes on. "Finally, the Romans built a ramp and were preparing to attack the fortress. The Sicarii knew they were going to, at long last, be defeated."

A headache is starting, and the continued lesson doesn't help.

Avi continues. "They refused to die at the hands of the Romans, and knowing they would be attacked at dawn, they drew lots. Ten men were chosen. These ten killed the others. They drew lots again and one of the ten killed the other nine. After completing this task, he killed himself."

Ruth covers her mouth. "Oh, my. I knew the story, but, being here, seeing this place—"

"Were they already dead when the Romans got here?" I interrupt.

Avi answers my question. "Yes. They found everyone dead."

I spread my arms in a "what gives?" gesture. "How do we know what happened?"

Caleb answers for Avi. "Josephus."

"Who?"

"Josephus. He wrote about the events here."

I shoot right back. "How did he know? Was he in the fortress?"

Avi takes over. "There were two women and five children who hid in the underground cisterns and survived. They told about what happened."

I want more. "Was Josephus a Jew?"

"Josephus was a Jew who became a Roman citizen. He had a complicated background and wrote extensive histories."

My energy is spent, and despite my interest, my head drops forward until I'm staring at the ground, playing with a small rock between my feet. People are chattering away with Avi, but I either can't or don't hear.

Who is this Josephus? Is he reliable? As a Jew, he would have wanted to create a legacy for his people. He was also, however, a Roman citizen, and history tells us the Romans were an unforgiving lot. A fabrication or embellishment, if discovered, would probably have caused problems for Josephus. There must be some truth to his account.

"You okay?"

Boy, Addy's vigilant.

"Yeah. Fine." My lie is as big as any I've ever told.

In addition to the other symptoms, I'm shivering, which is unexpected given we're perched about five feet from the sun.

Her hand is on my back. "Are you hungover?"

"No."

"Are you sure?"

"I haven't had a drink since before dinner last night."

"Do you always have a drink after dinner?"

Does she need to know this?

"Ben, answer me. This is important."

"Why?"

"Because I was watching you yesterday. You were hungover, sure, but I could see you recovering and I knew with time, you'd be fine. If you're not hungover today, we should consider if there's something else going on."

I start moving away. "You're on vacation. Take a break."

"Do you?" Addy squeezes my chin between her thumb and fingers, forcing my head to move. "Usually have a drink after dinner?"

There's no escape, and I succumb. "Drinks."

"Drinks?"

"Yeah." I'm nonchalant. "I have a few drinks every night. Usually during the day too."

"For how long?"

"As long as it takes to drink them."

She shakes her head. "No, no. For how long have you been having those drinks every night?"

"Since I was fifteen."

While her follow-up is calm, her eyes give away the alarm. "Fifteen years old?"

"Yes."

"With no break?"

"None I remember."

"Here." She pulls out a banana and bottle of water. "Eat this and drink this."

"I can't. Bad stomach."

"Get them down." It's like I'm reasoning with a seasoned mother of five. "And don't get too far away from me."

While I'm working my way through the banana, I turn my attention back to Avi. He's wrapping up the program. "... and for us Jews, Masada is a symbol. A symbol for our nation." His finger points, emphasizing each word. "We will not fall again."

$$\infty \quad \infty \quad \infty$$

Addy sits next to me at lunch, making sure I eat protein and fresh fruits, saturating me with Coke and water. I'm too busy following her instructions to participate in any conversations.

Afterward, as we start driving north, Pastor Marcus takes the microphone. "Tonight, we sleep in Jerusalem!" He pumps his fist while a cheer erupts. "Before we get there, I want to remind you today is Friday and encourage us all to respect the Jewish Sabbath." Everyone nods. "At the hotel, one of the elevators will be programmed to stop at every floor. This way, Orthodox Jews won't have to work by pressing the buttons. There will be a sign to indicate which elevator this is."

Caleb's ahead of him on the second point. "Tomorrow's breakfast will be slim, folks. There'll be coffee and breads and fruits. Don't bother looking for the buffet or anyone making omelets."

Avi takes his turn. "Tomorrow's sparse breakfast is one reason we're making our next stop. Up the road is a *kibbutz*. A dairy producer. Delicious ice cream. There's also a store selling drinks and snacks. I suggest fortifying yourselves before tonight's concert and maybe pick up food to supplement the hotel's breakfast."

Gerri and Addy are excited about the prospect of a midafternoon ice cream break, but I'm more interested in something else. Holding the top of the seats for balance, I move forward to Pastor Marcus. "There's a concert?"

"Yes. A big festival."

"After we get to the hotel?"

"No. Before. We'll be arriving in Jerusalem late tonight."

What? No Happy Hour? I feel the blood drain from my face—and my knees give out.

Pastor Marcus is up, Addy's beside me, and they ease me into a seat. I try to ward off their concern. "No, no, no. I'm all right. Sorry, lost my balance."

"Stay there." Addy won't let me back on my feet. "You haven't been right all day. Take a few breaths."

I push against her and stand. "I guess I'm nervous."

"Nervous?"

"The concert."

"The concert makes you nervous?"

"I don't enjoy crowds." I have no problem with crowds, but I need an exit strategy. "Don't worry. I'll be okay."

I force myself past Addy's protective hand and weave my way to the back of the bus. Missing the pre-dinner bar stop terrifies me. I thump down beside Joseph, who looks up from his reading. "My friend, what troubles you?"

"There's a concert."

"Ahh, yes, the Feast of the Tabernacles. We celebrate."

Before I'm able to explore further, I hear Avi. "We are getting near to our *kibbutz* stop. I should take the time to describe how these communities work. A *kibbutz* is a cooperative. Everyone contributes, and everyone supports everyone else."

Ruth's voice gently interrupts. "Do you live in a *kibbutz*?"

"Yes. A relatively new one. In most, income earned by members is put in a common pool. In mine, eighty percent of my earnings are contributed. I keep the rest. The *kibbutz* uses this money to provide what we need together as a group. Also, members receive income. All of us get the same amount, except for adjustments based on family size."

"Are you content living there?"

"Yes, Ruth." He nods while taking a sip of water. "These are wonderful places to live. Our kids do better than average, crime is lower, people are healthier. In my experience, they create better citizens of Israel." The bus is slowing down and starting to turn. "Ah, we are here. Time for refreshment."

What I was expecting is not what I'm seeing. A large, new, unblemished parking lot surrounds a gleaming, bright store, packed with shoppers. A green lawn stretches across to those shiny silver cylinders, the kind you see at every dairy.

Gerri speaks for all of us. "Wow. You gotta appreciate this. Especially plunked down right here in the middle of this dry-as-a-bone desert."

Caleb agrees. "Moses could have used this place."

Two dairy cows, one painted red and the other blue, guard the entrance. They're big, installment-art type sculptures—their shoulders are at the same level as my chin. I turn to Jeb. "These life-size?"

He shrugs. "Heck if I know, I'm a lawyer."

"Technically, you're a retired lawyer."

"True, but I still practice, although I don't get paid for it."

"Legal aid?"

"Guardian Ad Litem."

"What do you do?"

"I'm the lawyer for minors with legal needs."

"You work for free?"

"They pay an hourly amount, and I donate the money to halfway houses. To help people coming out of rehab." *Not again. Not another alcohol discussion.* Jeb keeps going. "I'm a specialist."

"Working with minors is a specialty?"

"No, I mean yes, but I'm a specialist as a Guardian Ad Litem. I only work with kids whose lives have been affected by alcohol or drug use. Not using themselves, but with abuse in their families. I make sure they get the support they need and, in certain cases, try to change their own path toward addiction."

"He's as ferocious as a Tasmanian devil, the way he fights for them," Ruth interjects.

Jeb gives a sheepish smile. "I do my best."

As we head through the door, Jeb tacks on a question. "You remember at the synagogue in Capernaum? The one where the new one was built on top of the old one?" I do recall but before I put all the pieces together, Jeb fills in the blank. "Christianity has built a new life on top of my old one, taking my past mistakes and helping me make something positive out of them."

Good for him. Not gonna work with my life.

"I do it for the kids," he adds.

"The kids?"

"The ones in the car. The two I hit in my hallucination the night I stopped drinking. Now I want to protect them."

We're inside, and the store is bustling. Jeb nods and heads off with Ruth.

The place is divided into two sections. To the left are tables with products the *kibbutz* makes or those associated with Israel. I explore and see cookies and cheeses and chocolate and all types of figs and fig products, including a fig syrup which, according to the surrounding chatter, is a great Thanksgiving turkey glaze. There's also an ice cream stand serving whatever flavors they make at the *kibbutz*. Gerri and Addy are in line.

The right side is similar to a regular convenience store with racks of packaged foods, pre-made sandwiches, and drink coolers lining the back wall. Maybe they sell beer? Israeli wine? Heck, I'd take a bottle of fermented figs.

I double time it through the aisles, swerving to avoid knocking over a woman and the baby strapped to her chest. Her startled reaction should cause regret. It doesn't.

Inside the coolers are sodas and juices and smoothies and fifty types of milk. Nothing to make me feel better.

I curse, and a minute later, I'm outside, heading to the bus. Addy is backpedaling a few steps ahead of me. She offers a cup. "Eat this. Chocolate chip ice cream. You need the sugar."

"Thanks."

While the ice cream is good, my hands shake with each spoonful, and my head won't stop pounding. How in the world am I going to survive an event called the "Feast of the Tabernacles?"

∞ ∞ ∞

The bus jostles along, and with each mile, I sink deeper. There are flashbacks—memories of missing Zach's All-Star game because I was "sick" and standing in the shadows on Halloween night to hide my drunkenness.

Coming out of a doze, Addy's face floods my vision. "What?" I ask, startled. "What are you ... what do you want?"

"Doing my monitoring. How do you feel?"

"I'm fine."

Addy and Pastor Marcus are conversing while her hands embrace my forehead and cheeks, before they prod either side of my neck. I make out the words "clammy" and "pallor" and "dehydrated." When the phrase "hasn't had a drink" sifts through the fog, I blow a fuse. "Will you people stop talking about my drinking?"

All the noise, except the hum of the bus against the road, stops. I'm on two legs, shaking all over, and smelling my own stinking breath. My vision is distorted, and there's a panel of frosted glass in front of me—I'm viewing recognizable shapes instead of distinct individuals. The one I know as Jeb stands, says a few indecipherable words, and the whole crew faces front again. My stomach seesaws, and I drop to a sitting position, trying to calm my body down.

"Ben, do you hear me?" Addy's still there, her hand on my back. I nod. "Pastor Marcus and I are going to talk to Avi. Ruth is going to stay next to you."

I search for Joseph, but only for a minute. I'm concentrating on not getting sick.

∞ ∞ ∞

The bus pulls off the highway, stopping at a small white building. The sign is in a foreign language with two pictures on either side. One is of a mortar and pestle. The other is a snake twisted around a staff. We must be at a pharmacy.

Avi, Pastor Marcus, and Addy jump out and go inside. Through the glass doors and large windows, I see the man behind the counter, his hands protruding from a lab coat, pointing to various shelves and displays. While Addy gathers a few items, lab coat guy disappears and comes back with a Styrofoam cup. Addy opens a box and drops in a tea bag. Pastor Marcus hands over the cash. Transaction complete.

Once we return to the highway, Addy's bugging me again, carrying a vitamin bottle and the cup with the tea bag. "Ben, I need you to listen to me. I think you're in alcohol withdrawal." *Then let's get a drink.* "I don't know for sure, but I'm guessing you're a heavy user."

"I drink, I don't use," I say, trying to get her to stop talking.

Addy pulls me upright and looks at me directly. "Alcohol's a depressant." *There's no depression here. All you need to do is get me a drink.* "It slows down your brain function. As your intake increases and heavy drinking becomes a habit, your central nervous system adjusts, compensating by producing stimulating chemicals in bigger than normal quantities. The primary offenders are serotonin and norepinephrine." *Norepine what?* "The basic premise is after the booze stops, your body has trouble adjusting back to normal."

I'm skeptical about her diagnosis. "Without the booze? My last drink was barely a day ago."

"Specifics vary, but this condition sometimes starts in five to ten hours and peaks in twenty-four to forty-eight hours. I see withdrawal all the time at work." *Oh, right, I'm with Florence Nightingale, Emergency Room nurse.* Her voice goes soft. "Here, drink this."

"Drink what?"

"This is Kava tea, to help with the symptoms." She holds out a pill. "Also, take this. I got you a high-quality multi-vitamin. Among other things, you'll get some folate, magnesium, phosphate, and zinc—a bunch of stuff you've probably depleted. If not, no worries, you'll pee the extra out."

I shrug, pop the vitamin in my mouth, and wash the pill down with a gulp of the tea. "Thanks for the cup of dirt."

"What you need now is rest. Keep your body still until we get to the concert. We've got about an hour." She returns to her seat.

I listen to the bus move, my gut in chaos, grieving over the missed Happy Hour. Through a crack in my eyelids, I see Joseph. "Time for sleep, my friend."

I don't disagree.

∞ ∞ ∞

When I wake up, I need a few minutes to figure out we're sleeved between two other buses.

Addy's back. "Here, drink some more Kava. This time you're having concentrated juice mixed with water."

"Where'd the juice come from?"

"Same place we got the tea. Come on, now. Down the hatch."

Oh, great, more liquid grit. She holds out another of the vitamins. I protest. "Again?"

"I've already told you, if you take too much, your system will filter the excess out. We've got to make sure you'll survive this concert."

We're being overly dramatic here, aren't we, Addy girl? However, in case she's right, I propose staying behind to avoid troubling anyone with my lifeless corpse.

Addy shakes her head. "Not a good idea. The way these buses are packed in, you'll feel as if you're trapped in a tunnel and probably get claustrophobic. Plus, I want to keep an eye on you." She points to the bottle and hands me the pill. "Drink it."

The bottle is half empty, the dirt juice washing down the pill, when Avi starts to talk. "You're a lucky group. You are here during the great Feast of the Tabernacles, an ancient celebration outlined for us by God in Leviticus."

"Chapter twenty-three," Gerri explains, pointing to her Bible.

Avi continues. "For seven days every year, Jews gather to remember God delivering us from Egypt and protecting us in the wilderness. The Feast is also a time to prepare for when the Messiah will be here, walking the earth."

Caleb interjects. "When the Christ comes at the end times, during the Apocalypse."

Avi smiles. "Yes, and when he does, all the nations of the world will be united. This is the Jewish celebration inviting all countries to join in."

Pastor Marcus takes over, outlining the flow of the evening's events and passing out tickets. We start moving off the bus.

Addy hustles over to me. "You okay to go?" After I nod, she hands over a plastic bag filled with nuts and dried fruit. "Eat as healthy as possible."

Outside is a sea of buses and people from every age group. I see matching T-shirts, flowing colorful dresses, hats with all kinds of paraphernalia sticking out, and flags from dozens of countries.

After about a half hour, I find myself sitting in one of a thousand plastic seats, holding a paper plate with a stale roll, watery coleslaw, and what I'm assuming is an Israeli hotdog. Not the feast I was expecting. There's also a ginger ale, courtesy of Addy.

I'm sweating in the late day heat, picking at my food, and worrying about the massive bank of lights next to the stage. I'm pretty sure they'll blind everyone after the sun goes down. There are two huge TV monitors playing a slickly-produced fundraiser, asking for donations to a Jewish relief fund.

Groups are being introduced by country and waving their flags, parading to the front and around the perimeter. I don't pay much attention, except to the group from Texas. Their representative is big, his cowboy hat bigger, and he's carrying the state flag, not the US flag. The Master of Ceremonies announces them as the Republic of Texas.

Caleb nudges me, pointing to the sky. I see three or four drones circling around. He explains with one word. "Security."

The music starts. I'm assuming these are the warm up bands, but they're talented enough and sing in both English and Hebrew. Members of the audience join them, following the words shown on the monitors, clapping with the beat, and dancing around in a long conga line. Enough is happening during the first set to make me forget I'm feeling rotten. After the music stops, a guy gives a sermon type talk, maybe ten minutes worth. At the end, he points to the TV screens, and they play another fund-raising commercial. As my interest slips away, two words jump into the void—Happy Hour.

Saliva starts to circle my mouth, held in by shaking lips, and tremors begin moving down my arms and legs. Normally, my it's-time-to-think-about-a-drink discomfort progresses at a steady pace, allowing me to adjust as the day passes. This, however, is a train roaring down the tracks.

My vision becomes lopsided, undulating in and out of my field of sight, expanding sideways, and contracting again. All the lights combine into one big blob. The upset stomach intensifies, reminding me of the time I got seasick as a kid.

Hands grab my arms. After they half carry, half guide me away from the music, I'm eased to the ground, my back resting against a tree. Someone scurries off while another person, who I observe is Pastor Marcus, kneels next to me.

Addy jogs up with a plastic cup of ice cream and a bottle of water, ordering me to consume them. I submit, and after a few minutes, I sit without shaking. The train, though, is still running rampant.

I hear the word "hospital" and practically jump through my skin. "No hospital!"

"Ben," Addy objects, "you're in serious withdrawal and the symptoms are only going to get worse. You need medicine."

I shake my head. "Nope. You take me there, I'll refuse treatment. Force me in, I'll walk out. I'll feel better once I slow down and sleep this off."

They huddle again. I hear words along the lines of "try again later."

Spit flies from my mouth. "Try all you want. It ain't happening." I close my eyes and rest my head against the tree. "Go on back to the concert. Pick me up on the way out."

I have no idea on the who, what, or how, but I'm back on the bus, rolling from side to side, constantly adjusting to avoid toppling over. Joseph's next to me, reading a magazine, and Addy's across the aisle, riding along. I have no doubt she's watching.

I'm assailed by images of mixed drinks, my family, and those fund-raising commercials from the concert. There's a soundtrack too, a medley of Aerosmith's "Dream On" and Queen's "Bohemian Rhapsody," both weaving through the chaotic "Revolution Number 9" from the Beatles' White Album. I pick up external conversations, most notably Addy telling Pastor Marcus "his pulse is good and I managed to take his blood pressure. If anything, it's low," and "let's see how he does through the night."

After a long ride, we stop at an overlook. Addy slides open the window, suggesting I "get some air" and joins the rest of the group outside the bus. The city lights are fully visible, and Joseph touches my arm, encouraging me to listen along. I can't explain the feeling I have, but in an instant, my head clears and my thoughts become lucid.

I'm in a good spot to hear Avi clearly as he declares, "We can't simply drive into Jerusalem. First, we must understand." He opens his Bible and, using Pastor Marcus' cellphone as a light source, begins to read. "'As the mountains surround Jerusalem, so the Lord surrounds his people, from this time forth and forever more.' This is a passage from Psalm 125."

Pastor Marcus gestures, moving his arm in a panoramic arc spanning the city's lights, cars, and buildings. "Behold. The magnificent city. Brilliantly illuminated for us on a crystal-clear evening. Before we continue on, we must appreciate where we are. This is the city David captured and named as the capital of Israel. This is where his son,

Solomon, built the great temple. Pontius Pilate lived here. Our savior, Jesus, was crucified and, of course, rose here. Jerusalem stands today, once again, as our capital."

I can't see Caleb, but I hear his voice crack. "It's also where Peter denied our Lord."

Avi reads again. "Jerusalem staggers, Judah is falling; their words and deeds are against the Lord, defying his glorious presence. The look on their faces testifies against them; they parade their sin like Sodom; they do not hide it. Woe to them! They have brought disaster upon themselves." The light reflects off the page, embracing his face. "Isaiah speaks of how we were an unfaithful people. For this reason, Jerusalem has risen and fallen many times throughout history."

He goes to a new passage, this one at the back of the book. "I saw the holy city, the new Jerusalem, coming down out of heaven from God, prepared as a bride beautifully dressed for her husband."

"The Book of Revelation," announces Gerri. "Amen."

Avi is solemn. "Yes. Amen. This city you are about to enter is the city where the Lord will return and reign."

He closes the Bible and returns to the bus. The group follows. The instant the door closes, I start to feel bad again.

PROGRESS REPORT # 7

Peter,

While there are ample details to share, the most important factor at the moment is Our Man's physical vessel. He is in a vulnerable position, making him receptive to an experience beyond the earthly plane.

In reviewing options, I believe the most beneficial approach is to present two distinct choices, utilizing vivid imagery and the room analogy. As you know, I have experienced previous success with this method. Moreover, I feel connected to Our Man and am confident I understand what will and what will not motivate him.

I have performed preliminary work to ensure our timing is appropriate. A brief intervention, at a stop prior to arriving in the Holy City, successfully removed the impacts of his physical malady and cleared his head. After a short period, I restored his ailments. A supplementary factor—his human mind is conjuring unusual and unexpected images which should stop him from any immediate rejection of our efforts. In addition, our marvelous caretakers are prepared to help. As dictated by protocol, they will be unaware of their contributions during the spiritual component of events.

Of course, the ultimate success or failure of this venture will hinge on Our Man making an independent decision.

INTO THE ROOM

I will update you immediately upon completion.
I stand ready and optimistic,
Joseph

DAY 8

I'm in front of Sarah, Zach, and Olivia, watching them eat at our kitchen table, knowing I should be the one sitting at the vacant spot, when all three of them make eye contact. Zach responds by throwing a steaming plate of pasta onto the empty chair. I thrash and wake up, pain stretching from temple to temple, wishing I could end the gag reflex. Squirming in a cocoon of sweat, I notice Joseph on one side of the hotel bed. Addy and Gerri are sitting on the other, but they're unmoving and inanimate, reminding me of department store mannequins.

"My friend, you are uncomfortable."

I point at the two women. "Joseph, don't let them take me to a hospital."

"Ah, do not worry. At the moment, any such decision is out of their hands."

My eyes close and I'm in a hallway. Caleb and Daniel and Jeb appear, a dome of light penetrating the darkness. When I call out, there's no noise. I try walking closer to them, but with each step they move away, keeping the distance between us the same.

He doesn't seem to talk, but I hear Jeb's voice. "We can't help. Not right now."

I respond. "What do I do?"

"Dig inside. Deep into yourself," Daniel replies.

"How?"

This time Caleb answers. "Think about what's been discussed."

"Me and you?"

"You and everyone."

The three men dematerialize, beamed to the Starship Enterprise, and an archway opens to my right. Ruth's there, sitting on a wooden bench, Bible open, her lips moving in the candlelight. She's praying. For me.

The archway goes dark and little vignettes appear above my head. I see myself, drinking as I help the kids do homework, sneaking out for my wedding night bar trip, holding a water bottle filled with vodka at a church picnic, and sitting in a movie theater, nestled between Zach and Olivia, sipping a spiked Coke.

Another event appears, and I know I'm seeing the last night I spent at home, with little Olivia in front of me, Sarah pleading with me to stop yelling, and the horrible event about to happen. Before it does, I scream.

The resounding "No!" wakes me up and I'm back in the room, my saturated clothes wrapped tightly around my shaking, shivering body, staring at Joseph.

"Joseph, I need Addy to help me. A cup of dirt tea, maybe."

The women are there, but they're still stationary statues, their concerned expressions fixed in place.

He sits on the edge of the bed. "No, I'm sorry, there's no tea right now. We have arrived at the time for a one-on-one conversation." As Joseph lifts me to a sitting position, his lips are moving, but I don't hear any words. At the instant he stops talking, I fall.

When the descent stops, I'm encapsulated in a thick darkness, convinced I either have a bag over my head or am inside a cave. The only sound is my own breathing.

After I hear a click, I'm showered in a cone of light, a perfect circle illuminating the space around me. As I blink and try to focus, there's another click, and I see Joseph, about ten feet away, inside his own circle. We're both sitting in identical straight-backed wooden chairs. I'm practically hyperventilating, my head swiveling from side to side.

"It is okay, my friend," Joseph says, and with his crossed legs and gentle smile, I picture him at a neighborhood party. He starts reading a book.

My reaction is immediate. "What the ...? You're *reading?* We're sitting here in the dark, God only knows where, and you're studying up on making cabinets?"

He rests the book on his lap. "Ben, while not germane to our discussion, please know God does indeed 'know where.' As for my reading, I'm merely filling the void until we begin."

"And when will we begin?"

"Commencement of our activities is entirely at your discretion." He's reading again.

This whole trip is getting tiring. I stand and move away from the chair. After two steps, all the light disappears and I lose my nerve. "Joseph!"

"It's okay, Ben, turn around and come back."

With the first move toward the chair, the light returns. I hurry to sit down. "Where are we, Joseph?"

"We are where you put us."

"I put us here?"

"Yes, with your thoughts and actions."

Folding my arms across my chest, I shake my head. *What's going on? Am I sick? Fevered?* I press a palm against my forehead. Maybe I'm having a dream.

Wait, what had Addy described earlier? I'm in withdrawal, meaning I'm probably having a hallucination. Vodka or beer should make all of this go away. I offer a solution. "How about a drink, Joseph?"

"There is no alcohol available, my friend."

I want to argue, but I know his position is non-negotiable. "Okay, let's agree I put us here. What do we do now?"

"We talk."

"Talk. Okay. About what?"

He puts the book underneath his chair. "Why are we here, Ben?"

"I don't know for sure, but I'm guessing this whole tableau is a hallucination."

"No, hallucination is a byproduct." He asks again. "Why are we here, Ben?"

"Because I'm traveling and my diet's off and my schedule's all mixed up and, because outside of this place, my life's a mess."

He shakes his head and stands, talking as he approaches my chair. "Those, again, are byproducts. Results. They are not the 'why.' I must ask again. Why are we here?"

When Joseph puts his hand on my shoulder, there's a shudder, followed by a flash, and I know. In fact, as I utter a three-word response, I realize I knew before he asked. "Because I drink."

Satisfied, he moves on. "Now, let us talk about your drinking." He returns to his seat and observes me for a while. "You are hesitant?"

"I am."

"Do you know why?"

"The truth? Because I get the feeling you already know everything I'm going to say."

"What I already know is inconsequential. Here, right now, we are concerned with what you know." He moves the conversation along with a question. "Do you remember what a Tell is Ben?"

"Of course, they're all over this place."

"To unearth a Tell, what do you have to do?"

"Dig through the layers, I guess?"

"Exactly. What you need is to dig through the layers."

"Dig through the layers." As I repeat his words, I'm watching the fingers of one hand scratch the knuckles of the other.

"Yes."

"How do I start?"

"A person's layers form an intricate apparatus. You begin by talking. Please, do not worry about what you say. We are safe here."

Since I can't compare "here" to anywhere I've ever been, I greet his comment with skepticism and decide to stall. "What if there's too much garbage to remove the layers?"

He doesn't break stride. "I'd suggest you start by taking the first piece off the top. The rest will follow."

I inspect our surroundings. There doesn't seem to be a way out, and even if there was, I've already learned I can't get up and walk away. Plus, Joseph, who's reading again, is over-the-top patient.

I cave and spill my guts, outlining my daily schedule and giving details about how I lied and snuck around, deceiving family, friends, and strangers. As I talk, I'm overcome by grief and regret, but I don't stop until I've disclosed everything. Well, practically everything.

When I'm finished, the combination of catharsis and revulsion leaves me fully depleted, causing me to sprawl out in the chair, head flopped back, arms uselessly dangling by my sides.

Joseph indicates we are not done. "I'm curious. You are describing a lifetime pattern of behavior. What is new? Why are we here now?"

I know precisely what he's talking about. "Please, Joseph. Don't make me say it."

"You must. To move forward."

I hear the silence.

After a while, I get ready to talk. Before any words come out, I stop. When they try to exit a second time, I can't bring myself to say them. I glance at Joseph, desperate for help, but he's an unemotional rock. Back and forth I go, about to speak and then holding back, until, like a man who is drowning and involuntarily draws in his last breath, three words tumble out. "I hit her."

"Hit who, Ben?"

"You know who."

"Tell me."

My response is half spoken, half groaned. "Olivia, my little girl."

"When?"

"On the night. The last horrifying night I was with my family."

"Tell me, my friend, tell me what happened."

I open the floodgates, explaining to Joseph about the unsuccessful dinner meeting and the dying business relationship. Upon arriving home, I had instantly downed three shots of vodka, followed by a beer in four gulps. All on top of the cocktails and wine at Ruth's Chris steakhouse.

How I yelled at Zach to stop playing his stupid video game and find a useful activity, snapped at every question Sarah asked, and complained about weekend plans and school assemblies. How little Olivia, in her brother's hand me down T-shirt nightgown, asked me to read her a book. I told her no and started back in on Sarah, who ordered me to "find a place and sleep things off" and I responded with "sleep what off?" and she started with the "impact I'm having on the family" guilt trip. While all this was going on, Olivia tugged at the bottom of my suit coat, asking me to read.

When the unthinkable happened, everything moved in slow motion.

My arm rose in the air, crossing in front of my face, providing me a split-second opportunity to stop, a split second I ignored, before descending. The back of my hand didn't hit her face flush, but there was enough force to bump her back a few feet before she thumped onto her bottom.

For one tick of the clock nothing happened. When the mayhem erupted, Sarah screamed, and my little girl's eyes grew into large liquid pools of terror. Sarah scooped Olivia off the floor and moved across the room, but I couldn't see her because standing between us, holding a baseball bat, was my son, ready to protect his mother and sister, cursing me with words I didn't even know were in his vocabulary.

I collapsed onto a couch. The rest was a blur—Zach standing guard, Sarah making a call, the blue lights in my face while I walked, handcuffed, to the patrol car. The ensuing ride, while short, was a voyage to a new world, as the silent officers took me away from my old life and deposited me in a cold, dark cell.

∞ ∞ ∞

I wake up in the hotel room, with Gerri holding my arms and Addy cradling my head, urging me to settle down. I spasm and turn, managing to jerk free and roll off the bed. After my head smacks the floor, I'm back in the chair, across from Joseph.

∞ ∞ ∞

He resumes his inquisition. "After this sad event with your daughter, what happened?"

"They made me get help. Going to rehab kept me out of jail."

"Did getting help work?"

"I'm not incarcerated, so, yeah."

"No, my friend. Did rehab work?"

"We both know the answer."

Joseph shifts in his chair. "Fair enough. I believe we both know why getting treatment was not effective."

"Tell me, O Wise One, tell me why."

Joseph examines the folded hands resting on his stomach. "A better approach is for us to talk and discover together. I would prefer beginning with a few inquiries."

"Shoot."

"What is your problem, Ben?"

Here we go. I'm in the Outhouse all over again, spouting rehab drivel designed to cure me. I didn't want to do this nonsense there, and I sure as heck don't want to do this nonsense now. I study my fingernails, aware the question won't dangle between us for long. Trying to wait out this guy is a failing strategy. "All right, I'll come clean. My problem is I'm a drunk, which isn't news to anyone. I don't want to talk about this, and if I did, we'd be engaging in a hopeless exercise. I've proven I can't stop being one."

The tireless one keeps going. "You're a drunk?"

"Yes. As I told you, approximately two seconds ago, I'm a drunk."

"Isn't there another word to describe what you are?"

"You want me to be more refined in my description? Okay, I will. Joseph, I'm an alcoholic."

"Did you admit this when you were getting your help?"

"I said the words."

"What has been the consequence of your being an alcoholic?"

"Joseph, do we have to do this?" He sits, waiting, until I answer. "Whatever. Fine. I've lost everything."

"Yet you still drink." *Ladies and gentlemen, Captain Obvious is in the room.* "Why does your habit continue?"

My back stiffens. The one question I don't want to answer. Except for THE night, everything else I've talked about, saying I'm a drunk, admitting I still am, and telling stories about what I've done wrong, is hard and emotional, but for me, my actions represent academic, check the box stuff. I don't, in any appreciable way, believe I need to change my behavior.

Joseph, of course, already knows this. "This is your chance, Ben. There's the possibility there won't be another one. You must dig." He starts reading again.

To get away from this place, I guess I'm going to have to do the digging. Do I want to?

"What did you mean by your comment?" I ask.

He inserts a bookmark. "Which comment?"

"When you said, 'this is my chance'?"

"Ahh, my friend, I assure you it's never too late to be forgiven. There is, however, a point when a life becomes unproductive, wasteful, and out of sync, denying fulfillment of purpose."

"Joseph, I hit my little girl. There was no injury, not a mark on her, but I still hit her. Not by mistake and not because she misbehaved in any way. Is there anything I can say or do to change my actions?"

"Unfortunately, no."

"If that's the case, I don't care about being out of sync with my purpose or life goals or whatever else I'm supposed to be doing."

"We've discovered the center of our problem, have we not?"

I shrug. As far as I'm concerned, the only way out of this hole is to forget, and for me, there's only one way to forget.

Joseph stands, picks up his chair and walks over, the light moving along with him, until he sits again, this time about two feet away. He bends forward, bringing himself closer. "It is true you cannot change what has happened, but I advise you to honor the present. Build a future from your past."

"You're giving the same advice I heard in treatment." *And here, too, courtesy of Jeb.*

"Ben, do you believe change is possible?"

"I'm not sure. Sometimes I think so and even consider trying, but then I stop."

"Why are you hesitant?"

I know the answer but don't reply. After Joseph puts his hand on my shoulder, I listen to my breathing, considering what to do. When I speak, I'm barely able to hear myself. "Because if I changed, I would have to admit what happened."

"Finally, my friend, we have arrived at the crux of the matter." He leans back, his index fingers resting against the bottom of his chin, and he waits.

After concluding I can't end the conversation, I choose to reveal more of the truth. "I could move past all the other history, the years before this one. I'm mortified, though, about what I did to my daughter. All she wanted was for her daddy to read a story. I hate what happened, and I hate it wasn't enough to make me stop drinking."

Joseph gives a small smile. "There is irony there, is there not?"

"Please, Joseph, I'm too wrung out."

"Yes, yes. Your fatigue is evident. I am sorry. I did not mean to frustrate you. I ask because I find myself considering an interesting contradiction. What happened with your daughter put you in a position to receive assistance, and the same event is also preventing you from benefiting from the available help." He ponders before moving on. "Ahh, not a consideration for right now. The important step is to admit what is hindering you. You have done so. An excellent development."

My eyes ease open, and I'm back on the bed, battered as if a bus hit me and tasting bile in my throat, lying still. Addy's standing over me, saying she believes I'm past the worst part. I feel a soft, cool cloth on my head and squeeze out a "bless you" before drifting off.

Joseph and his chair have returned to their original spot.

"What now?" I ask.

"You choose."

"I choose?"

"Yes. You choose whether or not you want help."

This seems too easy. "Where would this help come from?"

"From the only one who makes a difference. God."

"Joseph,"—I'm rolling my eyes—"we've plowed this ground. I don't believe enough for God to help me."

"Let me ask you this, my friend."

There's no way to evade. "Go for it."

"Why not try? Make the first step?"

"If I thought it would make a difference, maybe I would. Although, the real issue is I don't know where to start."

Joseph becomes a negotiator who's figured out he's going to win. "Ben, do not worry. Helping you get started is part of my assignment."

A low-level illumination, not enough to read by but enough to make my way around without stumbling, fills the room. Turns out we're in the middle of a perfect square, and I see two closed doors, one on either side, facing each other.

"I present you with a choice." Joseph points to the door on his left. "You are in there now."

It opens and a reddish, black light emerges. There are people screaming, crying, and pleading for help. Wolves are growling and the odor of rotting carcass drifts out. I recoil, my next sentence muffled by the hand covering my mouth and nose.

"Ah, Joseph, I'm not in there. I'm here with you."

"While no one is physically inside, humans exist there every day, living hopeless, tortured lives."

"Does it always sound this way?"

"I cannot answer the question. I don't know what you're hearing."

I unmask my face. "You can't hear those noises?"

"For me there are noises, but they are not the same as what you hear. Much depends on your perception."

"Of?"

"Distance. Estrangement. Separation."

"From?"

"God."

This whole experience is getting way above my pay grade. I move on. "What about the other door?"

"The other door represents the room."

"The room?"

"The one Daniel and Addy mentioned to you."

"How do you know about our conversations?"

He gives a wave of the hand. "Not a pertinent consideration. Think, Ben, think about what they told you."

I spin back to my conversations with Daniel. I have a vague memory of him describing, while he was in New York, entering the room. Addy told me to step inside the room if I wanted to discover a faith. "What's behind the door?"

Joseph, for the first time since I've met him, is impatient. "Have you learned anything from me at all?"

"Right. Discovering what's behind the door rests on me."

"Combined with how you view God."

How I perceive God produces a dilemma. Other than the pre-established old-guy-with-a-beard-in-the-sky stereotype, I haven't given the topic much, or any, sincere thought. "Joseph, at my best, I'm cynical, and at my worst, I don't believe he exists. What the heck am I going to see or hear?"

"I assure you there will be something. For most people, there's a vision, a strong one, buried underneath the clutter and confusion humanity creates. Only the most hardened of unbelievers don't respond. I am certain you are not one of those."

The door swings open.

I don't hear any noises but do see a light. While I'm expecting the bright and blinding LIGHT from the conversion stories, this is the warm glow created by a comfortable fire.

"If you feel compelled, examine more closely," Joseph tells me.

I shift my position, craning my neck as if I'm peering around a corner. Whatever I'm seeing folds into itself and pulls away, reminding me of giant waving palm branches, except the leaves shimmer and radiate, and I would swear they're beckoning me.

I take three long strides, and while there's still no sound, the cloak of warmth pulls me closer to the door. I turn around and face Joseph. "What happens if I go inside? Will I be safe?"

"Of course. I promise, if you go into the room, a new life will become possible."

"Why not save the time and chuck me in there?"

He shakes his head. "I cannot. Others can attest to what's in there, offer assistance, or coerce a peek inside, but you must take the final steps over the threshold."

While the prospect is enticing, I remember Daniel's comments about the room, calling his entrance the beginning of a journey. *Do I want a journey?* Based on what he described, there was hard work, changed behaviors, and, given how honest he was, accountability. Worst of all, a new life would not include alcohol, an appalling concept.

The light from above disappears, further emphasizing the unmistakable contrast between my two options—the reddish-black, sound-filled first room and the silent, golden second room.

The choosing should be easy, but isn't. The first room feels familiar, and I know how to function there. All I need to do is take a short journey, hunt down a liquor store, and I'm back where I belong. The sounds from behind the door get louder, and along with the noise, glowing eyes stare outward. The temperature fluctuates between searing heat and bone-chilling cold. The strange thing is, I'm not deterred by this collage of misery. There are ways to deal with anguish—I can always hide under a blanket of vodka. I raise my foot, ready to take the trip, knowing I shouldn't, certain I will. The foot hovers, shaking in midair, when I hear different noises or, to be more precise, voices. Six of them. Caleb, Ruth, Jeb, Daniel, Addy, and Gerri. They're talking all at once but the words filter to me as distinct conversations. A compilation of questions asked, answers given, and kindnesses offered. I know they're not coming from the room in front of me.

I remain perched on one foot, fighting the tug-of-war created by the two rooms. My balance subtly shifts each time I oscillate between my two options—continuing the life I know or embracing the potential to become a better man. I argue with myself, weighing the costs and perceived benefits, until, after a few minutes, I succumb, deciding a new approach to living requires too much sacrifice.

Then there's another sound. My hand. Hitting flesh. I'm confronted with Olivia's terrified eyes, Sarah's screams, and Zach holding his baseball bat. There's no question this all emanates from the dark light beckoning me forward.

I put my foot down, moving backwards, shaking my head and speaking softly. "No, no, no. You can't go back there, Ben. You can't go back there. The worst will happen again." Another image is before me. My high point as a husband came the day Olivia was born. The doctor had ordered an induced labor, a delivery by appointment, and we were scheduled to be at the hospital around six in the morning. As we woke up, Sarah slid across the bed and gave me a light kiss, resting her lips on the corner of my mouth, a gesture I still feel today. With the kiss, she murmured the kindest words anyone has ever spoken to me, "You're good at days like this."

Turning, I look at the other room. Maybe I should try, once again, to be a good man. I move with more confidence, encouraged because the light is still there, and although I have no idea why, is willing to accept me.

I notice the door is different, maybe halfway closed. I stop, five steps away. *Does the door closing mean I can't go in? Is my time running out?* I turn to ask Joseph but his chair is empty. Not surprising. He did say this one is my call.

Rushing forward, I crash through the door, clearing the threshold.

The room pulls me in, encasing me in something I'm unable to define. The best description is to say I've entered a radically inviting universe—a big, open heart pulling me deep into a loving core.

My brain shifts gears, and I try to calculate the cost, the price I'll have to pay for an experience this magnificent. The potential answer generates anxiety over what will come next, lets loose a new wave of Olivia shame, and releases my habitual obstinance, the chronic pigheaded desire to handle my life on my own. For a second, I deliberate going back outside, but an isolated thought, similar to something Joseph stated, emerges through the heap—based on the way life had gone out there, why not stay in here and give this a chance? I reach, and after my gentle kick, the door swings shut.

∞ ∞ ∞

I'm conscious again, back on the hotel bed, with my hips thrusting into the air, my body still sheathed in sweat, and a groan escaping my lips.

Addy's voice is forceful. "Ben, it's okay, you're with friends." She's holding one shoulder, Jeb the other, and someone else is clutching my ankles.

As I continue to struggle against them, I see Joseph standing to my left. "Welcome to the room, my friend, welcome."

I realize only I see Joseph. My body flops all over the bed, bucking against the people holding me down. At the same time, someone or something is infusing itself into my being, creating a sensation similar to sitting next to a warm fire or the reassurance offered by my grandmother's embrace. What I'm feeling is much more than an external perception. I'm being injected, through a figurative whole-body IV, with a tranquility I can't possibly translate into words.

I see Joseph's hand come forward as if he's going to help restrain me. However, inches before making contact, his index finger reaches out and touches the middle of my forehead. In an instant, the shaking stops, my stomach settles, and my brain clears.

I lay still.

Jeb and Addy let go and Gerri and Caleb release my ankles. I fill my lungs and my eyelids start to fall.

No one says a word until I break the silence. "I'm better now."

PROGRESS REPORT # 8

Peter,

I'm happy to report Our Man took the all-important First Step.

We engaged in a lengthy process. As suspected, his physical condition allowed for openness to interaction, and following the necessary prodding, essential details were eventually uncovered. These revelations were, for him, deeply painful. However, they effectively removed a layer of emotional crust, allowing a time for questions and discussion. This, in turn, led to the recognition of a potentially more advantageous approach to his earthly walk.

The situation was the most tenuous at the final decision point. As we often witness, he was extremely close to succumbing to the comfort of the known. However, at the penultimate moment, our caretakers' work bore fruit while, simultaneously, enemy forces, as they tend to do, overplayed their hand, choosing to trust regret and despair. Fortunately, our Man was not tempted to pursue further misery.

The next major task is to reduce skepticism and establish a base of belief. To prepare the path forward, I took the liberty of restoring his health, hopeful he will awake fresh, energetic, and attentive.

INTO THE ROOM

I must confess, my energy is drained.
With thanksgiving for rest,
Joseph

DAY 9

When my eyes snap open the clock reads 5:32 a.m. I sit propped against the headboard, sorting through a montage of bizarre memories—a jumble of dark rooms, chairs, clashing noises, doorways, and people holding me down on a bed. There's also a single finger pushing against my forehead. *A dream, right?* Had to be.

I try to change the channel and eavesdrop on the hotel room, hearing the air conditioner humming, a few vehicles moving around outside, and Joseph sleeping. Except, I realize, I don't recognize the breathing cadence. I listen again. Nope. Definitely not Joseph.

My legs slide to the floor. The city lights, sneaking around the edges of the curtain, gently illuminate the space. There are facecloths on the nightstand, empty bottles of water strewn around, the bedsheets all kicked loose, and, sleeping upright in a chair, Addy. A blood pressure cuff is resting on her thigh and a stethoscope is draped around her shoulders.

I start to wonder. The vignettes. Did they arise from a fevered delirium? I run through them again, and as the events fall into sequence, the whole night registers as more real than not. Plus, I feel as good as I've felt all week. Rested. No shaking. A settled stomach. There's not a single thought about my first drink. I always start the day planning the first sip.

I should care about the time, but I don't, and I call out. "Addy."

$$\infty \quad \infty \quad \infty$$

"You gave us a scare," Addy tells me.

We're at breakfast, and I'm devouring a mound of eggs, fresh fruit, and breakfast meat. She's playing with her yogurt and granola. "Toward the end, you were convulsing. At one point, we had to pick you up off the floor." Her face reflects every bit of last night's strain.

"How long did all this last?"

"For the entire day yesterday. A few of us missed the touring."

"Addy, I'm sorry to put you through all of this. If it helps, thank you for being there."

"It does."

We focus on our food, until after a few minutes, she blurts out, "You know the strange part? Everything stopped stone cold. I've seen withdrawal, which I'm sure you were experiencing, come on quickly, but I've never seen the symptoms end with a snap of the fingers. There's always been a slow come down, a tapering off."

I decide not to mention my experiences or dreams or whatever all those things were, especially Joseph's finger touching my forehead.

Addy completes her prognosis. "Either way, I'm optimistic you're moving forward. Still feeling good?"

"Yeah, I do. Honest."

"Okay. Stay hydrated and pace yourself. Skip an activity if you're getting run down."

After a few more mouthfuls, I point at the medical equipment on the table beside her. "What's with the blood pressure cuff and stethoscope? You travel with those?"

"I told you a couple of days ago. Being an emergency room nurse is my calling, and yes, I take them everywhere. You never know when they'll be needed."

"Lucky for me." I give her a grateful smile.

∞ ∞ ∞

As the bus pulls out, Caleb says the morning prayer and rallies the troops. "This is not a drill, people! We're in The Holy City, the hub of our faith."

Right away at our first stop, I notice the temperature is much cooler than in the desert, and since we're on city streets, there's no dust. Instead, I see flowers, trees, cats milling around, and people, lots of them, living their everyday lives.

Avi leads us along a large wall to a door imbedded in an archway, reminding me of the entrance to a castle. "This, the Wall of Jerusalem, was built in the 1530s, during the Ottoman empire."

The 1530s? A heck of a long time for a structure to stay in place, and unquestionably, the construction is sturdy. The wall must be at least two feet thick, and as I crane my neck, tilting my head skyward, I estimate the hand-carved stones are stacked forty feet high. Avi keeps talking. "The wall is about four thousand meters long—"

"For us ignorant Americans, we're talking about two-and-a-half miles."

Avi nods to Caleb and continues. "There were originally seven gates. This one is called the Zion Gate—"

"The wounded gate." The dry cleaner is on a roll today.

189

"Ah, yes, Caleb, as usual, you know your history. Now, everyone, let me guide you to these pockmarks around the archway." Avi points at a series of small indentations where the rock has been chipped away. "During the 1948 War of Independence, there was a harsh battle here to break a siege. What you see are bullet markings, remnants from the fight."

Ruth wants to know more. "Did the Israelis win?"

"Yes and no. The militia got through but was forced back. They did, however, get the Jews out of the neighborhood as they retreated."

She shakes her head. "So much bloodshed."

"True. Yet, for us as Israelis, necessary."

We continue along the street, which was clearly established before modern vehicles needed a wider berth.

Everything is made of a tan-colored stone, accented by brown veins and patches. As we walk, I run my hand along the walls, experiencing the wear created by centuries in the elements.

We stop in a small plaza facing a large house, a beautiful building with arched windows, and a courtyard in the back.

Avi gathers us around. "This is one of Pastor Marcus' favorite stops. Let's ask him to explain where we are."

The Good Pastor steps forward and points at the house. "The second floor here, according to tradition, is the Upper Room, the location where Jesus and the disciples had their last supper. The room is also, again according to tradition, where the disciples hid after the crucifixion and where Jesus appeared to them—"

"And Thomas doubted," interjects Jeb. He shrugs. "Sorry to interrupt. I'm a big Thomas fan. He appeals to the lawyer in me."

We climb a flight of stairs. As we step inside, Avi's next to me, and I'm reviewing a phrase Marcus used. "What does according to tradition mean?"

"With these types of locations, places where significant events occurred, there is a verbal tradition informing us where they happened."

"There's no conclusive proof?"

"Although nothing definitive verifies this was the spot, we have written accounts of the events, including the Gospels and other independent historical records. There is also oral history, passed down over time."

I remember a stop from earlier in the week. Caesarea. Avi showed us the Pilate Stone, which presented clear evidence Pilate lived. A couple of days later, we saw the Dead Sea Scrolls, and I recognized there had to be something there, given all those source texts for the Bible. This tradition concept feels less substantial. "Isn't verbally based history more suspect?"

Avi stops. "You are an interesting one. On these tours, I rarely have to convince a visitor about authenticity. They come here assured, full of faith, eager to put a name to a place, and affirm a lifetime of beliefs. Not you, though. You are searching."

Searching? I'm simply passing time, tolerating the trip.

As groups of people funnel around us, he provides additional explanation. "During Jesus's time, no one knew what was happening. At first, Jesus was special. He grew and became a prophet, and a great one, but controversial. He was not teaching in ways people had been taught before. There were those who loved him, but others wanted him dead. He was a threat. He was a blasphemer. As we know, they did kill him and put him in a tomb. Then a small group witnessed him alive again. Still, no one, including his closest friends and ... how do you say this ... yes, I remember now, confidants, knew what Jesus's life meant. None of them knew they were at the birth of the world's greatest religion."

Gerri, who I hadn't noticed had stopped with us, adds her viewpoint. "Let's not forget, those early Christians weren't exactly the toast of the town. Between the stonings, the arrests, and the lions, I'm not sure I'd hang a plaque to commemorate my newfound faith."

Avi joins back in. "Allow me to explain another way. We, all this time after, know the ending. The story's packaged in a single book, there are thousands of other writings to explain what's written there, scholars to teach us, theology to explain what happened. There've been two thousand years of a church growing and expanding. They had none of this perspective."

I have to admit, he's making sense.

Avi puts his hand on my shoulder. "Do you mind if I offer advice?"

"Uh, sure."

"Don't question as much as you do. Appreciate Jerusalem. What we have here was real in Biblical times and is real now. See, touch, and smell. Let the experience lead you, spark your thoughts, tell you the story."

I remember Joseph, those two doors, and what I chose. Real or imagined, there was a decision there. *I should at least give the place a chance.*

The actual Upper Room surprises me. I was expecting a cramped wooden hovel. This room is spacious and bright, with elegant pillars and stone tiled floors. In my everyday world, I could subdivide, make two luxury apartments, and double my investment. A real estate guy's dream.

I also sense an aura or energy, or as weird as this sounds, a type of presence, permeating the space. As I invest a few seconds searching for a description, I'm surprised I would try, given my habitual cynicism. I am curious though and ask Gerri, "Do you feel something?"

She nods. "You could cut it with a knife."

"Cut through what?"

"The Holy Spirit."

I glance over to see if she's joking.

She's not.

$$\infty \ \infty \ \infty$$

Addy's on nurse duty as the bus navigates Jerusalem traffic. "How are you feeling?"

"Fantastic." I'm being sincere. I don't know how or why, but I'm gliding through the day.

She's suspicious. "Okay. Don't get too crazy. Pace yourself. Your recovery speed is highly unusual."

"Stop worrying."

I see the blood pressure cuff in her hand. "Let me do a quick reading?" I hold out my arm. The results are good, and she heads back to her seat, muttering to herself. "I'll never see this happen again."

Avi's at the microphone. "As we head to our next stop, let's learn more about the Upper Room."

Gerri stands, and before Avi continues, she points at me. "You know what, honey? I'm not comfortable with you sitting away from us all. You been back there since this trip started, and I think it's high time you scooted forward."

Caleb agrees. "Yeah. Come on up, pilgrim."

I can't say no, and in a way, I'm happy to be asked. I walk the ten rows, settling in behind Jeb and Ruth.

Gerri's satisfied. "Much better. Avi, please continue."

He doesn't miss a beat. "Several of you noticed Muslim men and women visiting the Upper Room. This is because Jesus is a major figure in the Islamic religion." I find myself listening closely. "To Muslims, Jesus is the ultimate prophet. A direct messenger of God. There's disagreement about his divinity and the resurrection, but we must not mistake this for disrespect. In fact, they believe he will return at the End Days and rule for a seven-year period."

I hear someone mumble about his rule being for forty years, but I dismiss the difference as semantics.

Avi expands his explanation. "Muslims are a reverent people. Those you saw today, they wanted to witness Jesus. To honor a significant part of their religion."

The ever-inquisitive Ruth asks a question. "I don't want to be mean-spirited or bigoted here, but I thought they wanted to eradicate us."

"Muslims do believe Islam, in the end, will rule," replies Avi, "and they are waiting for their time to come. There is a more extreme sect, those on the edges, who wish to fulfill the prophecy now."

We creep along the city street, advancing maybe half a mile, before Ruth asks another question of Avi. "Do you have Muslim friends?"

"Of course. They are warm, wonderful people. Those I know are exceptionally devoted to their families. I'm afraid you are judging an entire group of people based on the extremists. The crazy ones who commit evil acts. Hatred dominates their hearts."

What Avi's saying makes sense. Regardless of affiliation, the nutjobs get all the attention—regular folks aren't provocative enough to make the news.

Avi has more to say. "Don't misunderstand me. Those who want to kill and maim and terrorize should be tracked down, exposed, and eliminated. I see no mercy for them."

I love the Israelis. They don't take anything from anyone.

Daniel slides in next to me. "How are you feeling?"

"I'm confused."

"What I mean is, how are you doing physically? I heard yesterday was a rough one for you."

"I feel great. Thanks."

"Truly?" He sounds unconvinced.

"Truly."

"Okay, good."

He peers out the window for a block or two before following up. "What are you confused about?"

I've shared enough face time with Daniel to know this could get involved. However, my head's clear, and I'm feeling fit. *Why not answer the guy?* "Jesus."

He plays with his whiskers. "You've introduced an expansive topic. Could you narrow down your concerns for me?"

"What Avi told us about Muslims and Jesus, is, I don't know, contrary to any understanding I had. No, no, not contrary, it's additional."

"Additional?"

He lets me cogitate. "What I'm struggling with is ... we're discussing a different construct about Jesus than the one I had."

"Construct is an interesting word to use."

"There's something wrong with using construct?"

"No, no, not at all. However, construct, the noun, reflects an image, an idea, a theory you have. A construct is not necessarily based on anything real."

I massage my forehead. "And?"

"This tells me Jesus is a notion, a concept to you. Not a tangible being who walked the earth." Since I don't have the mental and emotional energy necessary to unpack his observation, I'm grateful when Daniel keeps the conversation going. "Tell me about your confusion concerning the Muslims."

"I had no idea they acknowledge Jesus lived, let alone recognize him as a prophet."

"How does this affect your, as you say, construct?"

I answer from behind closed eyelids. "Additional information is added to the data base, I guess."

He's quick with the next question. "What does the information add?"

"A level, or, maybe ... a layer? Yeah. A layer."

"What does the layer do?"

"Creates more on top of the history I know."

Daniel goes full Socrates on me. "But didn't you use the word construct?"

"We've been over all this."

"I believe, a moment ago, you used the word history."

"I did, yeah."

"Doesn't history imply an assumption of authenticity?"

"Uh-huh."

"Wouldn't you agree the two words, history and construct, when applied to the same matter, are contradictory?"

Fortunately, I'm not on trial here. "Are you saying I believe more than I'm letting on?"

"I'm not drawing any conclusions. I'm responding as you answer questions."

"Maybe, I don't know. I'm getting twisted up here."

"Are you? Let's simplify. You revealed today's experience created a layer. On top of what you already know."

His summary makes sense. "Agreed."

"And the new layer confuses you?"

"Yes."

"Why does the new layer confuse you?"

"Because I now have information I didn't know before."

"You're not responding to my question."

I'm surprised when the answer occurs to me. "The new layer, this new information, makes all of this more"—I pause before I say the word— "real."

"Y'all coming along or not?" Gerri is standing next to us. The bus has stopped and everyone's unloading.

Daniel's ready. "We sure are. Our friend needs fresh air."

∞ ∞ ∞

Real. Real. Real. The word bounces around inside my head.

"Oh, my goodness." Ruth stares at the sign.

HORTVS GETHSEMANI.

Everyone's studying the words, itching to get inside. Reaching back into my brain, I remember this is a big stop, but I can't recall why. A place where Jesus did a miracle? A place where he preached? Based on how deferential everyone is, I'm too embarrassed to ask.

Once we're inside, Avi bails me out. "Welcome to the Garden of Gethsemane. This is where Jesus came after the last supper, where he agonized about the challenge he was about to face, and where the leaders tracked him down and arrested him."

Pastor Marcus leads us to a quiet spot and asks us to take our Bibles out, pointing us to Luke, chapter twenty-two and reads, "Jesus went out as usual to the Mount of Olives ..." He stops after those ten words, rests the Bible on his hip, and continues. "This is where we are. At the base of the Mount of Olives. Take a moment and rotate in a circle. See what's here. Within your line of sight, Jesus walked, talked, sat, and prayed."

Do I believe Jesus was right here? Wait. No one has used the descriptor "according to tradition." Is this unequivocally the place? No debate?

Pastor Marcus is talking again. "Addy, could you read verses forty-one and forty-two?"

She thanks him for the opportunity to share on such sacred ground and recites the words in a respectful, subdued tone. "He withdrew about a stone's throw beyond them, knelt down and prayed, 'Father if you are willing, take this cup from me, yet not my will but yours be done.'"

When she's finished, Ruth offers commentary. "An indifference prayer."

"Exactly," responds Pastor Marcus, "Jesus wasn't trying to influence the outcome of his actions, all he wanted was to fulfill God's will."

Gerri jumps right in. "Let's not forget, he was pretty darned stressed about what was about to happen."

Pastor Marcus agrees. "Which is exactly what we're going to read about next. Afterwards, I encourage you to experience the Garden. Consider what this setting means to you."

He asks Gerri to read verse forty-four. She doesn't use the book. "And being in anguish, he prayed more earnestly, and his sweat was like drops of blood falling to the ground."

While the sentence floats over us, eyes are closed, mouths are moving, and the entire group is participating in a moment of silent reverence. Except, of course, me. I'm shifting from one foot to another, feeling little beyond discomfort. I guess when you go to church for show, this is the outcome.

Once people start peeling away, I move closer to the olive trees. While the trunks have uneven, coarse, grey-black layers, the branches are young, fresh and covered with leaves, a series of houseplants sprouting from ancient, arthritic hands. Apparently, the exact age of these particular trees is unknown. However, a guide nearby is telling his group they were probably all planted after the Roman conquest in AD 70. I have to admit I'm impressed. These trees come across as positively pre-historic.

I amble along the paths, conscious of all the visitors. They are either walking along quietly or utilizing benches and rocks to pray and read their Bibles.

"Will you help me?"

The voice comes from my right, where an older woman sits, a Bible opened on her lap, gesturing to me.

"Uh, sure, what can I do for you?"

"Would you mind reading this to me?" She points to her book, which I notice is a large print Bible. "My eyes, when I'm looking close, betray me. I hope, though, to be in the Word while I'm here."

I slide onto the bench beside her.

"What is your name?" she asks.

"Ben."

"Ben, I am Isabella."

"Nice to meet you, Isabella."

She smiles, deepening the folds in her face, and repositions a pair of thick eyeglasses on the bridge of her nose. Her light golden-brown skin blends beautifully with her off-white cotton dress. "Are you an American, Ben?"

"Yes."

"I am also. My family emigrated there when I was a young girl. I became a teacher and raised three boys who grew into strong men. Now, though, I am old and need help at times."

I take the book off her lap. "What am I reading?"

She points to the Bible. "The Gospel of Matthew. The part enclosed in a red square. I had my grandson use a Sharpie to mark it."

I read to her from Matthew. The section is in the twenty-sixth chapter, verses thirty-six to forty-five, and is similar to the Luke passage from earlier, with Jesus agonizing before he's arrested.

When I finish, Isabella gently takes my hand and is quiet for a moment. "Thank you, Ben. This means more to me than you could possibly understand,"

"Should I read more? I'm happy to keep going."

"No, I've heard enough for right now." She points down the path. "Besides, someone's waiting for you."

Addy's on a rock, waving me over. As I leave, Isabella, still holding my hand, pulls me close. "You have a good heart, Ben."

If she only knew.

When I get to Addy, she's curious. "What was going on there?" After I tell her, she's pleased. "That was lovely of you, Ben."

I shrug. "I enjoy reading to people."

She pivots back to being a nurse. "Are you physically okay?"

"Yep. Feeling good."

I notice her Bible's open and head the other way, saying, "Hey, I don't want to bother you while you're reading."

She shakes her head. "You're no bother at all. Tell me your impressions."

I stop. "Of?"

"This place."

The truth is, I'm stumped. If what we read is historically accurate, Jesus was physically present, possibly on the spot I'm standing, roughly two thousand years ago. Accepting the premise puts me at odds with the abstract construct Daniel and I discussed. "Do people sweat blood?"

"Absolutely. The condition is called hematidrosis. The capillary blood vessels feeding the sweat glands rupture. They exude blood."

"Have you ever seen this happen?"

"Sure have. One time I treated a cop who was in a shooting situation. He sweated blood during a standoff and right after they captured the gunman."

"Did he get grazed?"

"Oh, no. One of the possible causes of hematidrosis is extreme physical and emotional stress."

"Which I guess he had, huh?"

"The cop? Definitely. He was at the front of the line. Ended up being the one who tackled the guy." She stands, checking her watch. "Oops. Time for us to head back."

"Do you believe it's true?" I ask, as we walk along.

"What?"

"Did Jesus actually sweat blood?"

"Of course. The story's in the Gospels."

"And you believe the Gospels are true?"

She shrugs and says, "What else could they be?"

"A legend based on myth or an allegory or an inaccurate depiction of oral history."

She keeps walking while she responds. "There's not enough space between us and the bus to lay out all the historical foundations for the Bible. I will admit, though, there was a time in college when I questioned. I got through the phase pretty quickly."

Of course she did, although I ask for more. "How do you know? How are you sure?"

"I just am, plain and simple."

When we get to the gate, Gerri's waiting for Addy, and hands her a packaged ice cream cone. Gerri must notice I'm perplexed. "What's eating at you, sweetie?"

"He's wondering about the Book," Addy answers between bites.

Gerri takes my arm, turning me around. "Benjie, mull over where we are. All this was here back when the Book was written and all this is still sittin' here now. Nothing got covered with all kinds of archaeological sediment and no one says they *believe* this is the place. This *is* the place. As Pastor Marcus told us—there's a strong chance your feet crossed ground where Jesus—JESUS—actually walked."

If she's right, things are as real as they're going to get.

$$\infty \quad \infty \quad \infty$$

Our next stop is Bethlehem. Before we cross into Palestinian territory, the bus driver has to call the Israeli military and get permission. The call must go okay, because we keep lurching along the tight streets.

While we're moving, I remember the woman Hannah in Nazareth. She was convinced she would see us all in heaven, expressing her belief as a statement, not a question. In the Last Supper room, Gerri demonstrated similar confidence, telling me the Holy Spirit was present. Now, a few minutes ago, Addy flat out accepted the Bible as true.

"What bothers you, my friend?" It's Joseph.

"Huh? Oh, ah, nothing. All good here."

"You were staring at the back of the seat with such ferocity, I thought you would bore a hole through the fabric."

Evidently, I was chewing my thumbnail too. There's a spot of blood on the cuticle. "You know something, Joseph? I negotiate and make deals for a living. One definitive talent I have is recognizing a false front, knowing when something's phony." I pause and consider my fellow travelers. "These folks here on this bus, they're sincere. They believe what they see and say."

"Yes, this is most assuredly true."

I refocus on the back of the seat, concentrating on the Garden, those geriatric olive trees, and the reality of sweating blood. I review my conversation with Daniel about constructs and history, and the discussion with Avi and Caleb about what the words "according to tradition" represent. Heck, until today, I didn't know there were Muslims who believe Christ existed. As my eyes lift and I see the people sitting in front of me, I marvel at their persistent faith. The word I thought earlier returns.

Real.

∞ ∞ ∞

As Caleb starts digging into his lunch, our first meal with a waiter since the trip started, he checks on my health. "You're still feeling okay, huh?"

"Can't complain. All good."

I don't know the name of the restaurant, but the food is great. The only problem has been the language. Fortunately, thanks to Avi and Caleb's translation skills, no one's eating any unusual local delicacies.

I'm wolfing my food, a steaming plate of chicken, rice, pita bread, and humus, consuming calories at post-marathon levels. There's also a cup of dirt tea, a maintenance dose, prescribed by Addy.

The lunch banter is light, more informal than usual. Jeb notices the difference. "Lots of emotional energy this morning. Those were two big stops. Folks are taking time to unwind."

I'm perfectly content listening to the clamor around me. Pastor Marcus and Caleb are discussing football, debating a wide range of topics, including whether or not watching a game is more enjoyable live or on TV. Caleb describes a home entertainment room in his house, which includes a massive TV, surround sound, recliners, and a small kitchen. Ruth and Daniel are comparing television sitcoms, which surprises me. Neither one of them has struck me as interested in pop culture. Turns out their taste is pretty mainstream. *Seinfeld* and *The Goldbergs* for Ruth, *The Big Bang Theory* for Daniel. Off on the fringe, I half listen to Gerri and Addy argue the merits of various ice cream flavors.

During a brief lull, Gerri takes the dispute public. "Addy, sweetheart, your mama's a sister to me and I love her, but, and bless her heart, she messed you up. No one eats pistachio ice cream anymore." A controversy erupts, and the whole table starts debating flavors. When Daniel claims frozen yogurt belongs in the discussion, Gerri blows up like Mount Vesuvius, and Ruth, of all people, raises her voice.

Jeb catches my eye and gives me a head nod, pointing to a big picture window where Avi is staring out, his Bible opened, oblivious to the restaurant's activity.

When he sees us, Avi motions to the open landscape below. "What we're seeing is the Shepherd's Field. Where the angels appeared and announced the birth of Jesus."

The field is a massive tract of land, sloping at various angles, covered with grass, rocks and scraggly trees.

Avi hands me his Bible, already opened to Luke, chapter two. The passage describes an angel proclaiming to the shepherds "a Savior has been born to you. He is Christ, the Lord." The words also include the famous swaddling clothes reference. Avi explains that the shepherds decided to go check things out and finishes with how they went to Bethlehem, saw Jesus and, according to Luke, "spread the word concerning what had been told them about this child ..."

As Avi takes the book back from me, he addresses his absence from the lunch table. "I've been to this place hundreds of times, and I always have to stop and gaze at the field. These shepherds, they were not respected at all, a group positioned at the absolute bottom of the social order. Yet, God chose to tell them before anyone else."

Jeb puts his hand on the window. "Right out there?"

Avi nods. "Yes, right out there. As the Book tells us, the shepherds were the first to let the world know. You see, shepherds were the town criers, the internet of ancient society."

I try and imagine being outside, in the dark, on a remote stretch of land, looking at an angel. I stop myself. *Do I actually believe these events happened?* Before settling on an answer, another question crashes into my head. If, as Avi says, shepherds were on the lowest rung of the social ladder, why would they be chosen for a job this important? I shake my head, trying to rearrange the overload in my brain.

When we get back to the table, everyone's talking about the vast philosophical divide related to home ice cream makers. For most, hand cranking is the only acceptable method. Addy and Ruth are the strongest holdouts, seeing no loss of authenticity in using electric—Addy because "you more mature folks need to get out of the dark ages" and Ruth because "I'm too old to be gyrating my hands for forty-five minutes."

As we pay for our meal, Jeb leans in. "Why do you suppose you're feeling good today?"

Based on the last twenty-four hours, I could offer a million hypotheses while, at the same time, there's a strong argument I should be physically and emotionally exhausted. I mean, Joseph put me through one grueling night. I go with the easiest explanation. "No drinking yesterday."

"Feeling energized?"

"I am."

His lips purse and he studies my face. "A word of advice?"

"Shoot."

"Be careful."

"Careful?"

"We've all been where you are. We drinkers. You can't do everything at once."

"Do what?"

Jeb doesn't answer directly. "Right now, you're riding a wave. Enjoy the wave but be aware you're probably experiencing a temporary high. The tests will come." He ends the conversation with a slap on the back.

∞ ∞ ∞

After lunch, we stay in Bethlehem to go souvenir shopping.

I was expecting the shop to be a dark hovel, jam packed with cheap junk. Instead, the showroom is spacious and bright, with spotless white walls, polished wood floors, and plenty of room to move around. In addition to the usual collection of trinkets and baubles, there's plenty of high-end jewelry, paintings, and intricate wood carvings.

"Interested in buying anything, honey?" Gerri's next to me, holding a pile of olive wood figurines and a bunch of coaster sets.

I shake my head. "No, probably not. I'm not much for souvenirs." My comment is inaccurate. On any other trip,

I'd search for a memento or two. However, despite today's positive surge, this particular expedition comes with too much baggage.

"We've only got a few minutes. You need to make up your mind soon," she advises.

I browse, stopping at a jewelry case, admiring a collection of beautiful pendants attached to silver necklaces, their dark blue stones accented with green, gray, and sky-blue flecks. Addy walks past admiring them but quickly moves on when she sees the price, commenting "too pricey on a nurse's salary."

Watching her move away, I remember the event earlier in the week when she lost a necklace. I subsequently learned the pendant was a sentimental piece given to her as a college graduation gift. I get an idea and decide, after all, to make a purchase.

After selecting a necklace, I walk to the main counter and approach a person who I assume is the guy in charge. He matches the prototype of every male shopkeeper I've ever seen—slightly harried, deep circles under the eyes, not sloppy but fashionably unkempt, complete with the requisite five o'clock shadow.

His arms open wide as I move closer. "Hello, American Pilgrim! Welcome to Bethlehem and welcome to my establishment." We shake hands. "My good friend, Avi, he takes care of you, no?

"No. I mean, ah, yes. Avi takes great care of us."

"Ah, delightful!"

He holds the pendant, nodding his approval. "Ah, the Eilat Stone, also known as the King Solomon stone. Our people believe the Eilat Stone heals both the physical and emotional state."

He goes quiet while he finishes what I presume is a mail order. Watching him wrap a ceramic plate in tissue paper, I consider what Avi told us on the way in, about this being a difficult place for Christians. I blurt out a question. "What is living in Bethlehem like?"

There's no hesitation before he answers. "Bethlehem is glorious! I am here, am I not?"

I can't argue with his logic. The plate goes into a box and he continues talking, his hands moving automatically to the next item, a wooden cross. "What is your name?"

"Ben."

"Ben, I am Yussef." He switches to a language I don't understand, directing a teenage girl into a back room. "Did you ask because we are in Palestine?"

"I did. I'm sorry to be intrusive."

As he swipes my credit card and puts the necklace into a bag, he shakes his head. "No, no. No worries. Many who visit are curious about us living here. What do you want to know?"

My image of interpersonal relations in the Middle East has been shaped by three-minute news clips and espionage novels. All I picture are Christians being beheaded. From this narrow viewpoint, I ask a simplistic question. "Do you feel safe?"

Yussef stops what he's doing. "Conditions here are sometimes challenging. More and more of our brothers and sisters are leaving. Getting work is difficult and we are not integrated. Maybe a better word is united. We are not united with our neighbors."

"Would you say living here is uncomfortable?"

"At times, yes, but we also must maintain perspective. My Palestinian neighbors would tell you they are oppressed, and their land was stolen from them. They call the country of Israel Occupied Palestine. As you see, my friend, life is difficult for everyone." He points to the back room. "Let us consider the girl working in the room behind me. She was a Muslim. Now she believes in Jesus as the Messiah. Her family has shunned her."

"Shunned her?"

"Yes."

"Thrown her out of the family?"

"Yes."

"Where does she live?"

"There are rooms. Right above us. A few of my workers reside there."

"Why do you stay? Why not leave?"

"Leave?"

"Yeah. Move away. Go someplace you'll be more accepted."

He shakes his head. "No, no, no, no. I cannot leave. This is my home." I'm sure he notices the confused look on my face. "We all have our crosses, do we not? For me, being here is worth some discomfort."

I can't help myself. "But why?"

He leans in, rests his hand on the back of my neck, and talks in a low voice. "I cannot ignore the holiness, the history. This town of Bethlehem is where our Savior was born. His first earthly breath, drawn here. In a dirty manger, surrounded by animals. Me? I am warm. Fed. Clean. Any risk I have is nothing. I am blessed to be close to his beginning."

There's a tap on my shoulder. "There you are. Ben, buddy, hop to it. Time to load up."

Before Caleb grabs my arm, Yussef offers a farewell. "God be with you and thank you for your business."

Back on the bus, I slump in the seat next to Joseph, impressed by Yussef's intensity, his convictions, and how, in all my life, I've never encountered anyone, including my fellow travelers, with less bull in him.

After the bus starts moving, I slide ahead a couple of rows and hand Addy the bag from the shop. "I bought you this to replace the one you lost the other day. Thank you for all the care you've given me."

Addy's eyes brighten, and she holds the necklace close to her chest. "My goodness, Ben, the stone is beautiful, although I'm not sure I should accept a present this extravagant."

Gerri's looking over the top of the seat in front of us. "You sure should, honey. When a person shows gratitude, simply say thanks and enjoy the gift."

Addy gives me a light kiss on the cheek. "Thank you, Ben."

∞ ∞ ∞

"Change of plans, folks." Avi is on the phone while Pastor Marcus talks. "How about we visit the Garden Tomb today?"

Before anyone responds Avi ends his call. "There has been a cancellation with my favorite tour guide. As he has limited availability, we should head there now."

There's clapping, murmuring, and a couple of enthusiastic squeals. Pastor Marcus raises his voice over the growing clamor. "Everyone, could I have your attention? Folks? Please?" He repeats his line twice more before the pilgrims settle down. "You all know I've been here three other times. On each trip the visit to the tomb was, of course, a highlight. After the first visit, I'd wished I'd done more study up front."

He opens his Bible. "I suggest we make this short ride in silence, individually pray, and maybe visit with our Bibles. Prepare ourselves for what we are going to see." He quickly flips to the page he wants. "Chapter twenty of the Gospel of John is an excellent preparatory scripture reading."

Over the next few minutes, remaining conversation dies down, Bibles open, and eyes close. After locating John 20, I try a paragraph, but there's no connection, and since prayer's out of the question, I distract myself by counting what I have left for money. Opening my wallet, I see Caleb's business card, the one for his dry-cleaning business. I turn the card in my hand, noticing his company's emblem, an anchor and a cross combined, which was connected with the early church.

The bus worms through the city streets until I see another one of those high rock walls and a sign sticking out parallel to the sidewalk. The Garden Tomb.

∞ ∞ ∞

The place is mobbed, and from what I'm observing, people are wandering aimlessly, bumping into each other, trying their best to move around. As we maneuver along, I hear talking, singing, chanting, and the occasional burst of laughter. Every twenty feet or so, one or two people are sitting, eyes closed, meditating or praying, seemingly oblivious to the chaos around them.

We stop underneath a small canopy covering a few stone benches, part of an elevated level perched above an open courtyard. The courtyard runs to the base of a masonry wall. There are gardens here and there. I'm guessing the whole place is about half the size of a football field.

Our guide's name is Dale. He's got a classic American Guy appearance—half bald, glasses not completely snug against his nose, bit of a paunch, khakis, wrinkled blue button-down shirt. I'm guessing he's a corporate middle manager who spends his weekends as a Boy Scout leader. When he starts talking, I realize I'm way off. While he is American, from a small town in Ohio I've never heard of, he hasn't spent more than two weeks there since 1998, the year he turned thirty. Referring to himself as a "Missionary Pastor"—the title is accompanied by air quotes—Dale explains he moves around the world starting Christian churches. Once a parish is established, he moves on to another. His current home is in the Ukraine. "Every year, there're four weeks of vacation. I spend two in Ohio around my mother's birthday, and I come here as a tour guide for the other two."

"Seriously? This guy's idea of time off is to give tours in Jerusalem?" I whisper to Gerri.

She provides the perfect response. "Honey, whatever he has to say, I'm listenin'. He's carrying bona fide Christian street cred."

Dale starts explaining the surrounding area. "From where you're sitting, you're able to see where tradition tells us Jesus was crucified, buried, and rose from the dead. I won't tell you this is definitively the location, but I am going to provide the evidence and let you decide."

Addy interrupts. "Do you, personally, believe this is the spot?"

"Would I come here every year if I didn't?"

After a nod from Dale, Pastor Marcus stands and reads. "Carrying his own cross, he went out to the place of the skull (which in Aramaic is called Golgotha.) Here they crucified him, and with two others—one on each side and Jesus in the middle."

As soon as Pastor Marcus is finished, Dale shows us an old black and white picture. "This photo was taken around 1900. Let me pass it around."

I'm right in front of him and get the picture first. There are camels walking along the base of a steep hill. My eyes zoom in. No, not a hill but a sheer cliff, all rock and, imbedded on the side of the cliff I see a forehead, two dark eyes, and a nose. There's no struggle recognizing the image. I'm looking at a skull.

After passing the picture along, I open my Bible. Gerri must be reading my mind. "John, chapter nineteen, verses seventeen and eighteen."

I reread what Pastor Marcus recited. "The place of the skull ... here they crucified him."

Dale starts talking again. "What you see in the picture is over there, right across the street." He motions to the right, and I see craggy white rock and the cliff. While the image of the skull is not as clear as the old picture, I make out black eyes and the nose. "There's been geological settling since 1900, but most still identify the features present in the historic photograph."

For a few minutes, the group compares, points, and discusses. Everyone eventually gets there, but a few people need to have the similarities pointed out. I don't participate but, instead, try to process the connection between the Bible, a hundred-year-old photo, and what I'm seeing now in real time. The effect is the impact of Ein Gedi on steroids.

Dale continues. "The custom is to assume Jesus was crucified on the top of the hill. This was probably not the case. The Romans preferred to put their victims where people could see them, to set an example, as they say. If you'll notice, behind you, there's a road." We all turn. "The road has been there, in one way or another, since the time of Christ. My hypothesis is he was crucified there."

I circle my head back to the skull and around again to the road. They can't be more than a quarter to a half a mile apart. Hill or road, it's still safe to link the crucifixion to the Place of the Skull.

"After Jesus died, his body was claimed by Joseph of Arimathea. Now, because a good portion of the legend around Joseph originated in the Middle Ages, I'm going to stick to what we know from this." Dale's holding his Bible. "Matthew tells us Joseph was a rich man who went to Pontius Pilate and asked for Jesus's body. Mark tells us he was a member of the council, the Sanhedrin, and characterizes Joseph's request as 'bold.' Luke provides additional information, telling us Joseph did not agree with the decision to persecute Jesus."

I, of course, attended enough Easter services over the years to be familiar with the name Joseph of Arimathea.

Dale keeps going. "As for John's Gospel, let's read what he has to say."

Pastor Marcus opens his Bible. "We'll start at chapter nineteen, verse thirty-eight, and read to verse forty-one." After we all find the spot, he starts in.

> Later, Joseph of Arimathea asked Pilate for the body of Jesus. Now Joseph was a disciple of Jesus, but secretly because he feared the Jewish leaders. With Pilate's permission, he came and took the body away. He was accompanied by Nicodemus, the man who earlier had visited Jesus at night. Nicodemus brought a mixture of myrrh and aloes, about seventy-five pounds. Taking Jesus's body, the two of them wrapped it, with the spices, in strips of linen. This was in accordance with Jewish burial customs. At the place where Jesus was crucified, there was a garden, and in the garden a new tomb, in which no one had ever been laid.

Dale lets the words sink in before talking again. "Given our time commitments, I'm going to focus on three aspects of the reading. The first is spices."

Spices? Really?

"During Biblical times, bodies were anointed with spices to control the smell during decomposition. John says Nicodemus brought about seventy-five pounds of myrrh and aloes. When a Gospel writer is specific with a description, especially a quantity, we should pay attention. There's a definite reason." I imagine a standard one-pound sack of flour. Hauling seventy-five of those to a grave site does not sound fun. "This amount of spices would be used to anoint a king. We're not talking about a small gesture here."

If this were a debate, I'd concede the point—these men didn't believe they were entombing a random, insignificant guy.

"Next, let's talk about these two men, Joseph of Arimathea and Nicodemus. We already know Joseph was a member of the Sanhedrin. As for Nicodemus, in chapter three of John we learn he was a Pharisee. Neither of these men were members of the working class or the general masses and, as we learned a moment ago, at least one of them, Joseph, was afraid of the Jewish leaders. My assumption is Nicodemus was also, but either way, their actions tell us Jesus's influence went beyond his traveling band of disciples."

This guy Dale is good.

"Of course, we have to tie all these factors to where the body went. I'll ask you to follow my finger, down to the left, into the courtyard. Through the door in the wall is what we believe to be the tomb."

I'm not sure why, maybe because of the crowd, but I hadn't noticed the long line of people leading to the door. Maybe this place isn't as disorderly as I thought.

"Now, let's review why we believe this door in this courtyard leads to the tomb." Dale holds up an index finger. "First, geography. We are near the Place of the Skull, Golgotha. We could draw a triangle from the tomb, to Golgotha, to the place along the street where I surmise the crucifixion took place." He points and turns. "The distance between these three points is close enough to move a body quickly. This would be true whether Jesus was killed on the hill above the skull or down there near the road. Luke mentions the Sabbath was about to begin. There would not have been time to move Jesus's body a great distance."

Two fingers go up. "Second, the section of John Pastor Marcus read states there was a garden at the place where Jesus was entombed. Now, I assume we all agree there're gardens in and around where we are now, but the ones we see weren't here two thousand years ago. They've been added. However, archeologists discovered a large cistern and wine press, providing strong evidence there was, in the past, a garden here."

Three fingers. "The Gospel of Matthew says Joseph of Arimathea gave his own tomb."

Gerri's getting excited. "He sure did. Chapter twenty-seven, verse sixty!"

"We know Joseph was a wealthy man. The tomb here is spacious with a small weeping room, or crying chamber, for mourners. There's a window up above. The burial room has a raised platform, a place of honor for the body to rest. Plus, this tomb was designed to be protected. There's a trough for a stone to be rolled across the opening, an event the Gospel of Mark tells us happened. This is definitely a rich person's burial site."

Four fingers. "Fourth, the tomb below is cut out of rock. It was not a cave or other naturally made space. This is consistent with how several of the Gospels describe Jesus's tomb."

Five fingers. "Now the fifth point is going to move us outside the Bible. To the left of the tomb entrance, etched into the wall, is an anchor cross. This was a symbol of the early church. A declaration someone was a follower

of Jesus. I'm aware of this one and one other in Turkey."
I'm already alert, but I perk up and listen closely as he
finishes the thought. "Archaeologists have dated the cross
back about nineteen-hundred years, to the first century."

Daniel interrupts. "Jesus was killed around AD 30. If
you do the math, the cross was put there within seventy
years of his death."

"Exactly!" Dale punctuates his exclamation by jabbing
a finger at us. "Which means the cross was carved inside
a time frame when recent oral history would be, at most,
a generation old. Said another way, the history was once
removed from its original source, people who were alive
when Jesus was killed and resurrected. Actual eye witnesses
to events."

"I'd take that evidence to court," whispers Jeb.

Dale's still talking, but I'm focused on his comment
indicating the actual events weren't a hundred years
old when someone marked the spot. This spot. From my
viewpoint, there's only one reason why—they knew this
was the place. Before I ponder any further, we're moving,
heading across the courtyard.

Dale takes us right to the anchor cross and shows us
the outline on the wall. The shape chiseled into the rock
is not blatantly evident to the naked eye. which to me is
reassuring. Roughly two thousand years of weather and
wear would have an impact. My innate suspicion had me
asking if an overzealous believer carved the cross there
more recently.

I'm thinking Dale must be an influential man, because
we get to cut the line at the tomb. I still estimate a fifteen-
minute wait, giving me more time to process.

I dig the Roth's Cleaners card out of my wallet,
reflecting on the cross Caleb added. At the same time, my
peripheral vision catches movement. Caleb's looking at

me with a see-I'm-onto-something-here expression while he points to the logo and nods at the wall.

Gerri, who's next to Caleb, notices, and when she realizes what the emblem is, her eyes get wide and she states simply, "There are no coincidences in life."

As the first person from our group enters the Tomb, Dale offers an additional fact. "On the back wall, you're going to see a reddish or rust-colored cross, accompanied by Greek letters referencing Jesus as the Alpha and Omega. We estimate these were added in the fifth or sixth century." Dale's work is done, and we start to file in.

While we're inching forward, Gerri scoots back in the line, kidnaps my Bible, and draws a square around a section of text. "I avoid dictatin' to people what they should do, but if you're feeling inclined, read this passage when you come out."

"Okay, thanks." My reaction surprises me. In the recent past, meaning less than twenty-four hours ago, I would have responded with a nod, mumbled a condescending response, and ignored her suggestion.

Jeb, Ruth, and I go in together. We crouch to fit through the door, stepping into the room Dale called a crying chamber.

My line of sight rotates, taking in a series of images. The metal bars protecting the burial area ... the rock shelf, about the size of a twin bed, where a body would be laid ... the red cross Dale had described ... Ruth's hands roaming across the walls and ceiling ... Jeb holding his camera but not taking pictures, his eyes wet, and him saying, "I can't, I won't. This is too sacred" ... the door, made of a rich, dark wood, and the simple engraved sign— "He is not here, for He is risen."

A minute passes in silence.

"I'll never be the same."

Ruth responds to Jeb with a nod, stands on her tiptoes, and gives him a kiss on the cheek. "I know what you mean."

My legs take me into the bright sunlight, still holding my Bible, left index finger marking the page Gerri recommended. There's a short wall next to the door, and I sit, opening the book. The section is the Gospel of John, chapter twenty, starting with verse ten. I read.

> Then the disciples went back to their homes, but Mary stood outside the tomb crying. As she wept, she bent over to look into the tomb and saw two angels in white, seated where Jesus's body had been, one at the head and the other at the foot. They asked her, 'Woman, why are you crying?'
>
> 'They have taken my Lord away,' she said, "and I don't know where they have put him." At this, she turned around and saw Jesus standing there, but she did not realize that it was Jesus.
>
> He asked her, 'Woman, why are you crying? Who is it you are looking for?'
>
> Thinking he was the gardener, she said, 'Sir, if you have carried him away, tell me where you have put him, and I will get him.'
>
> Jesus said to her, 'Mary.'
>
> She turned toward him and cried out in Aramaic, 'Rabboni!' (which means Teacher).

I picture a woman, racked with grief, stooping to see through the door. Walking into the courtyard, I stop about twenty feet in front of the tomb entrance and turn myself slowly in a circle. If I were holding a ten-foot pole, the scene I read would probably have happened within this circumference.

I stop, startled. *You don't believe this do you?* No, I can't. At least I know I never have, not in any tangible way. Yet

219

here I am, visualizing a reality based on the Bible. I scour my brain, digging for the cynicism, the doubt, the *'yeah, but ...'* Amazingly, I don't sense my usual disdain. Instead, I keep weighing one simple word. *Real.* The resounding theme of the day.

The people around me, the ones praying, singing, and waiting in line, have become an amalgamation. Colors and shapes are indistinctly blended together. All I see clearly are my feet, the door to the tomb, and my imaginary ten-foot perimeter.

I read again.

When I get to Jesus saying "Mary," I close the book. *How did Jesus speak the word?* I imagine hushed, compassionate syllables, a verbal embrace.

I feel a breeze. The gentle gust swirls around my feet and a whirlpool of dust ascends my legs before enveloping my torso. The "good" feeling arrives, escalating at a furious pace, becoming a sensation I can't explain or quantify. An incomplete description would label the sensation a warm, tender shroud, but the impact is more than external. This being, for lack of a better word, is saturating me, penetrating deep into my bone marrow.

I can't say how long the feeling stays and am disappointed when the euphoria drifts away. After returning to the wall, I see clearly again and sit, watching the world.

As a Chinese couple exits the tomb, their friends snapping pictures, I know why, a few minutes before, I couldn't drum up my usual cynicism or doubts.

I believe.

On the bus, Daniel comes to see me. "We've experienced, I must say, a complete day."

I agree with a nod, but my energy is sapped.

"Physically okay?"

"Doing good, Daniel. Thanks."

What I've told Daniel is true. Physically, I'm feeling stronger every hour.

If he'd asked about my emotional condition, we'd be having a different discussion. At best, I'm confused. At worst, I'm what they call a hot mess.

This whole believing concept is hard to reconcile. A lifetime of doubt, contempt, and hypocrisy can't instantly disappear. While I know my experiences will take time to sort out, every new thought clashes with an old one, reminding me of those two rams on the nature shows, running full speed, smashing horns, and bouncing back to try again.

Daniel studies me over his folded hands. "I'm not sure you're being completely truthful."

His comment is a lifesaver thrown to a drowning man. As the rams collide again, my thumb points to the seats behind us. "You okay if we move back there for a couple of minutes?"

"Of course."

We settle in, and I immediately begin a verbal purge, telling him about the day, front to back. This includes reiterating the conversation about the Muslims after the Upper Room, my impressions of the Garden of Gethsemane, Avi showing Jeb and me the Shepherd's Field, and the sincerity of the Bethlehem shopkeeper. I bend his ear revealing my thoughts about the skull, the anchor cross, and the time inside the Tomb. I pause. "I'm not sure I should share the events after the Tomb, when Jeb and Ruth and I came out."

"Ben, do you remember when I told you about the night I infiltrated the banker's email?"

I nod, remembering he had read those messages from the guy's wife.

"Is what happened to you more unusual than finding Scripture readings in a hacked email account?"

He's made a good point. I grimace and offer a few uhhs, hmmms and yeeshes before fessing up. "No."

"Why not tell me?"

"Too embarrassing I guess."

"Interesting. Any more embarrassing than me and Jeb transporting your impaired body to the hotel the other night?"

Wow. Hardball. The answer is simple. "Not even close."

"Shall we continue?"

I wave my arms in mock surrender and continue talking, telling him about my Bible reading, the circle, imagining Jesus's tone, and the breeze. I swallow hard, describing the "good" feeling, followed by the moment I no longer doubted if things were real.

When I finish, he doesn't try to interpret for me. "Thank you for sharing."

I'm not done, though. "Earlier in the week, Gerri and I discussed this thing she called a God Whisper. Could today have been one of those?"

"Today, for you, was no whisper. Today was a shout."

"Okay, say I agree. What do I do next?"

"You wait."

"Wait?"

"God has been busy with you since breakfast. I imagine he's finished for today. I'm guessing you need some time to process. Also, I'd recommend you be careful."

"Careful?"

He nods. "You're on a high. Once the day settles, you'll be tired. Physically and emotionally. This could create vulnerability."

I remember Jeb offering a similar warning. "Vulnerability to what?"

"The Bad Guy, as I call him. He's not going to let you go without a fight. I'm guessing you'll feel his presence soon."

The rams keep hammering each other. I'm not ready, in any way, to ponder what's going on at the other end of the spectrum.

∞ ∞ ∞

At dinner, Daniel and Addy sit alone at a separate table. They're looking stylish, at least for this trip. Addy's in a flowered sun dress, she's put on "going out" make-up, and her hair's curled at the ends. I also notice she's wearing the necklace I bought her earlier in the day in Bethlehem. It looks great on her.

Daniel, for his part, cleaned up good—he's wearing dockers, an ironed, blue button-down shirt, and his beard's trimmed. They're laughing and talking while Gerri, across the table from me, beams. "My girl's on a date."

Here we go again. They've got me ruminating about Sarah. Our first date was going out for Mexican food, and we talked about her love of hiking, camping, and bird watching, which she'd do with her father. I told her about my love of card games, reading, and do-it-yourself projects. She made fun of my English and philosophy double major, and I cross-examined her on what would motivate a person to study math for four years. Other recollections pop up—the time I made her cookies, the date when she took me to the circus, a canoe trip on the James River. While I enjoy the ride down memory lane, my reminiscing also generates the usual remorse and sense of loss. As dinner breaks up, I decide to go for a walk.

I roam around for about forty-five minutes, keeping to brightly-lit streets, and enjoy the cool night air. About a hundred yards from the hotel entrance, I see Addy and Daniel, holding hands and strolling along the sidewalk. They turn to face each other and he leans over, giving her a kiss, one she clearly returns, and when they pull apart their eyes hold for a second before they continue walking.

God, I want to feel that way again. With Sarah. I wonder if there's any way.

PROGRESS REPORT # 9

Peter,

We hit Our Man hard today, focusing, as promised, on removing his skepticism and doubt. The itinerary was well suited to this purpose. We began with the Upper Room, moved to the Holy Garden, and continued on to Bethlehem. There, we were assisted by the ever-faithful shopkeeper, Yussef.

The day was advancing better than expected, and sensing a possible breakthrough, I intervened, creating an opportunity to alter the schedule and visit the Tomb a day earlier than expected. As an added benefit, we were blessed with one of Brother Paul's most gifted missionaries.

At the Tomb, the relationship between the site itself, the Holy Book, and evidence left by early disciples, when combined with the morning's activities, invited a direct communication from the Spirit. This, in turn, cracked the shell, releasing Our Man's belief. As always, the moment was magnificent.

At the day's conclusion, he was consumed by confusion and questions. Not a surprising development, considering his earthly journey to date. However, this mental status, combined with physical fatigue and the probability of a forthcoming spiritual battle, puts Our Man in a precarious position. To help prepare for what is to come, two of our caretakers provided warnings, suggesting he be vigilant as events move forward.

As you know, my custom is to report on the seemingly minor happenings to provide additional evidence our work is gaining a foothold. In this case, there are two promising developments. First, Our Man was encouraged to sit in closer proximity to his traveling companions, an invitation he accepted. Second, he has stopped referring to those around him using a snarky moniker meant to debase their faith and diminish their influence. To this point, he hasn't recognized this change and, perhaps, will not consciously do so. Regardless, these are positive steps, and they will assist as we move forward.

One additional and unexpected item—Our Man engaged with a stranger and read to her from the Book. This was the result of a chance meeting. I dare say, given the volume of items on today's agenda, I would have never, out of fear of overload, planned such an encounter. However, the interaction was a success, releasing a portion of the virtue buried in Our Man's heart. While this particular event will, in all probability, not be a factor over the next few days, his actions will serve to bolster future progress.

With hope for tomorrow,
Joseph

DAY 10

I wake up exhausted and refreshed at the same time. I'm feeling fine physically, expectant about the day, and I'm not bothered when Avi, following the morning prayer, warns we will be busy. "There's construction going on, making certain Old City sites unavailable. In response, we've made a few adjustments to our itinerary. Rest assured, we have a full schedule."

Caleb, as usual, is ready to roll. "Of course our schedule is packed! This is Jerusalem. Plenty to see!"

Avi continues. "Now let me tell you why we're on the bus at six in the morning. Today starts at the Western Wall, an exceedingly sacred location to us Jews, perhaps the most holy of all Jewish places. I want us to arrive early and for you to experience people praying in the morning, visiting the Wall as they begin their day."

He's holding a picture. "The Wall has a long and complicated history. Allow me to simplify. The original structure was built by King Herod in 20 BCE and fell out of Jewish hands following the Roman conquest in the year 70 CE. After the Six-Day War in 1967, we Jews got the Wall back, excavating and reclaiming the site, creating this area around the Wall, this Prayer Plaza." He's pointing things out in the picture. "The Wall itself is sixty yards in length and sixty feet high, if you consider the part submerged below ground level."

Pastor Marcus stands. "Okay, folks, I know we went over this at dinner the other night, but let's review etiquette. The Wall is a divided location. Women to the right, men to the left."

I've heard this already, but I'm still surprised. Israeli women are all subject to being drafted and getting their heads blown off in combat. You'd assume the country would be past this type of segregation.

The good Pastor continues on. "Women, your shoulders and knees should not be exposed. Men, your head needs to be covered. You could wear a baseball hat, but I'd suggest a yarmulke. If you don't have one, there are disposable ones available for you to wear."

Have one? Who the heck packs a yarmulke? Despite my question, a few of the guys rummage through their backpack and pull one out. Caleb's has been around for a while. Probably left over from his pre-Christian days.

"The Wall is a place for petition to God. The tradition is to write a prayer and then wedge the folded-up paper into a crack between or around the blocks."

"Will we have a problem getting close enough?" asks Ruth.

Pastor Marcus shakes his head. "I don't think so. You'll have to be patient with those praying in front of you, but the crowd moves along."

A few minutes later, we're on the plaza. After we get instructions about meeting up, I head straight for the Wall, picking my way through the throng of people. At a wooden cart, I gather my yarmulke, which fits snugly over the crown of my head.

Caleb touches the fabric. "Huh. Pretty good quality for a temporary item. I was expecting paper not cloth."

As we approach the Wall, moving through a thick crowd, the majority of the men are in the traditional Jewish black suit, white shirt, and hat. Most have beards, except the teenagers.

Caleb points. "All these guys are here for morning prayers. You'll see them reading from the Book, reciting prayers, and mediating."

A man is walking backwards and hits me straight on. He doesn't change course, but keeps moving while I shift to the right and let him through, although not without a protest. "Hey, what the heck?" As he passes, I hear rhythmic murmuring.

Pastor Marcus helps clear up my irritation. "Out of respect, he won't turn his back to the Wall. You'll see others follow the practice." Sure enough, I observe several men acting in the same way and start to pay more attention as I move forward.

As we get closer, the crowd diversifies. I see men wearing robes, praying silently. Several are in all white outfits, eyes closed, heads bowed, hands folded at their waist. Others are reading from a Bible, dressed in regular street clothes. There are also the obvious tourists, snapping pictures and posing for selfies. A wide range of ethnic backgrounds are represented.

Since I can't identify any protocol for approaching, I squeeze my way through to the base and bend my neck back, straining the muscles, creating an unobstructed view upwards. The picture Avi had doesn't do the Wall justice.

Around me, men are either sticking folded papers into crevices or, as I see Caleb doing, standing, palms against the Wall, eyes closed, head down. I'm no expert at praying, but the last few days have me mulling over the possibility, and what better place than the Wall to try?

Except, of course, for the indisputable road block. I don't know how.

The most logical approach would be to write something uncomplicated on a slip of paper. Of course, I'd have to identify the something. One option is to search through my Bible, but where's the starting point? Should I close my eyes and deliberate, waiting for an idea to present itself? *No, meditation isn't for me.* How about I simplify my approach? Touch the Wall and see what happens?

As I reach out my hand, I hear a voice, not out loud, but in my head, barking out a series of statements and questions. *These people around you, they are authentic believers. You? You're a fraud. You've paid real attention to God for, what, a day? Why would he listen to you, after the life you've lived? What qualifies you to ask for anything? After what you did to Sarah and Zach and Olivia?*

Olivia. I see my hand again, against her face, and remember the Psalm Ruth read— "I am a worm and not a man"—before the voice gives me a final sentence. *You don't belong here.*

I turn my back to the Wall, the yarmulke drops to the ground, and I walk away.

∞ ∞ ∞

The funk persists. As we move through the tunnels under the Wall, I notice nothing, except seeing women standing in darkened corners, praying with a fervor I've never seen. *Perfect. More genuine faith from people who have no qualms about showing their devotion.* I slide deeper into the trough.

Stop number two is the Holocaust Museum. Our private guide provides detailed explanations of pictures, exhibits, facts, and figures. He also tells stories of individual struggles, relayed by survivors, not only of the concentration camps but of the ghettos where Jews were segregated. We stop at miniature models showing the flow of people from railcars to the ovens and watch a video of Nazi leaders talking about extermination. The whole thing is horrifying enough to deepen my bad mood.

Afterward, I need sunlight and head outside to unwind on a stone bench. Daniel offers me some water.

"Thanks."

He sits. "Impressions?"

I sip before answering. "Mind boggling."

Daniel nods.

I continue. "You know what got me the most? The stories of people being shot and falling right into mass graves. Learning a few survived by laying under bodies or faking death." I shudder, feeling a sudden chill. "How could the soldiers follow those orders?"

"For me," Daniel counters, "what resonated was the efficiency, which is an appalling word to use, of the camps. The sorting process, the gathering of belongings, the deception, and the orderly entry to the showers. The way a system was developed to exterminate quickly and, to use another repulsive word, productively."

I'm playing with the cap of my water bottle. "This place helps me understand the people here. The security. The commitment to service. I believe what Avi says, they're not going to capitulate again."

Daniel leans back, puts his hand on my shoulder, and asks. "Do you believe me now?"

I'm not sure what he means. "About?"

"Evil. Will you accept there's a force of evil at work?"

"You mean the Devil?"

"Use whatever name you want. After what we learned here today, are you ready to acknowledge a malevolent power?"

"Possibly."

He stands. "I urge you to reflect further while the topic is still fresh."

It doesn't take long. Any honest assessment would lead to only one conclusion—Nazi Germany's attempt to exterminate the Jewish people had to flow from a malicious source. The Holocaust didn't occur because someone had a screw loose or was mean-spirited. Something, maybe an actual being, was urging them along.

If he was still sitting next to me, I'd turn to Daniel and say "Yes, I believe you now."

∞ ∞ ∞

Between the Wall and the Museum, we don't get lunch until about two in the afternoon. I'm churning on this evil concept and know the Holocaust is a radical example. However, Hitler's particular brand of viciousness is not what I'm deliberating. I'm guessing there are less severe cases than killing millions of Jews. Isn't this what Daniel has been talking about? Forces of evil and spiritual warfare?

"You seem preoccupied there, Benjie." I hear Gerri, my Bible quoting acquaintance. Actually, given our time together, maybe I should describe her as a friend.

"Ah, yeah. Sorry. How's the ice cream?"

"Not as good as yesterday. What's eating you?"

This issue's not ready for prime time. "Nothing. Doing fine."

"Hmm. I'm not sure I believe you. Feeling okay?"

"Absolutely." I pause, deliberating before I ask. "Do you believe in evil? As a tangible force?"

"Sure do. 'Your enemy the devil prowls around like a roaring lion looking for someone to devour.' The first book of Peter, chapter five, verse eight."

"You see evil as the devil coming to get us?"

"Now, sweetie, Peter used the word prowling, which I see as stalkin'. Nothing matters unless you open the door. You gotta allow him in before he brings on any harm."

"Allow?"

"Yes, sir."

"Can't a force strong enough to conquer Hitler get us whenever it wants?"

"Not from where I sit."

"Yeah ... uh, okay. Then how does the evil force get in?"

"Temptation. He dangles a donut in front of our face. If we eat the donut, he's got us. If we don't, he goes off and creeps around someplace else."

I challenge the metaphor. "Is it wrong to eat a donut?"

Gerri leans forward. "Honey, you ever know anyone who eats only one donut?"

∞ ∞ ∞

We're at the house of Caiaphas, the High Priest during the time of Jesus. Avi explains why we're here. "The High Priest was the chief religious official of Jerusalem. Two significant events in the life of Jesus are attributed to this, his palace. First, the Jewish leaders plotted to arrest Jesus here, and second, after Jesus was taken in the Garden of Gethsemane, he was brought here for trial."

Our tour starts inside where we see a guardroom with fixtures for attaching a prisoner's chains. I can't imagine spending a night in shackles.

Despite my curiosity, I'm only half engaged. Those moments at the Western Wall fired up my brain's negative thought factory, and I've been letting the machines run at full speed. Trying to sort through the concept of evil, combined with feeling horrible about who I am has me sluggish and distracted.

We step outside onto a courtyard, and as Avi and Pastor Marcus alternate back and forth, I perk up. This, apparently, is the THE courtyard. The one where Peter denied Jesus. You don't have to be a seminarian to know the story—Peter promises loyalty no matter what, Jesus tells him no, Peter will disown him. Not once, but three times. Of course, Peter does, and when the rooster crows, he weeps. Bitterly. Actually, I had forgotten the last part, but I'm reminded when Addy reads a Bible passage.

Avi walks us to the edge of the courtyard. "This is a two-thousand-year-old road uncovered by researchers. There is a strong possibility Jesus walked this path after being beaten and flogged."

"Are your conclusions based on tradition, or is this confirmed as the actual site?" asks Ruth.

Pastor Marcus answers. "Our conclusions are based on tradition. However, the presence of the road and other archaeological evidence supports this being the place."

Avi jumps back in. "I have two more things to show you. There is, of course, the big church right here. This is the Church of St. Peter in *Gallicantu*. *Gallicantu* is a word meaning 'cock's crow.' You'll notice on the roof, a golden rooster on top of a black cross." He points to the second item, a statue in the courtyard. "This sculpture is of Peter at the time of his denial."

Pastor Marcus carries on the tag team. "I'm always grateful when we visit here." He checks his watch. "We're planning one more stop, but before we leave, let's take a half-hour and ponder where we are. The residence, this courtyard, and the ancient road. In every story, there is a beginning, a middle, and an end. The events here made the end possible. Peter had to fail. Jesus had to be convicted. The Jewish leaders had to triumph. Here, right now, take a few steps and, using your imagination, become an eyewitness."

People disperse. I'm among a few lingering near the statue and move in closer. There's Peter, two girls, a fire, and a centurion. In the middle of the figures is a stone pillar with a rooster on top. I circle the statue, admiring the work but not overly impressed. We've been around statues all week.

The front of this statue, though, is different. Compared to the Peter statue in Capernaum, which depicted a triumphant, conquering hero, this Peter is resolutely ordinary, a man sitting between the two servant girls, his arms open, a man explaining himself.

When my gaze shifts to his eyes, I stop moving. They are wild, panicked, and lifeless all at the same time. Seeing them hits me hard, causing my knees to buckle, and I search for a seat. There's one across the courtyard, a bench, and I race over and sit.

Those eyes on Peter are a mirror, confronting me with a ghostly reflection of my failures. The events of the past two days hang before me. Joseph, the chairs, the dark, and me entering the room. Joseph touching my forehead and the euphoria when I woke up. Not drinking yesterday. Not *wanting* to drink yesterday. The inside of the tomb, standing in front of the entrance afterwards, and realizing I believe. Jeb and Daniel telling me to be cautious. Today's guilt at the Wall. Agreeing there is evil in the world.

I consider Jesus in the Garden of Gethsemane, the bloody sweat, the arrest, and his crucifixion near the awful skull. How his closest disciples, personified by Peter in this courtyard, abandoned him. As bad as their actions were, I'm ten times worse. As someone observed earlier in the week, we know the end of the story. The Disciples? All they knew was a contingent of soldiers had arrested their friend and leader. They couldn't possibly comprehend what was ahead.

Throughout my sorry life, I've heard the story of Jesus hundreds of times, creating uncountable opportunities to understand and embrace exactly who Jesus was and is. I didn't, though. I pretended, going through the motions, and humoring the world. I abused and rejected all I was given. In the end, I did the unimaginable.

I begin to cry. Not subtle tears, but the kind that shake your shoulders and make your nose run. They wash nothing, but instead they water the bitter, sad, and regretful garden I'm tending. My mood gets darker with each sob.

There's a hand on my shoulder, and another offers a small towel. As I wipe my face, Jeb and Ruth sit on either side of me, and my confession spills out. "Oh, God, help me. I hit my own daughter."

I expect to feel them both recoil, or at least show a reaction, but they're as still as rocks, offering the only thing available, their presence. I shake my head, disgusted with myself, knowing I don't deserve what these people have to offer.

The only sound is my sniffling. I sneak a peripheral glance, and after realizing both Jeb and Ruth are praying, I want to tell them not to bother wasting their faith capital on me.

Ruth speaks next. "You know, God will forgive anything."

"Not this, he won't, no chance," I respond.

Their expressions tell me Jeb and Ruth don't agree with my conclusion. They both have the good sense not to argue the point.

∞ ∞ ∞

Once we get back on the bus, I brood, and almost everyone steers clear. The exception is Daniel, who's sitting across the row. "He got to you, didn't he?"

Eyes closed, head resting against the back of the seat, my clipped answer shows little patience. "Who?"

"The Bad Guy."

Not now, Daniel, buddy. Please, not now. "I did have a rough day."

"After a good one."

I move to the back of the bus. Daniel follows, joining me in the last row. "When did he make contact?"

I've had enough. "Listen, I did what you asked. I stepped into the room, I visited the Tomb, and I read the book. I listened to tour guides, studied all those statues, and believe the stuff we've been seeing is real. I've talked endlessly with you and half the people here, discussing topics I don't want to talk about. I even tried to pray at the Wall this morning. The message is clear—I don't belong. I'm not right for this club. I'm a bad man who's lived a bad life. Please, don't waste your time on me."

"Thank you for sharing."

"Thanks for sharing? You're kidding, right? Who are you people?" I'm talking loudly. There's a good chance the rest of the bus has gotten the same earful.

"Ben, this is good, a reason for optimism. You've got the Bad Guy worried. Tell me the emotions you're feeling."

As with every other exchange we've had, Daniel isn't going to stop. As I answer, I'm hoping to give him enough information to end the conversation. "I don't know. Guilt, I guess. Frustration. Shame. The usual for a person who's ruined his life."

"He's coming at you hard."

"No one's coming at me. I've earned every negative emotion."

Daniel turns. "Ben, none of those words you mentioned, not one of them, originate from God. They showed up because you lost a battle."

"A battle?"

"In the spiritual war."

Oh, man. Here we are again.

My visible frustration doesn't stop him. "I trust, after the Holocaust Museum, you do believe in evil. Don't let him win."

"Okay, sure, there's an evil something." My admission is accompanied by a grudging nod. "Although, with me, he's already won. My life is what my life is."

"A life never has to be what a life is. What better example is there than me?"

When he stands, I'm surprised. "You're leaving?"

"I don't have to, but, yes. I should probably give you space." He points to my chest. "Your heart holds whatever you need. To open the gates, say a prayer."

I give a head shake. "Ain't gonna happen. A few words, a couple of rehearsed sentences, they can't fix what's wrong with me."

He snorts a laugh. "You're thinking too much, my man. Don't overcomplicate. All you need to offer is one word, one sentence."

He leaves me alone in the back of the bus. Feeling worse by the minute.

∞ ∞ ∞

We're given a choice on how to end our day. One option is to visit an open-air market in the Jewish Quarter. Avi describes three streets of stalls selling meats, cheese, fruits, desserts, and, based on the list he rattles off, whatever you'd ever want in the Jewish food category. The time is late in the afternoon, though, and, for those who want, there's a stop at the hotel to jump off and rest before dinner.

A few folks, the more senior members of our group, accept the offer. I do also, searching for relief, not from being tired, but from my cravings.

They began as a subtle nudge. I ignored them at first, until, as the day moved along, I considered reestablishing a routine. My routine. The nudge got stronger, taking a huge leap when I was sitting on the bench with Jeb and Ruth. Now, I'm excited about slipping into the hotel and getting a drink. Without anyone knowing.

As I walk along the bus aisle, I know I'm heading down a dark path. If I have one drink, I'll have a second, followed by a third and, in all likelihood, more. When I'm leaving the bar, I'll place an order for an evening delivery.

Passing my little cohort, I know they know. Ruth starts to stand, but Jeb pulls her down.

When my feet hit the pavement, I'm elated. It's about fifty feet to where I want to be, to who I've always been.

As I take the first step, I see a donut, hanging on a string, reminding me of Gerri talking about the word temptation. Before step two, I remember Daniel, a few minutes before, telling me to keep things simple and to pray.

I mutter a sentence about prayer not being worth the energy and continue forward.

Along comes another thought. *You could try.* The counterpunch comes immediately—*you don't want to and, if you did, the effort wouldn't matter. The car is totaled. No repair shop would take you.* For about thirty steps I volley conflicting thoughts and there's only one way to stop them. My reliable fix.

The lobby bar, as welcome a sight as I've ever seen, is clearly visible as I reach to pull the hotel door open. *Is going in there a true fix? You've been trying to solve problems this way forever, and they're still there.*

When there's no counterargument presented, I drop my hand from the door handle and have no idea what to do. Four words pass through my lips. "Please, God, help me."

The bus brakes squeak behind me. At first, I'm confused. Why is the bus still here? Then I don't care. I turn and run. My hand pounds the glass on the door until the bus stops and I hop on.

There's a cheer as I take the first empty seat, which is across the row from Addy.

"Changed my mind," I inform her, with a smile.

"I'm glad."

I'm puzzled. "Hey ... um ... why weren't you guys already gone?"

"Oh, I thought I lost my phone. We had to wait while I rummaged around."

Right. I've been watching Addy for days and there's a better chance her arm would fall off than she'd misplace her electronics. Either way, I'm grateful. "I don't know how you knew what I needed, but thanks for buying me time. I owe you an ice cream."

"I don't know what you're talking about." She goes back to playing a word game she downloaded early in the trip.

"Hi, ho! Let's hit the market!" Caleb is standing and waving, a wagon train leader in the old west. "Let's show Brother Ben a good time!"

∞ ∞ ∞

"Quite a day, my friend, no?" asks Joseph.

I'm sipping Kava tea and my indefatigable roommate is ready to talk. My body objects, begging for sleep, but I manage to push out an answer. "Today was crazy."

"Tell me."

I go through the whole day. The Wall, the Peter statue, the disgust, the guilt, the shame, and how I was about to go into the bar.

"But you didn't?"

"No. I turned around and jumped onto the bus."

He scratches his beard. "What happened right before all this?"

"Before?"

"Yes. Before you turned around."

"Nothing. At least I don't remember anything."

"Are you sure? You didn't say or consider anything in particular?"

"A few random words. Nothing special."

"What were they?"

I rewind the tape. "I mumbled a half-hearted sentence, God help me, or words along those lines. Out of desperation. My mother would do the same when she was exasperated."

He inspects a fingernail. "What came next?"

"I don't know. Heard the brakes squealing or at least a sound like it. Realized the bus was still there."

"You went back?"

"Uh-huh."

"Not into the bar."

"No. As I said before, I didn't go into the bar."

Joseph rolls his feet over the side of the bed, and he's facing me. "What you did was say a prayer."

I shake my head. "No way. I was desperate and arbitrary words came out. What I said wasn't premeditated."

"Lots of prayers are distressed pleas during times of distress. In this situation, you were alerted to the bus's presence at the moment you uttered the words."

Gerri's voice, telling me there were no coincidences, surges into my head. Still, I'm doubtful. "I don't know. I've said similar words millions of times."

"Ben, with this one, there is a difference."

I'm out of energy and beg for relief. "Joseph, please tell me what. I'm beat up and don't want to guess."

"You were in the room."

The room again. I've got a quick rejoinder. "I was in the room when all the bad thoughts were going through my brain, too."

"You were. This time, however, you won."

"Won?"

"The battle. You appealed to God and got what you needed, which is exactly what the room offers. Not release from struggles or temptation or pain but, instead, strength in the face of life's challenges. Actually, the room offers much more, but today you needed fortification."

"Are you saying being in the room helped me avoid going into the bar?" I ask.

"Exactly."

"Will the room continue to help if I stay in there?"

"Ben, today was a miniscule example, a tiny glimpse, of what the room provides. Living in God's presence will lead you to new life."

Although my fatigue is bone crushing, I continue with the questions. "How do I find my way into God's presence? What do I have to do?"

"The necessary steps are different for everyone. God will lead as he sees fit."

"But what's my role? I imagine I have to do more than muttering a few random words in desperation."

He waves his hand. "Ah, do not worry yourself anymore right now. These things take time. Let us keep this simple— all you have to do, at this moment, is stay in the room."

He turns off the light. Lesson over.

PROGRESS REPORT # 10

Peter,

As expected, today Our Man was tested. Standing at the famous Wall, he was reaching for a simple touch, a gesture others have found beneficial. Unfortunately, he was attacked with a basic but effective weapon—reminders of his own past failings.

The strategy was entirely effective, and following the encounter, I wasn't sure if he would recover.

Our Man isolated himself during the ensuing emotional gloom. Fortunately, our primary caretaker inserted himself, continuing the ongoing dialogue concerning spiritual warfare. He was masterful, utilizing the Jerusalem museum commemorating the Great Evil. The abject horror was enough to allow discussion and subsequent intellectual consideration.

Soon afterwards, there was another interchange concerning the power of darkness—this one emphasizing the role of temptation. One of our caretakers deftly highlighted evil's ineffectiveness until granted admission. She did this using a clever analogy, borrowing from the celebrated carrot and stick metaphor, replacing the carrot in her example with an earthly confection considered, apparently, irresistible to the human palate.

The next stop was the palace of Caiaphas. In the outer courtyard, as he studied the realistic depiction of characters present on the Last Night, Our Man saw his own imperfections. The result was a great outpouring of human emotion and a verbal admission, to two of our caretakers, of his greatest human shame. This vocalization generated immense pain while also opening a previously secure gate, allowing the possibility for healing.

Shortly after this event, Our Man faced a considerable challenge and was tempted to engage in his earthly vice. However, the input received throughout the day, along with his own growing desire for transformation, led him to turn away. This victory was due, in no small part, to his own direct petition for help. To be certain this did not go unrecognized, I invested time reinforcing what had transpired.

Going forward, our next steps are evident. First, we need to emphasize the necessity of prayer. Second, Our Man does not believe himself worthy of the Gift. He must be convinced of this fact. Tomorrow's agenda provides ample opportunity to accomplish these objectives.

I close joyous at our progress,

Joseph

DAY 11

Joseph and I are packing our suitcases before sunrise, preparing for an early start to the day. On the way in from the market last night, Avi explained we're going to work our way back to a hotel near Tel Aviv, putting us closer to our flight home, making stops along the way to visit a prayer house and a spot called Peter's Beach. For those interested, we would end our day with baptisms in the Jordan River.

As we park our bags near the door, Joseph hands me coffee and offers an invitation. "We are ready early. Join me on the balcony?"

"We have a balcony?"

Joseph opens the sliding door hiding behind the drapes, showing me two chairs and a view of Jerusalem in the early morning light. "We most certainly do. Please."

The sound of car engines starting, people talking, and a general start-of-the-day bustle rise from the street below. We sit silently, listening to Jerusalem wake up.

After about half my coffee is gone, Joseph starts talking. "I will be moving on today."

"Moving on?"

"Yes. Leaving the group. I am to begin another job."

"Job?"

"Yes. My assignment here is complete."

I'm instantly uneasy. "I thought this was a vacation for you."

"Not at all. This was a consulting gig, to use the American term."

"Uh, yeah. Sure." I adjust in the chair. "Will you tell me what the job was?"

"I believe you know the answer. Consider these last days."

I don't have to contemplate long. "Your job was me?"

His answer is a simple nod.

"Are you saying someone sent you?"

"Yes."

"Who?"

After draining his cup, he replies. "I am not at liberty to respond directly. Again, though, you should be able to determine the answer."

I have too many other questions. "What was your task?"

"To guide you. Hopefully steer you to one specific place."

"We've been to a million different places this week. Which one?"

"I am, technically, not supposed to share certain information. Although I do have a level of flexibility and ..." He slaps his knee. "Yes, knowing would be beneficial for you. While circumstances vary from case to case, my assignment was to get you into the room and ensure you stayed there through a challenge or two."

"You were successful, I hope."

"For now, yes."

"For now?"

"Ben, you are human. Humans face struggles. You will always be tempted to run, flee, escape, give in."

"Why not be with me until at least the end of the trip?" I argue.

"I follow orders, Ben. Mine are to move on."

"Who gives the orders?"

"Think, Ben, think."

Joseph sits, appreciating the brilliance of the morning sun. I get ready to answer, draw back, get ready again, and draw back again, reminding myself of a kid who doesn't want to admit the truth. Finally, a single word emerges.

"God."

His response is another nod, which is nowhere near enough information, especially because Joseph's story still makes me theorize he might be Jesus's father. I demand more. "You're a special envoy who does odd jobs for the man upstairs? If you are who I believe you are, you've been at this for at least two thousand years."

Joseph smiles. "You are right in saying I have been of service for a long time. However, details of prior undertakings aren't relevant."

I know Joseph isn't going to cough up any additional information and change tactics. "But why me? Aren't there close to seven billion people in the world? Why would God invest time in a broken drunk who's ripped his life to shreds?"

"The why, truly, is privileged information. Those details have not been shared with me."

"Will I ever know?"

"Your journey should tell you."

My confusion persists. "Am I not on a journey now? Or do you mean another one?"

"Let me offer advice. There is an old saying: 'A journey of a thousand miles begins with a single step.' Concentrate on a step at a time. Listen to your heart. God will show the way." He stands in front of me, putting his hand on my shoulder. "Time for you to get downstairs."

"You're not coming with me?"

"I have a few chores to tend to, final duties before moving along. We will say our goodbyes here." When I hesitate at the doorway, Joseph tries to reassure me. "I have left my caretakers in place. They will help you." He backs into the room.

"Wait. You have help in place? Who?"

"Peace be with you, my friend," he says as the door closes.

∞ ∞ ∞

Avi's true to his word. Our first stop is a place called The Jerusalem Prayer Center.

Based on the name, I'm imagining a large church complex or spacious conference center. What I'm seeing is neither of those. The Prayer Center is a beautiful square building, the size of an upscale home, made of the same oversized, off-white bricks I've seen around Jerusalem. As we approach the archway surrounding the front door, I admire the elevated gardens on either side of the walkway.

When we get to the low porch, Avi talks before we enter. "This house was built as a residence in 1890, later became part of what was called the American Colony of Jerusalem, and has a long history and presence in this community. We don't have time to review all the background, but I would encourage you to pick up one of their pamphlets and read about it on the internet."

The door opens and a fiftyish woman appears, leading us to a room to the left of the front door.

We sit in rows, and she explains that the prayer center, built on the line between Arab East Jerusalem and Jewish West Jerusalem, is for all people. She also describes a link between the house and the family of the man who wrote the famous hymn "It is Well With My Soul." As she elaborates, I catch references to a shipwreck and daughters dying, but my attention is diverted. While we stand and sing the hymn, all I do is study a mural covering the front wall.

When the woman starts talking about the painting, I slip to the end of my row, improving my vantage point. Her hand points and gestures. "This was created by Pamela Suran and is symbolic of God's promise to the Jews fleeing Egypt, a reminder of his assurance they would inherit a bountiful land. She has painted what are known as the seven species listed in Deuteronomy chapter eight, verse eight. Wheat, barley, grape, fig, pomegranates, olives for olive oil, and dates for honey."

I move a few steps closer. "Here we have Scripture in English, Hebrew, and Arabic. And this beautiful passage from the Gospel of Matthew. 'The harvest is plentiful but the workers are few. Ask the Lord of the harvest, therefore, to send out workers in his harvest field.'"

"Chapter nine, verses thirty-seven and thirty-eight," Gerri whispers.

The woman shifts topics, describing the locations available for prayer—the room we're in, a second-floor individual prayer room, the gardens surrounding the house, and the kitchen. The kitchen has the added bonus of providing coffee, tea, and cookies.

The group starts to disperse, but I stay motionless, disappearing into the painting, taking in the trees, fruit, words, and colors. I move closer, running my hands over the appealing mix of yellows, oranges, and greens.

"This is an amazing scene."

I nod to Ruth, my fingertips tracing the images of leaves, and reply with, "I want to step inside which, I admit, sounds strange."

"Nothing strange there. This demonstrates God's provision. How he will care for us."

I have the usual knee-jerk reaction, silently considering if I'm worth God's effort. Based on what's been going on, there's a growing possibility I am. On the other hand, with me being an unmitigated disaster, there's no logical reason why. *None.*

Ruth gently takes my elbow. "We're headed to the second-floor room, the one for individual prayer. Would you join us?"

I stiffen. "I'd rather poke around here."

She positions herself between me and the mural. "Ben, it's okay to talk to God."

"I know. Truly, I do." My eyes are studying the floor. "But not yet. Not for me. I've done nothing to make him want to listen."

"God will always listen."

I bite my lower lip. "No, but thank you."

"This is all you have to do," she contends, pointing her finger at three words in the quote from Matthew. "Ask the Lord."

Jeb materializes on my left. "Come on, Ben. Let's go learn what the fuss is about."

I surrender, and we head to the second floor.

∞ ∞ ∞

Once we're in the prayer room, I grab a chair and watch. Daniel's on the floor, his back against a wall, with his Bible open. He reads a short passage, closes his eyes, and starts reading again. I notice other Bibles around the room, in various languages and sizes. Jeb is writing on small slips of paper and dropping them into a bowl of water where, I believe, they dissolve. I see a nearby table tent encouraging individuals to write their sins down, put them in the water, and watch them disappear. The process is a reminder of the complete forgiveness God provides. Good for Jeb. He must be far enough away from his sins for this to work. Any paper I put in the bowl would probably sprout back into a tree. A man I don't know is circulating through the room, reading all the banners with Bible verses on them. They're in different languages and I'm thinking he must be multi-lingual. I see Caleb, sitting on a low couch, silently reading through a small pile of laminated prayers. Others are drawing pictures, studying maps, or scribbling in journals. The only sound is pages turning and writing implements moving across paper.

The combination of soft lighting, muted colors, and wood tones has me in a reflective mood, and I start replaying the last week. At first, there's too much to sift through, but gradually, the stillness helps me sort out the disorder.

What do I know?

I know I haven't had a drink today or over the last couple of days. I know, because of what happened outside the Garden Tomb, that I believe. I know I've taken a step in God's direction by going "into the room." The problem is I don't know how to identify or make the next step and wonder if I've earned the right to try. I'm ashamed of, and don't know how to reconcile myself with, my past behavior and failures.

I slow the motor down and my thoughts drift to Joseph.

Our earlier exchange replays as more surreal than authentic. *God sent him? For me? Specifically? A special one-on-one intervention?* If I apply any reason at all, the conversation was absurd. There was the other comment too. He mentioned caretakers.

Ruth slides in next to me and speaks in a hushed voice. "I'm happy you joined us here, Ben."

I smile but don't answer. My mental gymnastics are still going.

"This is an easy place to pray. Comfortable. Reverent."

I shrug. My problems with prayer aren't the venue.

Ruth hands me a small pad and a pen. "If you write down your request and put the paper in the basket over there, the people here will pray for you."

"Thanks, Ruth, but, I'm not sure I want to."

"You could try."

I shake my head. "I know this sounds strange to someone like you, but I don't feel right about praying."

"Someone like me?" She's puzzled.

"Yeah, you know, lifelong follower, strong faith, one of those people they call prayer warriors. Belief must come easy to you."

"What makes you conclude my belief comes easy for me?"

"You know, with you being raised by missionaries and all."

Ruth takes a moment to smooth down her skirt. "Ben, I may be one of your so-called prayer warriors, but I got there after a long road. There were challenges along the way."

"Pardon me if I'm unconvinced."

"Believe me or not, I've drifted away twice."

"You drifted?"

"Yep. I drifted."

I respond with the phrase I hate. "Tell me about that."

She fiddles with her hair before continuing. "Yes, I lived around the world and was with my parents as they spread the Gospel. I was a model child—the adorable daughter helping with their mission, and at the time, my actions were sincere. The minute I got away, though, the first week in the dorm at college, I started a lifestyle you'd describe as, I guess I'd say, rebellious. I wanted to do all the things I'd been missing."

I'm speculating Ruth had a couple of beers and, after a rough semester or two, returned to the norm.

"I had a wild first two years. I partied three of four nights a week, experimented with drugs, and was intimate with any man I could find. My age, older, married, you name it."

Whoa, Ruth, TMI.

"I spent hours watching TV. Every afternoon and when I was free at night. When you grow up in the remote areas of Honduras, Peru, and Africa, you miss out on pop culture."

"Did you flunk out?"

"No, I managed to get enough done."

I can't picture Ruth, with her long skirts, sensible shoes, glasses, and hypnotically gentle voice, as the college party girl. However, despite my skepticism, I follow up. "What made you stop?"

"A married man."

I stay quiet, presuming she'll add to the story.

"I was in a bar, and I tried to pick him up. He was traveling on business. He told me no, he had vows, and though he was a long way from home, he'd honor them, adding he was there because he wanted to watch the Bills play on Monday Night Football."

"And?"

"I sat there, dumbfounded. Guys, especially married ones on the road, generally don't turn down women in bars. After a while, I left and walked around campus, mulling over his phrase 'a long way from home' and realized how far away I was from my home, the way I was raised, my former lifestyle. Over the next month, I used every free minute to read my Bible and pray. After you do enough reading and praying, eventually God gets through."

She's provided a good story, but, honestly, I'm not overly impressed. Everyone takes a wrong path or two in college, actions we're either ashamed of or have to stop doing. Most of us, eventually, grow up.

I remember she'd commented she'd drifted twice. "What was the second time?"

Ruth closes her eyes. "We lost a child."

"Oh God, Ruth, no."

"Edward. He was three months old."

Before she goes on, Ruth takes time to work through whatever the memory has conjured in her brain. "I didn't want anything to do with God after Edward was gone. No church, no prayer, no Bible, nothing. I shoved him as far away as he could go and sprinted in the opposite direction. I left poor Jeb alone for a summer and worked at a fishing lodge in Maine, making beds and serving meals. Running didn't help. I returned home more broken than when I left."

She takes a break to collect herself again. I fill the time by leaning over and pretending to adjust the lace on my sneaker.

"Over time, I found my way back, thanks to my friend, Annie. She'd come by a few mornings a week and sit with me, let me cry, hold my hand. Every time, she'd ask if she could pray. At first, I refused. I wasn't talking to God, and Annie, bless her, would nod and keep her mouth shut. After a while, though, I had one of my urges, telling me there was a way out if I would surrender, let God help me. I asked Annie to say a short prayer, asking for peace or rest, something along those lines. Over time, I let her say more and started inserting short sections myself. When Annie wasn't there, though, I'd fan the flames of my anger and end up screaming at God, telling him I hated what he did to us, pleading to know why. One night, I found myself all screamed out and fell on the floor begging for relief. In that moment, I remembered God had stayed with me when I walked away during college. I thought, maybe, he'd be there again if I sincerely tried to return to my faith. Right then, my heart softened."

Ruth? Screaming at God?

"So, no, Ben, my relationship with God didn't come easy. I never would have moved forward without those first, short prayers at a time when I thought I'd never be with God again."

As a parent, I don't want to imagine the pain Ruth felt. At the same time, though, if a couple of words to God helped her move from a deep abyss to where she is now, I should at least try to offer a prayer. "I guess I could come up with a few words."

She responds by standing. "I'll be right over there if you need help."

She moves next to Caleb and I sit by myself, legs straight out, ankles crossed. I revisit my time on the first floor, standing beside the mural, with Ruth pointing to the words about asking God. *I could, couldn't I? Make a simple, non-presumptuous appeal?*

My eyes close, and I see three words, writing them on the pad.

PLEASE ACCEPT ME.

Nope, not right. My life is way too messed up, and I'm nowhere near ready to ask for acceptance.

I cross the words out, knowing I'm not much different than one of those Tells we learned about—the crud covering me needs to be scraped away, one layer at a time. Bumping a fist against my chin, I shake my head. The only way out is to wipe away the past.

Jumping up, I circle the room, reading a few banners, my mental engine grinding away, reaching for whatever's floating around my brain. I catch one word, followed by another, and quickly add a third, creating the most basic plea out there. If granted, this wish would clean the past away.

I rest the pad against my palm and write.

PLEASE FORGIVE ME.

I give a dismissive grunt, knowing this won't be my prayer. I have no right to ask.

Chewing on the end of the pen, I think about the millions of germs left behind from visitors' hands and wonder if God will punish me with a rare and exotic virus, putting me out of my misery.

Despite my little pity party, I'm aware God does, and will, forgive. However, while there's lots of examples of him rendering mercy, my problem isn't solved. In this prayer room, nestled in the holiest of cities, I can't accept or believe I qualify for grace.

This time I write seven words, using a clean paper.

LET ME KNOW I CAN BE FORGIVEN.

Yep. I've found my prayer.

I drop the folded paper into the basket and head down to the kitchen for coffee.

∞ ∞ ∞

The bus has a we-want-to-see-the-next-thing-but-we're-tired-of-traveling feel. Heck, even Daniel appears weary. Addy must notice too, because she gives him a good-humored punch on the shoulder. "Time for you to get in a nap, old man."

"Hey, at thirty-six, I'm a veritable spring chicken. I must add, my lady, when compared to your youthful inexperience, my wisdom is evident."

"Keep talkin' tough guy," she retorts, "in the wisdom department, I'm twenty-eight going on forty. I'd recommend getting those old bones rested. I need you awake enough to take me out for a drink tonight."

Apparently, while I was embroiled in all the turmoil prompted by the Wall and the statue of Peter, those two must have kept the romance moving along. Maybe there was a second date.

Whatever happened, Gerri's ecstatic. She has an ear-to-ear smile and tells me about a gift Daniel bought Addy, a mosaic coaster decorated with a skyline view of Jerusalem. "He told Addy he was thinkin' she could use a memento at work. Then, last night, he took her to a legitimate restaurant, away from this crowd of geezers. I tell you, my girl came back to the room floating on air."

Once again, the two budding lovebirds take me back to Sarah. I'm not sure how, but Gerri knows. "Missing your wife, Ben?"

"Yeah. My son and daughter, too."

"Don't fret too much right now. Most problems work out the way they should."

"I don't know. I guess I'll see."

She gets animated. "Listen, sweetheart. I'm not blind and I can see you're haulin' around serious baggage. You're no lost cause, though. You've got plenty of sweet in you too, not necessarily a common characteristic for everyone. Plus, you two got kids to raise. You get rid of the baggage, there's a strong possibility she's waiting for you on the other side."

I'm unresponsive, not because I'm being rude, but because I have no idea what to say.

Apparently, Gerri does. "I bet you're reasoning you know I'm wrong, but you hope I'm right." She hit the nail on the head. "I say decide what you want and do what you have to do."

A few rows in front of us, Addy's resting her head on Daniel's shoulder. "What I want is that again."

"Now we've got ourselves a start." Gerri's tone changes and she leans in closer, whispering. "I do believe my Addy's falling in love. Her momma's never gonna forgive me for letting this happen when she wasn't around."

∞ ∞ ∞

I fall asleep as soon as we hit the highway, and when I wake up, we're back at the Sea of Galilee, parked outside a small church.

"My favorite Bible story was at this spot," Caleb proclaims, pumping a fist. He's ahead of the group, snapping pictures, running his hands along the church's large gray bricks, and pointing at the beach stretching about thirty yards to the water's edge.

Pastor Marcus pulls us together. "Our groups always name this stop Peter's Beach. According to tradition, this is where Jesus met the disciples and redeemed Peter."

Caleb protests. "Tradition, shmadition. Believing this is the location makes sense. Right near here is a sulfurous spring. Springs attract food for fish. Of course, the disciples would be here, casting out their nets."

Pastor Marcus leads us about halfway between the building and the water, explaining we're at The Church of the Primacy, which was founded by the Franciscans, and asks us to open our Bibles to John's Gospel, chapter twenty-one. I'm there in three seconds.

Gerri reads the passage, which is a post-resurrection story. The disciples are fishing when they see a man on the beach. When Peter realizes the man is Jesus, he jumps into the water and swims to shore.

When Gerri mentions a fire of burning coals, Pastor Marcus stops her.

"Read about the fire again, would you, Gerri?"

"When they landed, they saw a fire of burning coals there with fish on it, and some bread."

"Thanks. Now, could you read chapter eighteen, verse eighteen?

Gerri doesn't bother with the book. Instead, she recites. "'And the servants and officers stood there, who had made a fire of coals; for it was cold; and they warmed themselves; and Peter stood with them, and warmed himself.' Sorry, I recited a translation different from the one we're reading. Most of my early Bible was in the King James."

Pastor Marcus goes on. "The key word there is coals. Other versions use the word charcoal. Either is fine. Importantly, though, a coal fire is mentioned only twice in the Bible. This scene in John eighteen and the passage we read from chapter twenty-one. The scene in chapter eighteen is immediately before Peter denies knowing Jesus."

I don't know what Jesus intended when he built the coal fire or if Peter made a connection to the one in the courtyard. My mind, though, quickly links the two. I picture those wild eyes on the Peter statue, remembering the feelings they opened inside me. Before I know what's happening, the anxiety, shame and guilt are back, pushing me lower with each thought. Swallowing hard, I try to tamp down the reenergized regret.

I travel about ten steps away from everyone and turn, pretending to be interested in the water, anxious over how I'll overcome the harm I've caused those around me.

"Hey, hey, Ben, come back. You've got to hear the next part." Caleb is waving me over and waits for me to rejoin before he reads.

I listen enough to recognize the story. It's a famous one—the passage where Jesus asks Peter if he loves him and appoints Peter to head the church. I don't get much more engaged. The subsequent conversation reminds me of listening to the adults talking in the old Peanuts cartoons and all I hear is a set of random, out-of-tune trumpet-type noises.

I dial back in when Avi explains the nearby church is built around a limestone rock. This rock is purported to be the actual spot where Jesus laid out breakfast for the disciples. He leads us inside for a prayer and meditation time which, to me, is a good idea. At least I get to sit down.

Half-hidden in the back row, my eyes take in the stone arches holding up the whitewashed ceiling. At the front is the rock, sticking up through the tannish tile floor, protected by ropes. *"Mensa Christi"* is written on a sign. Addy plugs the phrase into her phone and provides the translation. "The Table of Christ."

Behind the rock is an enclave with a small altar, candles, and a cross. People around me are praying or reading or writing. A few take pictures.

My thoughts wander. I reminisce about my family, which makes me feel worse. I remember deceiving my parents, sneaking their alcohol or stealing their money. For the millionth time, I see all my other actions, my life nothing but a blob of waste, filled with disappointments too numerous to list. My eyelids are pressed together, trying to make the images all go away.

My backpack slips to the floor, and as my Bible tumbles out of the open pocket, the noise snaps me back to the present. I consider if the rock, the one at the front of the church, is THE rock, before deciding I don't care. I'm seeking a world I won't be allowed to join.

I notice the sun filtering through stained-glass windows. The light creates a pleasant ambiance, reminding me of the prayer room, my little piece of paper, and those seven words. I recite them, amused by their absurdity. "Let me know I can be forgiven." I catch a glimpse of my Bible, still open, resting on the floor. When I pick it up, I see the bold "21" and realize it's the same chapter of John we read outside.

"Hmmph," I muse, "what are the odds?"

Gerri, who's two rows up, turns around. "What's that?"

"What's what?"

"What you muttered about odds?"

"Did I say those words out loud?"

"Yes indeedy."

"Um, I dropped my book and the pages were opened to the same section we were reading before. I was commenting about the coincidence."

"Benjie, haven't we talked about this already?"

"What?"

"Coincidences."

"Yeah, I guess we have."

"You're darn right we have."

"And?"

"Don't ask me. Ask yourself. What are you going to do with this one?"

The pages stare at me. "I guess I should read."

"You know, Ben, sometimes you're as smart as you look."

I zip through the first fourteen verses quickly, recognizing the part I paid attention to earlier until, at verse fifteen, I slow down and start reading carefully.

> When they had finished eating, Jesus said to Simon Peter, "Simon son of John, do you love me more than these?"

"Yes, Lord," he said, "you know that I love you."

Jesus said, "Feed my lambs."

Again Jesus said, "Simon son of John, do you truly love me?"

He answered, "Yes, Lord, you know that I love you."

Jesus said, "Take care of my sheep."

The third time he said to him, "Simon son of John, do you love me?"

Peter was hurt because Jesus asked him the third time, "Do you love me?" He said, "Lord, you know all things; you know that I love you."

Jesus said, "Feed my sheep..."

The words slap me on the back of the head. *Is this saying what I believe it's saying?* There's an impulse to read again.

I run to the waterfront, the gravel pebbles crunching under my feet. As the waves lap against the rocks, I pore over the verses a second time, picturing Peter, conflicted between the joy of seeing Jesus and the grief over his denial, trying to convince Jesus he loves him. I envision Peter comprehending Jesus is asking him to lead and visualize Peter realizing he must be forgiven.

I read a third time, absorbing Jesus's words. I again see Peter's eyes as they were on the statue, crazed with fear and grief. I imagine a light gradually entering, bringing redemption. My thoughts hopscotch forward. If Jesus forgave Peter, who abandoned him during the most trying moments of his life, surely, Jesus will forgive me.

Won't he?

I say my prayer another time, uttering them with a sense of urgency. "Let me know I can be forgiven."

From somewhere nearby comes the sound of a rooster crowing. As the off-key warble passes over me, a dam breaks, and a blazing freight train knocks me to my knees.

I remain still, feeling the heat, surrounded by light, wetness from the damp rocks soaking through my jeans.

The rooster crows a second time.

With my head facing the heavens, the words spill out once more. "Let me know I can be forgiven."

For the third time I hear the rooster, followed by Joseph's voice. "Ben, you can be forgiven. The more important question is—will you allow yourself to receive forgiveness? God's mercy is offered as an unconditional gift. This gift, however, must be accepted."

The light and the heat recede, leaving only me, the water caressing the rocks, and a slight breeze. I put the Bible on a patch of dry gravel and again gaze upward. I start to say the words several times, unsure if I'm worthy to speak them, before I finally croak them out. "I accept."

My head falls into my hands, which in turn, descend until they rest on my folded thighs. There's an interlude before the tears come, but they do, as they did for Peter in the courtyard. Unlike him, my tears originate not from pain but from a place I haven't visited in a long time ... perhaps since childhood. I'm certain, if I tried, I could float across the lake in front of me, buoyed by the realization my life doesn't have to be a closed book, assured there are new chapters yet to be written.

$$\infty \quad \infty \quad \infty$$

As we settle onto the bus and move towards our next stop, Pastor Marcus is at the microphone. "It dawned on me we didn't pray as we headed out this morning."

"Dawned? Morning? Hah!"

Caleb's joke elicits a few groans before Pastor Marcus continues. "Would someone care to give us a blessing?"

Gerri raises her hand, but not to volunteer. "Ben should offer one up. He hasn't prayed us into a day all week."

She's right. I haven't. Of course, I don't want to either. Believing is one thing—standing in front of a group and professing my belief is another.

I slide lower in the seat, hoping the idea passes. However, based on the "yeah's" and "great idea's" circulating through the bus, I know my effort is wasted. I've been drafted. I stand, emotionally wrung out, but feeling the best I have all year. Maybe all century.

As I start to move forward, Ruth grabs me on the way by. "Don't overthink. Say what comes into your heart." Her whisper is accompanied by a tight hug.

I hold the microphone and close my eyes. Not to be reverent, but to cover my anxiety. *What should I say? Will my words be good enough? What would this crew want to hear? Heck, what does God want to hear?*

I sneak an eye open. All the heads in front of me are bowed, seemingly comfortable with the silence. Ruth tilts her head and offers a slight nod.

Remembering her advice, I open my mouth and choke out a sentence. "God, I, oh, I mean, we, uh, know you are there. We know you forgive. Lord, God, I, uh, we, uh, need forgiveness."

Boy, this is going awful. I appeal for help. "Please, God, help me to do this right."

No one reacts. They wait patiently for what comes next.

I focus on the back wall of the bus, take in a long, deep breath, and, as I exhale, words spill into my consciousness. I open my mouth and let them flow. "God, keep us safe. Help us to learn what you want us to learn. Help us enjoy our time together." I remember a phrase others have included. "And Bless this day." I pause. There's one other thought there. "What I guess I mean is, be present with us."

The string of words ends. I go back to my seat, staring at the floor, face burning red, armpits exuding sweat.

"Amen, brother!" exclaims Caleb, "I knew you had it in you!"

Ruth beams while Gerri gives me a thumbs up.

Relieved at not making a complete fool of myself, or at least seeing that no one is indicating I did, I start reading a beat-up paperback I found in the luggage rack.

Half a page in, Daniel joins me. "You're different today."

I have always responded to observations about me with a deflecting, sarcastic, or self-deprecating comment. This time I have nothing to say.

"I saw you at the beach. Most of us did," adds Daniel.

"Yeah, I kind of figured."

"Should we talk?"

I'm about to respond with "we are talking," but catch myself and, instead, chew on Daniel's question. He's happy when I answer "yes."

I give a detailed account of what happened on the beach, including the tears. When I finish, Daniel doesn't offer any analysis or critique and, instead, opts for a simple question. "What do we do when our hands are dirty?"

"Wash 'em."

"What about our soul?"

"Clean it, I guess."

The bus is turning and Daniel leans over. "Ah, excellent. Perfect timing."

As the bus weaves through a crowded parking lot, Avi gives us the rundown. "We are here, and I promise the long ride will be worth the time. This location is called *Qasr el-Yahud*, which translates to Castle of the Jews. We believe this is the location where the Jews crossed into the Holy Land after fleeing Egypt."

"One of the seminal events in church history," offers Caleb.

"True," agrees Avi, "but there is more. This site is also where Elijah was taken to heaven in a whirlwind."

Now Pastor Marcus stands. "This is also where tradition tells us Jesus was baptized."

Baptisms. Pastor Marcus has been telling us all week, either at dinner or on the bus between stops, about the chance to be baptized at the end of the trip. I have ignored the concept ... until now.

I turn to Daniel. "Jesus was baptized here?"

"Yes, sir. The River Jordan. Either right here or nearby." We start to unload and Daniel adds a sentence. "Baptism is the first step."

Buried away in what used to be my attic is a paper certifying my baptism as an infant. I was probably wearing a white gown, surrounded by my parents and godparents, while the priest offered blessings and prayers.

It's fair to say it didn't take.

I envision the road from little baby, squirming over a water-filled ceramic bowl, to where I am today, wondering if I should give the whole wash-my-soul-with-water strategy another try. "Am I too late to sign up?"

Caleb overhears me and shouts a question to Pastor Marcus. "Hey, Pastor, Ben here wants to join the baptisms. Have room to squeeze another one in?"

"As they say, the more the merrier." Pastor Marcus is nodding his head. "Glad to have him."

∞ ∞ ∞

Twenty minutes later, I'm wearing a white muslin robe, purchased for ten dollars at the gift shop, and zigzagging through the throngs of people. The sounds of singing drift from the pavilions, serenading the crowd. While small clusters of individuals sit and watch, other folks are either wading into the river or waiting for their turn. We take our place on a wooden platform and, when we arrive at the front of the line, Pastor Marcus grabs my arm. "Wait here. We're going to do yours in a separate ceremony."

He steps into the river along with about ten people from our group. They move out a short way, too far for me to hear the words, and Pastor Marcus starts talking. I watch, mesmerized by the steady flow of the muddy water, the brown color juxtaposed against the green vegetation lining both banks.

My attention shifts when I spot two Israeli soldiers, guns across their chests, surveying the opposite bank. Avi notices and explains. "On the other side of the river is the country of Jordan. Soldiers on their side are also peering over at us. This is nothing to worry about. There will be no problems unless an individual crosses into another country's territory."

"Where does the border start?"

"About halfway across the river. There is not much danger of getting there, though. A wooden barrier stops you from going too far."

Pastor Marcus, followed by ten wet but cheerful people, climbs back onto the platform. "Okay, Ben, your turn."

I follow him down the stairs, entering the river, and walk across a submerged deck. Despite the heat, the water's cold. After about fifteen steps, my hip bumps into a railing, which, I'm assuming, is the border Avi mentioned. I'm not taking any chances, though, and move closer to the Israeli side.

"Welcome, brother! Come next to me." I wrestle against the current and get over to Daniel. He squares my shoulders until I'm facing Pastor Marcus, who's standing, water lapping against his shins, on the bottom step of the platform. When

Daniel backs away, I'm confused for a second, until I realize I'm enclosed in a makeshift human horseshoe. In addition to Daniel, there're Jeb, Ruth, Addy, Gerri, and Caleb.

Pastor Marcus starts to talk. "Ben, baptism is a public declaration of your desire to join the family of Christ. You have made the decision to embark on a brand-new life, blessed by the Lord. Your old life will be washed away by the waters of the Holy Spirit." He runs his hands through the river. "Are you ready to be baptized into a new family? To become a follower of Jesus Christ?"

I believe I'm ready, but, at the same time, I want to be sincere. "Am I allowed to answer yes if I'm not sure exactly what being a follower of Jesus is going to mean?"

"Absolutely, Ben." Pastor Marcus is emphatic. "You most certainly are."

"I am. Ready, I mean."

Pastor Marcus raises his right hand above his head. "Ben Cahill, I baptize you in the name of the Father ..."

He stops. I wait for the next sentence.

"Dowse yourself, Ben, go under!" Gerri's yelling and gesturing for me to submerge.

Right. They told me to duck below the surface. I plunge. The current is a set of arms wrapped around my body, keeping me from drifting away.

When my head comes up, Pastor Marcus keeps going. "And of the Son ..."

I dive again. This time I count to ten, the silty water in and around my robe, filtering itself in my hair, washing me as the river flows by. I surge upward.

"And of the Holy Spirit."

With the third dunk, the water embraces me, and I float, suspended a few inches below the surface, until I burst back to the top.

"Amen."

The whole crew closes in, offering hugs and slaps on the back. Once I return to dry land, Pastor Marcus points me to the showers where the others are washing up. I tell him no—I want the River Jordan on my skin as long as possible.

$$\infty \;\; \infty \;\; \infty$$

Heading to the bus, I'm elated but unsettled. Jeb, who's walking with me, picks up on my restlessness. "What's wrong?"

"Huh? Oh, no, nothing's wrong. I'm in an awfully good place. I wish I could, I don't know—"

"You want to share it with someone." He finishes my sentence after he sees me watching Addy and Daniel holding hands.

"Yeah, you know, you guys are great and all, but telling Sarah about this would complete the experience."

Jeb stops me. "Sarah's your wife?"

"For now, yes."

He rubs his chin. "Why not call her?"

My response is instantaneous. "No. No way. She's not gonna want to talk to me."

"Ben, in the words of one of my old law partners, 'There's an old saying I just made up.' Mine for today is—don't assume there's no bridge until you try to cross the river."

I fold my arms, shifting my weight from foot to foot. "Good saying, Jeb. One I'll have to remember." I'm nowhere near ready to untangle my family's mess. "There's the practical consideration too. I don't have international cell service."

Jeb doesn't bother responding, but holds out his phone. His look tells me he's wondering how I ever got a business deal done. He turns to Avi. "Could we give our friend Ben here a few minutes to make a call before we leave?"

"Yes, we have plenty of time."

I'm stuck. After I reluctantly dial Sarah's number, she answers on the second ring. My jittery voice jumps across the miles. "Hi, it's me."

"Ben?"

"Uh-huh."

"Is everything all right? We're getting ready for the day here." *Right, I forgot about the time difference.*

"Yeah, I'm doing okay."

"Where are—wait." I hear her close a door. "Nick stopped by to check on us. Did you go to Israel?"

Good old Nick. I should have known my brother would make sure Sarah and the kids were okay. "Yeah. I'm still here." *Get on with it.* "Uh, listen, Sarah, how is everyone? You, Zach, Olivia?"

"We're all fine, thanks." Her voice goes cold with cynicism. "Ben, what do you want?"

I'm puzzled about what to say next. I hadn't developed a game plan before I dialed and I pause to toss around options. My deliberations must take more time than I thought.

"Ben?"

I'm afraid she'll think we lost the connection and jump right back in. "I want to tell you about this trip."

"You want to tell me about your trip?"

"Yes."

The proverbial last straw has hit the camel's back. "Ben, you got hauled out of our house by the police, drunk, got your butt handed to you in court, disappeared into rehab, and your first instinct is to tell me about your vacation? In case you forgot, let me remind you we're talking with lawyers about divorce, and you've had them separate our assets. To top things off, our son has a baseball bat in his bed, our daughter cries herself to sleep every night, and our family, which wasn't in great shape to begin with, is ripped to shreds. Hey, I know what. Send me a few pics, too."

Her eruption is a well-placed punch, hard enough I want to check and see if blood's dripping from my nose. The negotiator in me comes out, and I concede the point. "I know things are bad."

I hear her mutter "you're darn right they are."

"I've been sober for a few days—" I stop abruptly. She's heard this garbage before. "There's a load of history here. I've learned something every day." *Nice Ben. Powerful.* "I'm traveling with a great group of people."

I stop again, aware any more non-specific babble will end the call. Sarah confirms this when I hear an impatient sigh.

I decide to go with a simple and transparent response. "Sarah, I know there's no reason for you to hear or care about what I'm saying, but there's a reasonable chance I've found a way back."

"Back?"

"To myself."

She's quiet.

"I got baptized today."

After another silent interlude, Sarah answers. I hear the faintest wisp of affection in her voice. "I hope you do, Ben. I hope you find yourself again."

I go for broke. "And if I do?"

"Our kids need a father."

"A father? There's still a chance to be a father?"

"You'll always be their father."

"Right, yeah, I know. What I'm asking is, from where you sit, do you see me as a father who's part of their lives?"

"Ben, there're acres of ground between here and there. As I said, though, our kids need their dad." I hear her take a big breath. "I need their dad, too. Not the guy who was here a few months ago. The one I fell in love with."

A guarded excitement creeps into my voice. "I didn't dare imagine you'd ever consider us being us again."

"Ben, those are your conclusions, not mine. I want to be careful here, though. I'm not saying anything other than we need you, and if you find the man beneath all the sludge life has loaded on, maybe we'll talk more."

All the sludge. Like a Tell.

In the background, I hear a voice. "Mommy, I can't find my pink sweater."

"Hey, Ben? Hold on a second." Sarah muffles the phone, and I barely make out her telling Olivia to wait while she finishes her call.

My heart yearns to talk with my daughter, and I consider asking Sarah to let me speak to Olivia, but I stop myself. I'm not sure what I would say and my instinct tells me the next conversation with my kids needs to be carefully planned.

"Okay, Ben, I'm back."

I pick up where we left off. "Sarah, I know I've got a long road ahead. I know I need to prove myself. I'll try, with all I've got, to get there."

"I'm sure you will."

"I'm hanging up now. But first ..."

"Yes?"

"I'm sorry we've come to this."

"Enjoy the rest of your trip Ben."

I find Jeb and return the phone.

"How did the call go?" he asks.

I hold my thumb and forefinger about a centimeter apart. "I got this."

"What's that?"

"A tiny sliver. Of hope."

He grins. "Sometimes all we need is a sliver, enough to keep pushing us forward."

$$\infty \quad \infty \quad \infty$$

I'm sipping ginger ale at the last pre-dinner Happy Hour. People offered to skip the alcohol, but I told them no worries, I'm in a safe place tonight.

How, in essentially a week and a half, did this happen? Of course, there's Joseph. But there're also the people around me, an unusual collection of individuals who have supported, cajoled, listened, explained, and nursed me. If I didn't know better, I'd say they've been placed here.

Wait.

Placed here.

The words hit hard, and I step away from the group.

Caretakers.

I sip my ginger ale and wonder if they know.

"You okay?" Daniel's hand is on my shoulder.

"What? Oh, absolutely. Feeling good."

"I thought maybe the alcohol was causing a problem again."

"Nope. Needed to stretch my legs."

We both stare at a mass-produced landscape print, yellow flowers standing in a field, before Daniel says, "You know, Ben, I was jealous of you on this trip."

"Jealous?"

"Yeah, and this is super petty, but I envied you having a room all to yourself."

I give him a funny look. "All to myself?"

"Yes. A single. I'm an introvert by nature. I could have used the alone time to recharge. Also, as isolated as you seemed, there were a few times I would have enjoyed doing what you did, sitting alone in the back of the bus, away from the crowd."

Daniel, and I'm assuming everyone else, didn't know Joseph was around?

Given the conversation Joseph and I had before he left earlier in the day, what Daniel is saying isn't surprising to me now. Since there's no reasonable reply, I shake Daniel's hand and say, "Thanks for a great trip. Let's get back to the group. I want to thank them too." I head over to the others. My caretakers. My friends. When I get there, they all smile, offer a toast in honor of a wonderful trip, and I polish off the rest of my ginger ale.

PROGRESS REPORT # 11

Peter,

Somehow, someway, our project has reached a successful conclusion. I know you will respond with your usual and correct retort. We do, of course, absolutely know the somehow and the someway.

To determine Our Man was acting autonomously and making his most important decisions within the human realm, I followed protocol and removed myself from immediate physical contact. After a shaky spell, he reacted splendidly, and was provided direct, unsubtle input following a fully sincere and impassioned plea for help. During a particularly fevered moment, I chose to offer a brief verbal encouragement in order to ground him in the familiar.

He responded by acknowledging the Gift is available. To reinforce this, he made his most independent decision to date, electing to be washed in water.

While enthusiasm is warranted, there remains a long road ahead and we must remember his transformation is in the early stages. There will be numerous opportunities for regression and rejection.

On a personal note, I will miss Ben. Despite his life's path to date, he has a good soul imprisoned beneath his human faults and failings. I am certain, if he fully embraces the life before him, his soul will climb to freedom. This, combined with his numerous gifts, suggests a productive and satisfying future.

I close in curiosity. Given this project's ambitious timeline and the unparalleled quality of the assigned caretakers, I must ask the obvious questions. Why all of this for one person? What is he being prepared to do? I, of course, understand there is no need at present, or, if custom holds, in the future, for me to be privy to such information. I do, however, enjoy speculating.

Bless you my brother,

Joseph

DAY 12

I'm staring at a blank first page in a hard-covered journal. Jeb presented me with the journal, along with an olive wood pen, as we boarded the plane. They were a gift he bought me at Yussef's shop in Bethlehem. He also offered a simple recommendation—to use them to help figure out where I've been and where I'm going.

I'm not sure where to start. After a few minutes of thought, I decide to write what I know. *My name is Ben Cahill and I'm returning from a trip to Israel. These twelve days were, to say the least, eventful. One result is, for the first time in a long time, I'm not drinking every day. While I can't definitively explain how this change in behavior occurred, there was a mystical intervention in my life. No, "mystical" is not the right word. Divine is better.*

On this trip, I took an improbable first step into a world of faith, joining God's family when I was baptized. In the Jordan River. How many people are able to say that?

I've learned about spiritual battles and know prayer is available to help.

I've been shown I'm worthy of forgiveness, but also, I'm going to have to figure out how to let go of the things I've done. From there, I believe, I'll build on the past, creating a new life on top of the old.

On the practical side of the equation, I'm returning home to a fractured family, no job, and no place to live.

All of this creates an overriding truth—there's a formidable amount of work to do. However, and thankfully, I won't be alone. As long as I stay "in the room," God will help me. Plus, there's a whole new group of friends ready to assist.

The pen goes down and I chew on a thumbnail for a good twenty minutes before writing my last sentence of the day.

I wonder what's going to happen next?

ABOUT THE AUTHOR

Steven Rogers is a contemporary Christian fiction novelist. Steven loves the process of writing, especially exploring characters that are either broken or facing unfamiliar situations. They are usually ordinary people, confronting their own internal demons and the challenges of day-to-day living, being pushed to their limits. He also enjoys bringing his stories to a happy, or at least hopeful, ending.

After attending The College of the Holy Cross, Steven became a Certified Public Accountant and filled various roles in public accounting and private industry. A lifelong lover of books and literature, over the years he dabbled with writing fiction. Since retiring from the corporate world in 2016, Steven has fully committed to learning the craft. His short story "Deep Waters" earned an honorable mention award in the 2020 89th Annual Writer's Digest Writing Competition.

Steven, a proud father of three adult children and one incredibly lucky son-in-law, is happily married to his wife of thirty-five years, Kathy. They live in Richmond, Virginia.

To learn more about Steven and access the "Into the Room Discussion Guide," visit his website at www.steven-rogers.com.

Made in the USA
Middletown, DE
01 September 2022

72932531R00163